# HARD ROCK CRUSH

ATHENA WRIGHT

D1519889

Pure Passion
Ink

# BOOKS IN THE HARD ROCK ROMANCE SERIES

(ALL CAN BE READ AS STANDALONES)

## Cherry Lips

#0.5 Hard Rock Promise - Gael and Jessie's story

#1: Hard Rock Crush - Cerise and Liam's story

#2: Hard Rock Kiss - Nathan's story *(Coming late spring 2018)*

#3: *Julian's story*

#4: *Seth's story*

## Darkest Days

#1 Hard Rock Tease - Noah and Jen's story

#2 Hard Rock Fling - Ian and Hope's story

#3 Hard Rock Sin - Cameron and Lily's story

#4 Hard Rock Deceit - August and Cassie's story

#5 Hard Rock Heat - Damon and Faith's story

---

## Feral Silence

#1 Hard Rock Gaze - Jayce and Ailey's story

#2 Hard Rock Voice - Kell and Emily's story

#3 Hard Rock Touch - Ren and Ivy's store

#4 Hard Rock Heart - Morris and Natalie's story

## 1

The stage was empty. I tasted anticipation in the air. The band wasn't going on for another twenty minutes, and the crowd already buzzed with excitement.

"Who's playing?" I asked my brother. The launch performance for the city's Concert in the Park series always drew a big crowd, but the courtyard seemed busier than I expected.

"Don't know," Gael said. "Some local band."

"If you don't know, then why are we here?" I asked.

"We need to scope out the competition." Gael's bright blue eyes met mine as he grinned.

"Competition for what?" I asked. "We don't have a band yet. I'm not even sure I'm on board with the idea."

I had been, once. Singing in a band was all I ever wanted to do. My fiancé Harper and I'd had dreams of making it big.

But that was before.

A black pit in my stomach yawned open. An ever-present swirling mass threatened to swallow me whole.

I closed my eyes. Took a deep breath through my nose. Exhaled through my mouth. Did it again. And again.

The darkness was still there, but I was able to steel myself against it and shove it away. I refused to let despair consume me. Not anymore.

"Besides," I continued, my voice only slightly shaky. "Even if we wanted to start a band, there's only two of us. We'd still need a drummer and a guitarist."

"You play guitar," he said. "That's enough."

"I'm still not comfortable singing and playing at the same time," I said.

"Growing pains."

Someone jammed an elbow into my side with a muttered sorry. Another person stumbled into me from behind, this time without a sorry. The crowd was getting fuller by the minute. I'd never seen a Concert in the Park audience as packed as this one.

Gael glanced at me, eyeing the long hair that tumbled down my back in waves.

"That's a new shade of red," he said.

And with that comment, I knew the real reason we were here.

Gael was worried.

"Since when do guys notice when a girl gets a different hairstyle?" I asked.

Gael shrugged. "It's hard to miss when your lips are the same shade as your hair."

"So I bought new makeup to go with my new hair color. Why do you care?"

"It's different, that's all I'm saying."

That wasn't all he was saying. I heard his unspoken words.

*Why did you dye your hair again?*

*Are you feeling okay?*

*Have you been thinking about him again?*

*It's okay to miss him, but you can't let grief control your life.*

"I know," I snapped.

Gael's eyes widened in surprise.

"I mean, I know it's different," I said, trying to regain my composure. "That's the point."

Gael flicked his eyes away, focusing on the stage. "There was nothing wrong with the old Cerise," he said quietly.

I clenched my jaw. "I'm going to get a drink."

A wall of tented vendor booths surrounded the courtyard in a semi-circle, penning in the concert audience. Some were handing out water bottles branded with sponsor logos. I snatched one up and, before anyone could notice, slid my way between the small gap between two booths.

There were no crowds on this side of the tent wall. The noise and furor was muted.

I took in a deep breath. Then another. And another. Slowly my heartbeat calmed.

For someone who drank like a fish and brought a new girl home every night, Gael could be oddly perceptive when it came to his little sister.

He was wrong though. There had been something wrong with the old Cerise.

The old Cerise had been too sheltered. Too naïve. The old Cerise didn't know how awful the world could be.

The old Cerise couldn't handle losing Harper. She'd fallen apart. She'd let herself break. She hadn't been able to deal with the way he'd...

My chest clenched. Pinpricks of tears threatened to sting my eyes. I blinked rapidly and took a swig from my water bottle to wet my dry throat.

"Hey there, Cherry Lips."

I choked, sputtering, as a voice spoke up and surprised me. Droplets of water splashed down my chin and onto my shirt. I wiped at my face with the back of my hand, turning to face the voice.

I was confronted by a man with wavy brown hair and stunning green eyes. He wore a black and white *Our Lady Peace* band t-shirt stretched tight around broad shoulders. I inhaled a sharp breath. This guy was beyond good looking. I felt like an idiot for having made a fool of myself in front of him. I folded my arms over my chest, as if somehow that would hide my embarrassment.

"What did you call me?" My words came out strangled, still coughing water out of my lungs. So much for not looking like an idiot.

The man shrugged easily. "Seemed appropriate. Your lips are cherry red." He scanned me up and down, from the top of my newly dyed hair, to the toes of my black boots, to the ends of my bright red nails. "I'm sensing a theme."

That was two guys commenting on my fashion choice in one day. Maybe I was taking it too far.

"I like it," he continued. A hint of amusement glinted in those green eyes. "It's cute."

My heart did something I hadn't felt it do in a long time.

It fluttered.

My grip tightened on the water bottle, crushing it. I pretended to wrinkle my nose in disgust. "Don't call me cute."

"Wait, let me guess." He tapped his finger to his mouth as if he were in deep thought. His own nails were tipped with black nail varnish. "Dyed red hair, combat boots, thick black eyeliner... You're aiming for cool, powerful, and fierce, right?"

I scowled to cover up the flush on my cheeks.

His shoulders shook with silent laughter.

"And what would you know about cool?" I shot back.

The smile on his lips didn't fade. "I know that trying to look cool on purpose doesn't work."

I cast my eyes down, avoiding his gaze.

I couldn't deny it. By dressing like this, I was trying to be someone I wasn't. I'd never been that strong, take-no-shit kind of person. That had never been me.

"Listen," he said. "I get it."

I looked back up, meeting the man's gaze.

"The whole, I'm-a-bad-ass, don't-mess-with-me, thing?" His green eyes burned into me. "I get where you're coming from. But this?" He waved his hand, gesturing to my hair and boots. "This isn't the way to do it."

"Then how do I?" I hated how plaintive I sounded, how weak and uncertain.

He pinned me down with a stare. "When do you feel the most powerful?"

I paused, taken aback. "I... don't know."

"Think about it," he urged. "What makes you feel like you can do anything? Like you can take on the world?"

"I suppose..." I hesitated, but powered on. "When I sing."

His eyes lit up. "Yeah? You sing?"

I nodded.

"That's the key, then," he said. "Always be singing."

I let out a derisive laugh. "I can't go around singing all the time. Life isn't a musical."

"Not out loud." He tapped one finger against my chest. "In here."

My heart went into overdrive, beating madly against my ribcage. My ears turned hot. My lungs squeezed.

I hadn't felt anything like this since the last time Harper had...

"Think you can do that, Cherry Lips?" he asked with a grin.

I nodded dumbly, silently. He winked and sauntered off, ducking between the tents. I stared at the space where he disappeared. I fought to calm my rapid breathing.

My cell phone buzzed — a text from Gael, written in all caps, asking where I was and telling me the concert was starting.

I followed the mysterious green-eyed stranger's path through the tents, but I didn't see him on the other side. Disappointed but not surprised, I wandered back to my brother, elbowing my way through the crowd. The audience was reaching a fever pitch. Whoever this band was, they must have had a lot of local fans.

I poked Gael in the shoulder when I finally pushed my way to him. He nodded at me and jerked his chin to the side.

"The band's name is *Forever Night*," he shouted over the crowd.

My mind was elsewhere, still thinking about what that guy had said.

*Always be singing.*

Moments later, the screech of guitars hit my ears and the thumping of drums and bass thrummed in my chest. The first few bars of the song were catchy, but not enough to take my attention away from my thoughts.

A man began to sing.

I recognized the voice.

I turned my face toward the stage.

The stranger from before held a microphone in one hand, a guitar slung around his shoulders.

His voice was smooth and crooning at first, then turned deep and growling, switching off between soft and aggressive in turns.

It wasn't just a song. It was a litany, tirade, a prayer.

It was joy and anger and longing and pain and desire and regret and—

A million emotions flashed through me in the space of a five-minute song, the singer's voice wringing out every feeling I'd suppressed since Harper had been killed.

It was as if the man had taken every emotion in the world, as if he'd taken all the love and hate he'd ever felt, and turned it back onto the audience.

That's when I knew.

This was what I wanted to do.

He was what I wanted to be.

I didn't want to be the old Cerise, innocent and insecure and naïve.

I wanted to be someone who could take everything the world threw at her and spit it back out.

I wanted to be powerful. I wanted to be fierce.

I wanted to sing.

"I'm in," I yelled in Gael's ear.

"What?" he shouted back.

"The band thing. I'm in."

Shock crossed his face before he let out a whoop and fist pumped. "Hell yeah! Now we just need a name for the band."

"I've already got one."

He tilted his head, curious. "Yeah?"

I nodded.

"We're going to call ourselves Cherry Lips."

## 2

The bartender slid my drink across the counter. I caught it with one hand and brought it to my mouth, taking a sip. It wasn't as strong as I would have liked, but it was alcohol, which was all that mattered.

I never needed alcohol to soothe my nerves before a performance, but tonight was different. This was the first concert my band Cherry Lips was headlining since launching our first professional, non-indie album. This was the first night we'd play our new songs in front of a live audience. Tonight had to go well. There was no room for nerves.

Leaning against the bar, I rested my back against the rail. I surveyed the room, taking in the faces of my soon-to-be audience. Almost no one was paying attention to the band on stage. For good reason. They were less than impressive.

As I scanned the room, I caught a flash of wavy, longish, brown hair — a head I'd definitely seen before. It wasn't one of my bandmates or one of my friends coming to support me tonight. That hair was familiar in another way. I knew this guy from somewhere, but I couldn't place it.

He turned his head. I caught a glimpse of his face. A glimpse of his green eyes. My fingers went numb. I clenched my fist to keep from dropping my glass.

Liam Knight.

The green-eyed man was Liam Knight. The former lead singer of *Forever Night.*

The man who inspired me years ago to keep going after I'd given up on singing forever.

Cold liquid splashed over my trembling hand. I wiped it on my shirt absentmindedly, not taking my eyes off him.

I'd been staring at him too long. I was going to get caught. I had to look away.

I couldn't make myself.

I owed that man my career. My voice. My sanity, even. I hadn't had nightmares since starting Cherry Lips.

I owed him everything.

I could never let him know.

Darting my eyes to the side, I focused intently on the stage. The last thing I needed was for Liam to find me staring at him.

I found myself picking at the nail polish on my left hand. I rubbed my palms against my thighs to stop myself, the leather skirt smooth under my hands. The cherry red lacquer of my nails complimented my hair, and I didn't want it ruined the same day I'd put it on, especially before our set.

I tried to concentrate on the band playing, but my mind wandered back to the first time I'd ever met him.

Would he remember me the way I remembered him? That was unlikely. We only met the one time, years ago, and it wasn't like I was the famous one back then.

I was so absorbed in my thoughts, I didn't notice the crowd parting next to me, or see the person approaching me through the sea of people. I only noticed someone coming up beside me when a firm hand touched my arm.

My shoulders tensed. I made a motion to slap the hand away. I wasn't going to let those handsy club guys think they could get away with pawing at me without my permission.

I stopped, hand still in the air, when I saw who it was.

Liam was next to me, green eyes sparkling with good humor.

"Hey there, Cherry Lips," he said, mouth curling into a smile.

He remembered who I was. That was impossible. A five minute encounter years ago shouldn't have meant anything to a man like him.

But it had.

My left thumb scratched at the nail polish on my index finger. My musical idol was standing right in front of me. I wanted to play it off. *Oh, are you a fan?* I could say.

But from the glint in his eyes, he knew I recognized him.

"Hey," I said, my voice faltering. "Are you here to watch the show?"

"I'm here to watch you."

My thumb slipped, sharp nail jabbing into skin.

"You've done well for yourself," he continued. "A professional recording contract? Impressive."

I inhaled sharply. "You know about that?"

"Of course," he said, amused. "An indie band shows up on the scene called Cherry Lips and you think I wouldn't take notice?"

"I didn't think I'd made that much of an impression on you," I said.

"You did."

My heart reacted the same way it had years ago.

It fluttered.

Back then, that flutter had been the first time I'd felt anything in a long time.

This moment was only the second time. I'd never felt it since.

But the feeling wasn't unfamiliar — just long forgotten. I'd had those feelings when I was younger. Much younger.

Back when I didn't know any better.

Someone bumped into me from behind. Liam put his arm around my waist, steadying me. The heat of his palm pressed against the small of my back even through my black lace shirt.

Despite my better instincts, I allowed his arm to stay around my waist. I even let myself lean into him. He tightened his grip, hugging me to his side.

"So tell me about that contract," Liam said. "That's a pretty big deal."

"We really scored with that one," I nodded. "But I always knew Cherry Lips would make it."

"Did you?" he asked, amused.

"It's my band," I said. "I'm the driving force behind it all. I won't settle for anything less than world domination."

"Sounds like you've got big dreams," he said.

"They're not just dreams," I said confidently. "I'm going to make it happen. We're already well on our way with our new album and tour."

"You're going on tour?" Liam asked. "That's a big push for a new band."

"Well," I hedged. "It's a local tour. Only cities within a few hours drive. And only for a few weeks." I straightened my back. "But if this goes well, I don't see any reason why they won't sign us on for a second album. That's why tonight's performance is so important to me. It's our first headliner since we went pro. This is the first night we play our new songs in front of a live audience. We're going to blow everyone away."

The amused smile on Liam's face could have been considered condescending, but the glint in his eyes told me something different. He liked that I was boasting. He liked that I was confident.

He bent forward, putting his mouth to my ear so I could hear him over the noise of the club.

"I'm proud of you," he said. "You're really strong up there."

I took in a slow, shaky breath. Not because of lips brushing my skin. Not because of a hand wandering from my back to my hip. I was enjoying the physical sensations, yes, but that wasn't the reason I was so taken aback.

It was the words that were important.

Liam Knight thought I was strong.

The faintest sensation of tears threatened to burn the back of my eyes. I refused to let them fall. I refused to let him know how much those words meant to me.

It shouldn't have affected me that much. I was Cerise Moreau. I was the co-founder and lead singer of up-and-coming, soon-to-be hit rock band Cherry Lips. I was a fucking rock star.

And yet something inside of me, some small broken piece of me, began to mend itself. Sharp fragments began stitching themselves together.

"I should probably get ready," I said. "We're on next." Even I could hear the hesitation, the reluctance in my voice. "Will you be sticking around after the show?"

"I don't normally," he said.

"Oh."

"But maybe this time I will." He winked at me. "I'm going to start shoving my way to the front. I want a spot front and center for this performance."

I watched him disappear back into the crowd. Women everywhere threw lust-filled looks in his direction.

I brutally stamped down on any hints of jealousy threatening to take hold of me.

I headed to the far end of the club and climbed the stairs to go backstage, pushing through the doors. The bodyguard didn't give me a second look. The rest of my band members stood off to the side behind the curtains, waiting for the sign to take the stage. The opening act had filed out and our instruments were already set up. I had almost missed my cue.

My thoughts should have been on my upcoming performance, but I couldn't stop thinking about Liam being out there in the audience, watching me.

"Do you hear that?" My brother Gael, Cherry Lips's bassist, cocked his head towards the audience and cupped his ear in a comically exaggerated motion. "They're calling for us."

I turned my wandering thoughts from Liam to the crowd. Gael was right. The audience was cheering and chanting. Chanting for Cherry Lips.

Elation filled my chest. My veins began to buzz the way they always did before a performance. Our fans were out there, waiting for us. We were going to give them the show of their lives.

One of the crew members nodded, giving us our cue to take the stage.

I closed my eyes. Deep breath in through the nose. And out through the mouth. Again. Then again.

I opened my eyes.

I was ready.

Throwing my shoulders back and exuding confidence, I walked toward the dark stage. I grabbed my guitar with one hand from a waiting tech and I swung it around my shoulders.

I scanned the audience. I wanted to take a look at the faces of the people who so adored me.

I paused.

Off to the side, near the front of the pit but close to backstage, stood Liam. He was speaking to a bodyguard, his lips moving silently to my ears.

But his eyes were on me.

My heart jumped a quick beat. Then another. I almost missed my cue for the first song.

But I was a professional. I quickly and smoothly returned my attention to the stage, intending to put Liam out of my mind for the rest of the night. As long as I didn't look to the side, I could do that.

We finished our performance without any mishaps. The band didn't notice anything was off.

Before we left the stage, we threw guitar picks, water bottles, drumsticks, and other tokens to the audience. It was an ego boost, watching people fight over who got to leave with my guitar pick.

As I left the stage, I rubbed at my wrist.

"Is it bothering you again?" my brother asked.

"A little."

"We can always try to find someone else—"

"I'll be fine," I said. "We don't need any more members for the band. We're good the way we are. I'm just a little overworked."

"There's nothing wrong with hiring a session guitarist to go on tour with us," Gael replied.

"Can we not fight about this now?"

Gael put his arm around my shoulders and tugged me close. "Isn't everything always a fight with you?"

Before I could push my brother away, Nathan called out for him, getting his attention. With one last concerned look, Gael took off to join our bandmate.

Maybe my brother wasn't one hundred percent wrong. Maybe it wouldn't be bad to have someone else play guitar while I sang. I'd be able to have more fun running around on stage if I didn't have to worry about playing. But the band dynamic was great the way it was. I didn't want, or need, anyone else coming in and ruining that.

Now that the performance was over, I made my way back down the stairs, to the pit. A small glimmer of hope sparked inside me. I didn't want to get my hopes up, but maybe...

I pushed through the set of doors. The bodyguard nodded at me. The audience was slowly making their way to the exit. I scanned the room, looking for wavy brown hair. Nothing.

Disheartened, I returned to the backstage. Gael waved at me.

"Nate says we're heading up to that VIP lounge to party," he called out to me. "You joining us?"

"I will in a minute," I said.

First I needed to find the artist lounge and change out of my sweat dampened clothes.

The backstage of the club was like a maze, but since we'd played here a few times, I knew where to go. I maneuvered my way through the chaos, deftly avoiding crew members and equipment. I reached the closed door with a placard announcing it was the artist lounge.

I expected to find the room empty of people, with a few sofas, tables and dressing room stands, along with bottles of water and some snacks for the band members before the show.

I put my hand on the door, opening it.

I took in a sharp breath.

Liam stood in the middle of the room.

I stopped, frozen in the doorway.

The bodyguards and staff had let him through. They must have known who he was, just as I had.

He was waiting for me.

"You were great out there," Liam said. He quirked a half-smile, as if to say *great* wasn't the word he'd planned on using.

My hearted thumped madly. "Thanks," I replied numbly.

Liam scanned me up and down, gaze lingering in certain, more intimate, places. I was acutely aware of every drop of sweat soaking through my clothes, every stringy piece of hair clinging to my cheeks. I was a mess.

Judging from the heat in Liam's eyes, he liked that mess.

"What did you think of the show?" I asked, aiming for composed and utterly failing. At least I could chalk my labored breath up to the performance. I could pretend it had nothing to do with the way his searching eyes bore into me. "Was it up to your standards?"

"You blew the roof off. I've rarely seen a crowd go that wild for a brand new band."

"We've been hot in the indie scene for a while," I said. "We've got fans from our old days still following us around. They were really excited when we got a record deal."

"The fans sounded like they wanted a second encore."

"Not tonight. The guys are already upstairs on the second floor lounge getting trashed."

"Are you going to join them?" he asked.

"I need a change of clothes first," I said, slowly picking up my bag tucked away in the corner.

Liam's eyes narrowed, turning a dark forest green.

"You need some help with that?" he asked.

I knew exactly what he meant.

The tips of my fingers dragged against the rough texture of my chipped nail polish. I wet my lips, tasting the slick gloss coating them. I considered Liam's offer.

I was bold when it came to the stage, when it came to music.

I wasn't bold when it came to... *this*.

Liam seemed to sense how awkward I was feeling.

He stepped up to press against me, radiating warmth, his firm chest hot against mine.

I took a deep breath in to steady myself. A warm, woodsy, masculine scent filled my nose.

Damn. He smelled even better than he looked, which should have been impossible.

Forget the fluttering in my stomach. This was a swirling cyclone. A raging storm. This was the beginning of an armageddon ready to destroy every last inch of my resistance.

He tilted his head at me with a knowing smile.

I nodded.

He placed both hands on my arms. I felt every indentation of his fingertips, every whorl, as if it were branded into me. His palms ran up and down in a sensual, soothing motion, from my shoulders to my wrists.

I shivered, my insides turning hot and achy.

He took both my hands in his, lacing our fingers. I curled my fingers around his.

He placed a soft kiss on my neck.

My fingers clenched, squeezing his hands tight. "Wait."

I was surprised to find my voice was steady. No hint of the tempest racing through me.

Liam stopped, his lips still on my skin. I pulled away, untangling our hands. My heart jackhammered in my chest.

"I'm sorry," I said, avoiding his eyes. "I don't think I can..."

"Don't be sorry," Liam said. He tilted my chin up to meet his gaze. He studied me carefully.

"It's just—" I started.

He put a finger to my lips.

"You don't need to explain," Liam said. With a gentle smile, he pressed a kiss to my forehead.

I closed my eyes, breathing deeply.

It was just *what*? All I knew was that my fight or flight instinct had kicked in and I couldn't figure out why.

"I should go meet up with my band," I said weakly.

Liam nodded. I made a motion toward the door. I stopped.

"Will you be at our next concert?" I asked.

I couldn't just leave. I couldn't let it end like this.

Liam's expression turned regretful, as if he understood the true meaning behind my words.

*Will I ever see you again?*

"I'm only in town for a short gig," he said.

I could have invited him up to the lounge to party with us for the night.

I could have invited him back to my place.

I didn't.

"I'm glad I ran into you tonight," he said. "I'll be able to say, *I knew her when*, after you've taken over the world."

"You sound so sure that will happen."

"It will," he said confidently. "Just don't forget about us little people when you're rich and famous." He threw me a crooked smile.

My heart thumped. I quickly slipped out the door, closing it behind me. I rested my back against it. My chest felt tight, like I couldn't get enough air into my lungs, like all the oxygen had been sucked out of the room.

I was attracted to Liam. He was obviously attracted to me. I wasn't opposed to a random hook up, although it wasn't really my thing. I supposed a one-night stand could be fun. I had no reason to pull away. There was no harm in fooling around, no strings, no attachments.

But there were attachments, weren't there?

He wasn't some random guy I'd picked up at a club. He was Liam Knight, the man who'd saved me from myself. A crush didn't begin to describe the tangle of feelings I had inside me when it came to him.

If I had given in to him, if I had allowed myself to drop my guard...

Turning him down had been for the best, I decided.

All I had to do now was get my heart to agree.

## 3

The first concert after signing our contract had been wildly successful. Our fans were clamoring for more, so the label decided to push up the dates of our tour.

That meant Gael went back to bugging me about hiring a session guitarist to fill in for me.

"I don't know," Nathan said. "I like being the only male guitarist in our band. It scores me all the chicks."

Gael smacked him in the shoulder. "Hey, I used to score as many chicks as you."

"That was before you let some girl chain you down," Nathan said. "Now there's no more chicks allowed for you, isn't that right?"

Instead of getting mad, Gael puffed his chest out.

"There's only one chick I need in my life," he declared.

"Your girlfriend would have you by the balls if she knew you'd called her a chick," I said.

"At least I'm not calling her by a disgusting pet name," Gael said.

"Besides," Nathan drawled, "isn't that what our female fans are calling themselves? Cherry Chicks?"

"I don't know if that's cute or gross," I muttered.

"You think that's bad, you should hear what fans of Benedict Cumberbatch call themselves." Nathan gave me a lazy-eyed smirk.

I couldn't understand why all the girls flocked to someone like Nate. Well, I supposed I could, if I squinted and tilted my head. With his sandy brown hair, dark blue eyes and laid-back attitude, he had that cute boy next door thing going on.

Of course, behind all that boyish charm was a shark lying in wait. No one who really knew Nate would mistake him for anything else but a predator licking his chops as he waited patiently for his prey to appear.

"We've got a handful of guys out there waiting for their turn to impress us," Gael said. "We put the word out everywhere and got a lot of interest from guitarists in the local scene."

"One or two even decided to fly in from out of town to audition for us," Nathan added. "It turns out we're a pretty big deal."

"Where exactly did you put the word out?" I asked. "I haven't seen audition postings anywhere online."

"I didn't post the job description online," Gael said. "I spread the word among our musician friends."

"Keeping out the riffraff," Nathan said.

Gael shrugged. "If you want to put it that way. We still might end up with amateurs."

"Is that why Seth and Julian aren't here?" Nathan asked, referring to our drummer and keyboardist.

"No point wasting their time if these guys don't have what it takes. We'll weed out the ones who can't keep up with us."

Maybe that was a narcissistic way of putting it. Then again, no one had ever accused Gael of having too much humility.

Of course, I couldn't talk. I was just as bad sometimes.

I always said being an artist meant swinging between delusions of grandeur and crippling self-doubt.

"I'm surprised you're taking the lead on this," I told Gael. "You're not normally so responsible."

"My girl has turned me into a better man," he said with pride.

Nathan snorted.

Ever since he'd met Jessie, Gael had been much more reliable. It was odd to think of my older brother and the word reliable in the same sentence, but Jessie really had been a good influence on him.

"Are we ready?" Gael asked us. "Should we get started with the auditions?"

Nate and I nodded.

"Let's bring in the first one." Gael opened the door and waved a guy through.

The one who walked in first had a pale, washed-out look and wide eyes. He could have been a fan of ours, or maybe he always got nervous when auditioning. Gael asked the guy to introduce himself. He gave a long rambling speech about how he'd never been in a band before, but he'd been playing guitar forever and he was really grateful for the chance to audition for us and he hoped he impressed us. The guy didn't stop for air the entire time.

I didn't mind the rambling so much. It was the squirrelly way he darted his gaze between us that bugged me. If he looked this nervous performing in front of three people, how would he be able to play a live show?

He was a good guitarist but he didn't blow me away. Maybe that was the most I could ask for. I couldn't expect total genius from every session guitarist out there. Not everyone could be as talented as my own band members.

I wasn't being biased. I'd taken a while to gather the right group. Nathan, our guitarist, Seth, our drummer, and Julian, our keyboardist, were some of the best musicians to come onto the scene in a long time. I still sometimes wondered why they had chosen to join my band over all their other options.

Whenever we got together and talked about our future, about our ambitions, I was reminded. The fire in their eyes was the same as mine. We were all kindred spirits. World domination was in our blood.

The guy auditioning finished his song and lowered his guitar pick.

"Thanks," Gael said. "We'll let you know."

The guy bobbed his head and ducked out quickly, seeming relieved the ordeal was over.

Gael turned to face us. His expression was less than enthused. "Thoughts?"

"Not in a million years," Nathan said.

"I don't think he's the right guy," I said.

"That's it, then," Gael said. "One down, five to go."

"We don't really have to sit through five more of these, do we?" I asked.

"Only until we find one who fits," Gael said.

I was beginning to dread the process. I didn't want to have to sit here listening to mediocre musicians all day.

It turned out that that wasn't going to be a problem. Gael opened the door to usher in the second guitarist.

My heart stopped in my chest.

Liam Knight walked through the door.

# 4
---

L iam stood in the doorframe, guitar in hand.

He hadn't changed in the few months since I'd seen him. He had the same wavy brown hair, same green eyes, same gorgeous smile. He wore dark denim that looked artfully ripped, as if they had been designed that way. His tight t-shirt was some brand name logo I vaguely recognized.

His eyes scanned the room. They landed on me. He blinked. His gaze flicked back to the guys, then back to me.

"Isn't this the audition for Hairy Tits?" he asked.

"No," Gael said, sounding confused. "This is the audition for Cherry Lips."

Liam pursed his lips. "Huh." He flicked his eyes to me again. "Never mind." He shook his head. "It must have been a mix up. I didn't expect to be auditioning for a band like yours."

"What do you mean, like ours?" Gael spoke up, a frown crossing his lips.

"You're one of the most popular rock bands to debut in the last year," Liam said.

Gael and Nate tilted their chins up smugly. They liked having their egos stroked, my brother most of all.

But it was a lie. Liam didn't know Cherry Lips because we were popular.

He knew Cherry Lips because of me.

"Why are you here?" I asked.

"I'm auditioning."

"That's not what I'm asking."

"You're looking for a temporary session guitarist to join you on tour, aren't you?"

He was serious. Liam was actually here to audition. I didn't think he'd planned this. He had been just as surprised as I had been when he walked through the door.

I couldn't help but remember the way we had left things between us.

And now he was here, in front of me, asking to join my band.

This couldn't be a coincidence.

No. There was no way I was letting this happen.

I owed this man everything. There was no way I'd be able to keep my cool around him. I'd already let my guard down around him too much.

I couldn't let this happen.

"Liam, right?" Gael asked, unaware of my panic. "Why don't you show us what've you've got?"

Liam nodded and hefted his guitar strap over his head. "You guys mind if I play one of your songs?"

"Go ahead." Gael waved his hand easily, indicating for him to start.

The moment he began to play, I knew I was in trouble.

Because Liam was amazing. He played as if he'd been born with a guitar in his hands. His fingers spidered up and down the fretboard easily, perfectly mimicking the way I played.

Although I hated to admit it, he was better than me.

They were going to choose him.

"Thank you," I cut in over the music, long before Liam was done playing the song. "I think we've heard enough."

Liam stopped with a screech. He placed his hands flat on the strings to quiet them and looked at me expectantly.

"Thanks, we'll let you know," I said.

Liam stared at me. He nodded once. He turned to Gael. "Will you be making your decision today?"

"We'll need to discuss with the other members of our band," Gael said. "Would you mind sticking around?"

"No worries," Liam said. "I've got all the time in the world."

Without even looking at me, Liam left the room.

"Him," Gael immediately said. "He's the one."

"Definitely," Nathan nodded.

"We haven't listened to the others yet," I protested.

"Do we need to?" Gael asked. "This guy is even better than Nathan. Sorry, Nate," Gael tossed out.

"Ouch," Nathan said, deadpan. "My wounded ego."

"But—" I started to say.

I had nothing. They were right. No one was going to be better than Liam. If it hadn't been for their breakup, his old band could have rivaled some of the greats. They'd been that good.

"I recognize him from somewhere," Gael mused. "Wasn't he in some band before?"

"*Forever Night*," I said grudgingly.

Gael's eyes lit up. "Right. I know them. They were awesome." He looked to Nathan. "So we're in agreement?" he asked. Nate nodded. Gael looked to me. "Any objections?" he asked.

Yes. A million objections. A war raged within me.

"No," I said, giving up. "You're right. He's the best. But—" I held a hand up before Gael could respond. "We need to make sure he sounds good with the whole band. Seth and Julian have to work well with him."

Gael and Nathan nodded.

"We'll do a jam session," Nathan said. "See how we sound together."

"Agreed," Gael said. "I'll go tell the guy we need him to come back for another round."

"Let me," I said. "I'll tell him."

"Don't scare him away with some sort of, *you-better-not-fuck-up-or-else*, speech," Nathan said.

"I won't scare him away."

And it was true. I didn't want to scare him away.

Because Liam's audition had been awe-inspiring.

That was good for the band. It meant we could hire someone who could keep up with us.

It was bad for me. It meant we were hiring someone who turned my insides into knots. Someone who made me want to just go for it and fuck the consequences.

I had barely been able to resist him before. Would I be able to resist him again? Would I be able to keep myself together if I had to work with him, day in and day out, as we rehearsed for the tour?

I didn't know if I had the strength. The connection between Liam and I had been strong. Stronger than anything I'd felt since...

No. There was no way anything was going to happen between us. I would make sure of that. I would state my boundaries firmly and clearly.

I'd already let myself open up once before. I'd let myself become vulnerable. I wasn't going to make that mistake again.

I heard a familiar voice call out.

"Hey, Cherry Lips."

That was beginning to become a habit of his.

"If you're going to be in the band, you can't keep calling me that," I said.

Liam's eyes lit up. I tried to keep my face impassive.

"Your audition was impressive," I said.

"Did you doubt it would be anything less?" he asked.

I couldn't help but laugh inside. Liam's ego rivaled my band's.

"Did you really not know who you were auditioning for?" I asked him.

"My manager said the name of the band was *Hairy Tits*."

"I can see how he might've gotten confused."

"If I'd known it was your band..." he trailed off.

"You would have auditioned anyway?" I said, filling in for him.

A slow smile crossed his face.

"I definitely would've thought about it," he said.

"You didn't do this just to get close to me?" I asked.

"No." He slowly eyed me up and down. "Can't say I mind the perk, though."

His gaze lingered on my legs, on the skin exposed between the hem of my leather skirt and the tops of my knee-high boots. My stomach muscles clenched at the heat in his eyes.

His eyes snapped back to mine. "Does that mean I got it?"

"We want you to come back and play a few songs with the rest of the band. Make sure we all mesh. But if all goes well..." I took a deep breath in. "Yeah. You got it."

A triumphant look crossed his face.

"With a few caveats," I hastily added.

He turned solemn, looking at me expectantly.

"Laying down the ground rules?" he asked. "Let me guess. Rule number one: no dating within the band."

I nodded. "Band members being in relationships with each other never turns out well. I could go through a list of bands as examples if you like."

A predatory grin crossed Liam's face. "But I'm not in your band," he said. "I'm just filling in temporarily."

My heart thumped a heavy beat in my chest.

"Do you think that makes a difference?" I asked.

He shrugged easily.

"There's no risk of anything going wrong long term," he said, studying me. "You know just as well as I do there's something between us."

I pressed my lips together and looked away. He stepped close. He tipped my chin back towards him with one finger. I glanced into his eyes as they met mine, a bright green.

"I would really like to work with your band," he said, "but I'm not sure I can agree to your demand."

He took another step towards me. I took a step back. I hit the wall. There was nowhere to go. Liam leaned in. The masculine scent, that same woodsy smell that had so overwhelmed my senses that night in the club, washed over me. The heady scent turned me dizzy.

What was I doing, saying no to him? This was the first time I'd felt anything for another man since...

I shook my head internally.

This was such a bad idea.

I stared into Liam's eyes. He leaned forward, his face getting closer to mine. My lips parted unconsciously. His eyes fixated on my mouth. If I didn't do something, he was going to...

Liam flicked his eyes to mine, studying me. He pulled back. I let out a breath of air with a silent whoosh.

"I know your band members convinced you to hire me," he said. "There's no way you would have agreed to let me in the band if they hadn't pressured you. You're too—" he cut himself off.

"What?" I demanded. "What were you going to say?"

"You're too much of narcissist to allow someone who's better than you in the band." He laughed as I narrowed my eyes at him. "But if your bandmates have made the decision then I guess you're stuck with me, aren't you?"

"Don't forget about my rule," I warned. "We keep this professional."

"What if I also have a rule?" he asked.

"What would that be?" I asked.

"I always get what I want." His eyes flashed with wicked heat. "And I want you."

The glint in Liam's eyes, the deep rumble of his voice, was enough to send warmth flooding my system.

It was one thing to know there was an attraction between Liam and I. It was a completely different thing to realize he wasn't going to give up his pursuit.

"I'm not going to give in that easily," I told him.

"I don't expect it to be easy," he said with a crooked smile.

The butterflies in my stomach returned. I opened my mouth but nothing came out.

Liam backed away, releasing me from his hypnotic stare.

"So if I've got the part, I suppose that means I need to meet my new band members?" Liam asked.

"Our drummer and keyboardist aren't here today," I said. "We'll have you come back and meet them in a few days."

"I can be patient," he said.

The double meaning wasn't lost on me.

"You might as well take off now," I said. "I'll call you when we've got a date and time." I held out my phone for him to enter his details into my contacts.

"So this is all just an excuse to get my number?" His eyes twinkled as he thumbed the screen rapidly.

I grabbed my phone back the instant he was done. "I need to go tell the others they didn't make the cut."

"Let them down gently," Liam called out.

I stalked away. I needed to get away from him, to gather my thoughts and catch my breath.

Liam turned me upside down and no doubt took great pleasure in that knowledge.

I took long strides, not looking back. I knew that grin on his lips would still be there. He knew I was running away.

So what if I was? If Liam was going to push my boundaries, the only way I could survive was by putting distance between us.

Figuratively and literally.

## 5

When I walked into the rehearsal room on the day of our jam session, Liam was already chatting with the guys. He must've been telling some sort of joke or funny anecdote because Gael, Nathan and Seth were laughing. I thought I even caught a twitch of Julian's lips.

Liam eyed me as I walked carefully through the door.

"So this is the new band," he said, gesturing to the group of us.

"For now," I said. "You're only here for the tour. This is a temporary situation."

Gael shot me a look, as if to say *don't be so rude.*

"So is it true you were the founder of *Forever Night?*" Seth asked, his hazel eyes lighting up. He was practically vibrating with excitement. I had to wonder if he'd been a fan.

Liam's eyebrow twitched ever so slightly. The corners of his lips turned down. His expression soon smoothed out.

"Yeah, that was me." He didn't elaborate any further.

"So why did you guys break up?" Seth continued.

"Creative differences."

"Why don't you just start another band? Why just work as a session guitarist?"

Liam turned to me, ignoring Seth's question. "We should get started, shouldn't we?" he asked. "If we're going on tour soon, I'll have to learn all your songs and figure out how best to work with our different performance styles." He turned to Julian next. "You said you could provide me with sheet music?"

Julian gave a sharp nod. His dark hair fell over his eyes and cheeks. He went back to fiddling with Seth's drumsticks, no doubt eager to end the small talk and get started.

I hesitated in the doorway.

For now, Liam was keeping things professional. Maybe that was because we were in front of the guys, and he wanted to keep this — whatever this was — between the two of us.

He knew Gael was my brother. He would no doubt want to keep his advances a secret. The stereotypical protective older brother was a stereotype for a reason. I'd lost count of the number of guys Gael had almost punched in the face for trying to hit on me.

"Are you familiar with many of our songs?" my brother asked.

Liam nodded. "I know *Nineteen* and *Kneel Before Us* pretty well. Why don't we start with those to get us warmed up? Then we can move on to the songs I don't know."

I was impressed Liam knew any of our songs. He hadn't expected to audition for Cherry Lips, so he couldn't have prepared ahead of time. Maybe he really did like my band and didn't just pay attention to us because of me.

The guys gathered their instruments and got into place. I grabbed my microphone and put it in the stand. The atmosphere in the room turned tense, filled with nervous expectation.

Liam was good but we didn't know how he would mesh with the rest of us. Each band had its own unique dynamic. Bringing a new person into the mix always risked ruining that. That was one of the reasons why I'd been so reluctant to hire a temporary guitarist.

I shouldn't have worried. The instant the song began, Nathan and Liam wailed on their guitars in unison, perfectly complementing Gael's heavy bass. Seth pounded on his drums, keeping the band in time, as Julian joined in with the keyboard. As I sang the first lines of the song, the music vibrating throughout the room was in perfect harmony.

By the time I finished singing the first verse, our muscles relaxed and the tension melted away. It was early in the game and things were already going well.

The lyrics flowed from my lips easily. I knew this song even better than I knew my own brother. It was one of the first Cherry Lips songs I'd ever worked on.

One of the first I'd written after...

One of the first I'd written about how...

I dug my nails into my palms, refusing to dwell on those thoughts.

This song usually brought up a lot of unwanted emotions. I'd considered dropping it from our set list once we had enough songs for a full concert, but the audience loved it. Gael refused to let me cut it.

The words were painful. The lyrics used to dredge up awful memories. Memories of what I'd lost.

But after singing this song for so long, I had made new memories. Memories of me on stage with my band, cheering and chanting fans gathered around us. The lyrics no longer held as much heartache as they once did.

As the song wound down, I flicked my gaze to Liam, sensing his eyes on me. His head was cocked to the side, studying me closely with a concerned look on his face.

Without quite realizing it, the beginnings of tears had begun to gather along my lash line, turning my eyes shiny and glassy. Liam noticed.

I quickly turned my head to the front, focusing on the pretend audience in front of me.

Maybe I wasn't as unaffected by the lyrics as I liked to pretend. Showing emotion on stage wasn't a bad thing. It meant you were dedicated to the music. As long as I didn't let the tears fall, I could manage the feelings the music brought up.

The song came to a close. We put our instruments down.

"That was awesome," Seth said. "We completely rocked."

"Seems like we made a good choice," Nathan said. "We should go celebrate after. Drinks?"

"As if you ever need an excuse to go drinking," Seth laughed.

Gael was oddly quiet, staring at me.

If Liam had noticed my emotional reaction, there was no doubt in my mind Gael had as well.

My brother tilted his head toward me.

*You okay?* he mouthed.

I nodded sharply.

I didn't know why that song had affected me more today than it usually did.

"We were pretty good," I said out loud, "but pretty good won't satisfy our fans. We need to be fantastic."

I expected Liam to get offended with a blow to his ego like that. But he just nodded.

"We'll work at this until we're one hundred percent satisfied," Liam said. "I'm not afraid to put in some hard work."

"We'll be at it night and day," Gael warned. "This girl's a harsh task mistress."

Liam's eyes fell on me. "I have no problem with that."

The wicked smile playing on his lips was for me alone. My cheeks flushed pink. I looked away and busied myself with the cords and amps, not wanting the other guys to see me flustered.

If this was how I reacted to Liam when we were focused on playing and surrounded by my bandmates, I had no idea how I'd be able to keep myself together if he ever got me alone.

I would just have to make sure that never happened.

But from the determined look in Liam's eyes, I had a feeling that was going to be much more difficult than I thought.

## 6

After hours of practice, we left to go drinking. We were able to get into a club with special VIP access because I knew some people.

To say I had connections in the industry would be an odd way of putting it. I had a friend who was in a band that hit it big. Morris and I had been friends since we were kids, way back when Harper and I had first met.

I paused.

I'd actually said Harper's name out loud.

Or more like, I'd thought half his name. He always went by his last name, even though his first name was Jason. He'd been named after his deadbeat dad and wanted nothing to do with him. So even with me, he had always just been Harper.

And I'd thought his name. That was one of the first times in a long time I'd been able to make myself say his name to myself like that.

A sharp stab of pain, so familiar to me, shot through my chest.

"Hey. You okay?" Liam murmured quietly.

We were all piled into a cab on our way to the club. I was sitting next to Liam. I tried to maneuver myself to the far end of the vehicle, but Liam somehow slipped past the others to settle himself by my side.

The tips of his fingers brushed against the back of my hand as they rested on the leather seat. He looked to me with concerned eyes.

I made my lips curl upward, the closest to a smile I could force myself to make.

"I'm fine," I murmured back. I turned my head to stare out the window without another word.

Great, I was imitating Julian now.

"So what's with this VIP thing?" Liam asked the others, seeming content to let me keep to myself.

"We've got some hotshot friends," Gael said. "It gets us access to a special lounge on the second floor. We'll have privacy and space for just ourselves."

"We won't have to worry about hordes of fangirls flocking to us," Seth added.

"Since when do fangirls flock to you?" Nathan joked.

Seth made a face at him. "I get just as many girls as you, asshole."

Being the youngest, Seth often protested he was just as much of a sex god as the others. He had that kind of earnest enthusiasm that made you just want to ruffle his hair.

"You can stay in the lounge," Nathan told Gael. "I'm going to be on the dance floor with all those chicks you're not allowed to touch anymore."

When we arrived at the club, we took the back entrance that allowed us to reach the second floor directly, skipping the line and crowds.

Liam looked impressed when the bodyguard nodded and waved us through without more than a second glance. This was our usual place and he knew us by sight.

The private lounge had glass walls, so we could see the rest of the club, including the dance floor and small stage. The club was often booked for live performances. We'd performed here ourselves a few times, even.

"This is pretty swanky," Liam said.

"Your band must've played here a few times," I said.

"We never got special access to the private lounge like you guys." He nodded his head approvingly. "You really have hit the big leagues."

"Hell yeah we have," Gael said with a smug grin. "And you know what a private lounge comes with? Private servers." He gestured to the lounge entrance with his chin. One of the bartenders was there, ready to take our drink orders.

The guys each ordered rounds of beer. I thought about ordering a drink, but I wanted to stay clearheaded tonight, especially with the way Liam was staring at me.

"Just a seltzer water with lime for now," I said.

The bartender jotted down a note and looked to Liam, waiting for his order.

"You have twelve year Highland Park?" he asked.

I didn't know much about drinks, but I figured it was some top shelf stuff. I had to wonder how much money he had made with his old band.

"I've learned to enjoy the finer things in life." Liam winked. "I'm getting too old to drink cheap swill."

"Too old?" I said. "You can't be that much older than me."

"When you've been in the industry as long as I have and seen the things I've seen, it makes you grow grey hairs real fast," he told me.

"You've been doing music for a while?" I asked.

Despite myself, I was curious about Liam. That first time I'd met him, years ago, when he'd given me the idea for my band's name, he'd already been in the music scene. I'd just been starting out. Back then, the idea of being in a real band was simply an overly ambitious idea me and my brother had.

"My dad bought me my first guitar when I was twelve," he said. "I've been in bands since I was thirteen. Played my first concert at fourteen. Got my first fangirls and groupies at fifteen."

"Of course that's the metric you measure things by," I said. "Typical cocky rock star. All you care about is how many girls you can score with."

"You wound me," Liam said. "I care about the music just as much as you."

"If that's true, why did you quit your band and decide to go for a temporary position?"

His eyes turned dark.

"Like I said," he shrugged, flicking his gaze away from mine. "Creative differences."

That was a copout if I'd ever heard one, but I didn't want to push too hard. If I pushed on his past, Liam might feel like he could push on mine. That was a subject I wasn't prepared to touch. Not now.

Maybe not ever.

We settled on a pair of barstools with a high table. I perched on my stool, feet swinging, toes just barely touching the ground. The rest of my band seemed content to do their own thing for now, laughing and drinking and talking shit with each other the way guys always did.

"I'm surprised the other guys aren't pestering you with a million questions," I said.

"I asked them to give me a minute alone with you."

I shot Liam a look of disbelief.

"This isn't a come on." He held his hand up, palms out, as if in surrender. "You're the leader of this band. I want to find out more about the gig I just signed up for."

"What do you want to know?" I asked.

"Why exactly are you hiring a temporary session guitarist?" he asked with tilt of his head.

I exhaled deeply, annoyed that was his first question. I didn't want him to think less of me. I didn't want him to think I couldn't hack it. The other guys already worried too much about me. I didn't need that from Liam as well.

"It's nothing big," I said. "I'm perfectly happy to continue singing and playing guitar at the same time. My wrists just act up sometimes."

"You're overexerting yourself?" Liam guessed.

"I do tend to put one hundred and ten percent into my performances."

"But why a temporary guitarist?" he asked.

"My band and I already have a good thing going," I said. "We have a good rhythm. I don't need someone new coming in and ruining that. I'm sure you get what I mean. Bandmates reach a certain equilibrium with each other. You've worked with each other, you've grown up together. You've been through so much. It's always difficult to add a new person into that mix and have things stay the same. It's like a family."

"I do get that," he said, casting his eyes down.

The bartender returned with our drinks and handed them to us. I supposed I could have ordered something fancy and non-alcoholic but I didn't feel in the mood for some sugary sweet mocktail.

Liam took a sip. He eyed me over the rim of his glass.

"Have you been working with the other guys for long?" he asked.

"My brother and I have been playing together since we were teenagers," I said. "I've met the other guys along the way. I'd immediately known they were special. Everything kind of fell into place. All the pieces just fit together like a puzzle. I'm sure you've experienced the same thing with your other band members?"

He nodded shortly.

"Yeah. We used to have a great thing going." Liam took a quick sip of his drink. "So you and the guys are close?"

"They're like my brothers," I said. "We've been through a lot together. There's nothing I wouldn't do for them and nothing they wouldn't do for me."

"That's pretty great that you feel like your band is part of your family." Liam looked down at his drink, staring into it as if it held the answers to the universe. I waited for him to continue, but he didn't.

Seth came over and draped himself over my shoulders, resting his chin on the top of my head.

"What are you two doing sitting here all by yourselves?" he asked.

I tugged him down to poke him in the nose with my index finger. "We're talking business. You know, that stuff you always ignore?"

"You should join in on the fun," he said. "We're going to start a game of Poker Face."

"We'll be right over," I said.

"If you lose, I'm going to make your punishment even worse than last time." Seth grinned and pressed a kiss to the top of my head.

I blanched. I didn't think it was possible for anything to be worse than the shot he'd made me the last time we'd been in this club.

Seth made two fake finger-guns with his hands as he bounced off. He pointed them at me with a cheeky grin, as he was going to shoot me dead with whatever concoction he came up with.

I turned back to Liam with a laugh.

"Looks like we're going to have to join the party after all," I said.

"I thought you said they were like your brothers," he said. "Kid seemed pretty touchy-feely with you."

"He's like that with everyone. Why, are you worried you're horning in on someone else's territory?" I asked playfully. "Maybe I should have said I'm with Seth. Maybe that would stop you from coming on to me."

"Nothing in the world will keep me from coming on to you," Liam said. A slow grin crossed his face. "You're just too cute and sexy for me to resist."

"Use the C word to describe me again and I'm going to kick you in the nuts with my boots."

Liam laughed, not deterred in the slightest.

"Let's not join them yet," he said. "I want to talk some more shop. Let's go somewhere quieter."

Somewhere quieter. Was that his way of trying to get me alone?

I should have been alarmed. And a part of me was alarmed.

But despite my better instincts, I wanted to get to know him more.

Liam stood and took my hand with a gentle touch. The tips of his fingers against my wrist made my chest squeeze. His good-natured smile made my stomach flutter.

I didn't want to give in to him, but he was making it damn hard for me. Every moment I spent with him made my reasons for resisting seem less and less important.

That should have freaked me out.

That should have been the moment I shut him down and ran away.

Instead, the thought was almost freeing.

The feelings I'd experienced since meeting Liam had been long forgotten, but I was enjoying their return.

As much as it scared me, being around Liam was liberating in a way that I hadn't felt in a long time.

## 7

L iam held on to my hand as he led me to one of the sofas on the far side of the private lounge.

"You really do want to get me alone," I only half-joked.

"Just want some privacy," he said.

All my senses tingled.

"Don't worry, I'm not going to put the moves on you," he said.

A small, traitorous part of me felt a sting of disappointment.

"I wanted to talk to you about the details of the tour," he continued.

We took our seats on a sofa. I sat in the corner. Liam sat in the middle next to me.

"What do you want to know?" I asked him.

"When exactly do we start? Which cities will we be playing in? Do you have the set list confirmed yet?"

He peppered me with question after question. Maybe he really did want to talk shop.

"You really just want to know about the set list?" I asked.

He nodded. "I need to make sure I know all the songs before our first show."

"Most of them will be from our new album," I warned. "We won't be doing a lot of our old indie stuff. That's mostly what you know, right?"

"Good thing I'm a quick learner," Liam quipped.

"You better be. We've got more than a dozen new songs for you to memorize."

That familiar heated smirk crept across his lips. Liam shifted closer to me on the sofa.

"I suppose we'll have to work very closely together, won't we?" he said.

I braced myself against the cushions. "You ever heard of a thing called personal space?"

"I've heard of it." That smirk didn't falter.

"I thought you wanted to talk about work."

"We did," he said. "Now it's time to get to know one another."

"You've been following my career," I said. "You should already know everything about me."

"I don't want to know about Cerise, lead singer of Cherry Lips," he said. "I want to know about Cerise, the girl who choked on her water the first time she laid eyes on me."

I pressed my lips together firmly at the hint of laughter in his eyes. "It's not my fault you appeared out of nowhere like a ghost."

"Don't lie," he said. "You were mesmerized by my raw sex appeal, weren't you?"

I suppressed a snort of laughter. "Raw sex appeal? You really do think highly of yourself."

He shrugged easily. "I saw you eyeing me."

"I did," I agreed. "I distinctly remember thinking you were cute."

Liam looked taken aback. "Cute?"

I nodded. He grimaced.

"So you don't like the C word any more than I do?" I asked.

"I'm not cute," he said. "That kid Seth is cute. I'm a rock and roll sex god."

I couldn't help but laugh out loud.

Liam placed one hand on my knee. The laughter cut off. My stomach muscles clenched.

"Wait until you see me on stage with my leather pants and eyeliner," he promised. "You'll turn into one of those fangirls, swooning over me."

I'd almost fallen into fangirl swoons one too many times around this man already. He didn't need any help.

"I've been around self-professed rock gods for years," I forced myself to say calmly. "Leather and guyliner do nothing for me."

"So you go for the straight-laced type?" He raised an amused eyebrow. "Khaki pants and polo shirts?"

Liam chuckled at the face I made.

"So you don't go for straight-laced and you don't go for rock gods," he mused. "Who exactly do you go for, then?"

"Is there a reason why you're fixated on who's my type?"

He leaned back casually into the sofa stretching his long legs out. "Maybe I just want to know what kind of chance I have."

"Zero," I countered immediately. "I don't date band members."

"I'm not a band member," he reminded me. "This is just temporary. I'm not going to join Cherry Lips."

He shifted closer. His thigh pressed to mine. The rough fabric of his jeans scratched the bare skin exposed by my skirt. The heat of his thigh spread even through the dark denim. I inhaled a quick breath. His woodsy scent filled my nose. Blood flowed to my cheeks.

Damn. This happened every time that man got close to me. I'd never blushed this many times in one day. If I didn't get a hold of myself, Liam was going to think I was a schoolgirl with a crush.

I tried to scoot away. I was pressed against the cushion. I couldn't go any farther. I hoped Liam couldn't see my red, flushed face in the darkness of the club.

My head swam. He smelled so good. It was unfair. I'd always had a weakness for guys with that rich, earthy smell. Harper had always smelled like that. He'd take me in his arms and I'd be surrounded by a soothing, grounding feeling. I'd forgotten about that. It had been so long since...

My breath stuttered in my lungs.

Liam looked at me, concerned.

"You okay?" he asked.

"Yeah."

Liam took my hand. My nails were pressed deep into the skin. He took my fingers and loosened them one by one. He ran his fingertips along the small half-moon indentations left behind on my palm.

"Was it something I said?" He quirked an inquisitive smile.

"No. Sorry." I pulled my hand back slowly, putting it in my lap. "I just remembered something."

"Seems like it wasn't a very good memory."

I let out a shaky laugh. "No. It was too good."

That was the problem.

"I've got to go," I said shortly.

"Right now?"

I stood, smoothing down my skirt. "I'll see you tomorrow."

"You don't need to run," he said quietly.

"I'm not—"

Liam could see right through me. I couldn't lie. I was running.

"Be at the studio by nine," was all I said. "We practice every day until five."

"Cerise..." Liam started to say.

"If my brother asks, tell him I bailed early."

With quick steps I hurried out of the VIP lounge, making a beeline for the exit. A blast of fresh air hit me the moment I stepped through the door. I inhaled slowly. The cool night breeze helped steady my swirling head.

As I waited to hail a cab, I rubbed at the indentations on my palm, soothing them. I felt the phantom touch of Liam's fingers against my skin. I could still smell that warm, masculine scent of his, as if it were imprinted on my brain.

I knew choosing Liam as my guitarist was a bad idea. I hadn't known how bad. It was one thing to be attracted to someone I knew I had to stay away from. It was another thing entirely when that person kept on reminding me of what I'd lost.

I thought I'd set aside those memories, those emotions, years ago. If I hadn't exactly dealt with them, I'd at least been able to push past them and move on.

But being around Liam was stirring up a whole mess of stuff I didn't want to deal with. Not when I was so close to finally getting everything I'd dreamed of. I couldn't fall apart now.

I was Cerise Moreau, lead singer of Cherry Lips. I was strong. I was fierce.

I refused to let grief overtake me again.

## 8

I spent the night upset with myself and dreaded walking into the studio the next day after I ran out of the club.

After I ran away from Liam.

I didn't want to show my face. I should have had more control over myself, over my reactions. That familiar smell shouldn't have pushed me over the edge like that. It was distressing. I'd spent years trying to get over what had happened. I *was* over it.

I spent the night upset with myself and vowing to keep it together next time I saw Liam.

My resolve almost went out the window when he walked into the studio.

Liam was wearing a tight, black t-shirt, showing off his inked muscular arms. If I wasn't mistaken, he was also wearing the faintest hint of eyeliner.

Damn. That man was calling my bluff, wasn't he?

I stood frozen in the doorway.

Liam was talking with Seth. He didn't notice me for the first few seconds. He turned his head and caught me staring at him. I thought he would give me a knowing look, the kind that said *I'm-hot-and-you-know-it*. Instead, his eyes were only filled with concern.

That was almost worse. My bandmates already worried about me too much. I didn't need the same from Liam.

"Is everyone here?" I asked as I walked in.

"Just missing Gael," Seth said.

"He's probably still in bed with Jessie," Nathan smirked. "You took off early. Did you find some man-candy last night?"

My eyes flicked to Liam quickly without input from my brain. The look of concern in his eyes was replaced with a smug tilt of his chin, no doubt thinking that he was the man-candy Nathan was referring to.

"Let's get started without Gael," I said. "We've got to get Liam caught up with our songs. We don't have time to mess around."

"I agree," Liam said. "If we're going to be ready in time, we'll need to use every minute we have."

We had only just begun to set up our instruments when Gael breezed in, looking pleased with himself.

"Sorry I'm late," he said, sounding completely unrepentant. "Jessie and I—"

"Stop," I said. "I don't need to hear what you and your girlfriend were getting up to this morning."

Gael faked an affronted look. "I would never," he said. "A gentleman doesn't kiss and tell."

"Gentleman?" Nathan looked around the room with an exaggerated swing of his head back and forth. "I don't see a gentleman around here."

Gael just laughed, slinging his bass guitar strap around his shoulder.

"Let's start with one of the newer songs," I suggested.

The guys agreed. I shuffled through our folder of sheet music and handed the correct piece to Liam.

"Think you can play this on the fly?" I asked him.

"I'm insulted you would doubt my ability."

When we started playing, Liam was perfectly capable of keeping up with us. He was almost so good I had to wonder if he'd spent some time listening to our newer stuff. But he'd only auditioned less than a week ago. He wouldn't have had enough time.

Liam really was just that good. As much as I thought I'd personally made a mistake in hiring him, I couldn't deny that having this man in my band could only benefit us. We played through several songs without a hitch.

Maybe this would be easier than I thought. With Liam's talent, I had no doubt that we would be ready for our tour on time.

After a few hours, we took a break. I left the rehearsal room to get a bottle of water from the vending machine down the hall. I was halfway there before I noticed Liam following me.

I turned around in the middle of the hallway to confront him.

"If you're going to try and make me talk about last night..." I began to say.

Liam cut me off with a shake of his head. "If you don't want to talk about last night, you don't have to," he said. "I want to suggest an idea for the set list."

"What did you have in mind?" I asked "I've thought hard about our set list and carefully chosen each song."

"What if instead of starting with *Kneel Before Us*, we start with *Nineteen*?" he asked.

My shoulders immediately tensed. "We always start with *Kneel Before Us*."

Liam blinked at my strong reply.

"Any particular reason why?" he asked.

"It's a fan favorite," I said. "It gets the crowd pumped up."

Liam nodded. "Exactly," he said. "Your fans love the song. It's one of your earliest hits. That's why I think it would be a great idea to end with that instead of starting with it. Leave them on a high note, you know?"

I pressed my lips together firmly. It wasn't an awful suggestion, but something about Liam's confident tone made me bristle.

"We end with *Nineteen* because it has that emotional impact," I said.

Liam looked at me skeptically. "Ending with that song is kind of a downer, isn't it?" he said.

My eyes narrowed at his tone. Liam didn't know anything about that song. He didn't know anything about the meaning behind it, the significance of it.

"I think I know my fans better than you," I said.

"Maybe you're just too close to it," Liam suggested. "There's nothing wrong with an outside perspective."

A shivery coil of darkness slowly unfolded in my stomach. Of course I was close to the song. I'd composed it. I'd written it about—

I slammed shut the mental door keeping my memories at bay.

"Why don't you leave the creative decisions to me?" I said. "I didn't hire you for your input. I hired you to back me up on guitar. That's it."

"Are you always this resistant to new ideas?" Liam asked.

"When it comes from people who don't know anything about my band, yes." I crossed my arms over my chest.

I didn't know why I was so against the idea of switching songs. There was just something about the way Liam had suggested it. As if he knew more than me.

Maybe he did.

Maybe I was too close to the situation.

But now that my hackles were raised, I wasn't inclined to listen to him. I was being stubborn, and I knew it, but I couldn't make myself stop. The idea that someone might know my songs better than me, that he might know my fans better than me, was infuriating. The fact that it came from Liam—someone that I already felt vulnerable around—made it worse.

"We need to get back to rehearsal," I said. "The others must be getting impatient."

"Alright," he said. "I'll go back to being your silent backup guitarist. No more suggestions from me."

If it had been anyone else, I would have said the tone of his voice was sarcastic. Maybe that was just me projecting. I knew he thought I was being unreasonable.

Some part of me deep down agreed with him, but I'd already let my guard down around this man too many times. If I started giving in to him, even if it was just a song selection idea, I might start to give in in other ways.

I turned on my heel and as I walked back to the rehearsal room.

I felt Liam's eyes on me the entire way.

# 9

I had already made it back to the studio when I realized I'd never gotten a bottle of water. With Liam at my back, it was too embarrassing to turn around and backtrack. I'd just have to wait until our next break.

When I made it back to the music room I found Gael and Nathan huddled together, staring down at their phones with frowns on their faces.

"Bad news?" I asked, dread filling my chest.

Gael's head shot up, slightly panicked look in his eyes. "No," he lied.

I immediately pulled out my phone and checked my messages.

"Oh shit," I murmured, staring down at the newest email from the label's marketing department. All thoughts of Liam fled.

Nathan and Gael looked at me cautiously, as if waiting for an outburst. My heart sunk as I scrolled past the latest comments on a local music blog's latest post.

A cold nudge against my fingers startled me. Liam placed a bottle of water in my hand.

"Don't want you to strain your voice," he said with an imperceptible smile.

I took it from him gingerly with a muttered thanks before looking back at my phone.

"What is it?" Liam asked, noticing the tension in the room.

"It's just a bad review," my brother said. "Not the end of the world."

But it wasn't the review that had bile rising in my throat.

"They're trashing us in the comments," I told Liam. "Someone's saying our last performance was one of the worst they'd ever seen. That I—" I cut myself off, nausea taking root in my gut. I felt sick, queasy — and above all, angry.

"Cerise?" Liam prompted when I failed to speak. "What's wrong?"

I swallowed around the lump in my throat. I didn't even want to say it out loud. I turned my phone around and showed it to him.

Liam winced.

"Shit," he cursed. "You shouldn't read things like this. Don't listen to those kinds of people."

The commenter on the blog post had written that the only reason Cherry Lips got a record contract must have been because I'd—

And at this part, the anger in my chest turned into pure rage.

—because I'd fucked one of the music execs.

"Why would somebody say something like that?" I paced back and forth furiously. "Why would somebody write that for everyone else to see? It's horrible and disgusting and—" The more I continued speaking, the faster and faster the words tumbled from my mouth.

"No one would accuse any of you guys of sleeping your way to the top," I spat. "It's revolting sexist bullshit and—"

"Cerise." Liam placed a hand on my shoulder. I cut off my rambling with a snap of my jaw. His hand was soothing as it ran up and down my arm. It was similar to our first meeting, when he had touched me in the artist lounge. This time there was nothing sensual about the motion. It was meant purely for comfort.

My heartbeat began to slow with every stroke of his palm.

"Ignore those people," Liam told me. "They're just internet trolls. They're jealous of your success. If they could do what you do, they'd be the ones up on stage and not the ones leaving shitty comments on some stupid blog. Don't pay attention to them."

"But—"

"I understand wanting to know what people are saying about you, but it's only going to act as a distraction," he said.

A distraction.

Liam was right. It was a distraction.

And maybe it was a bad distraction, getting in the way of my work.

But maybe, angsting about what other people were saying was better than angsting over all the shit I'd been trying to suppress. It was easier. If I kept all my focus outward, I didn't have to deal with the creeping darkness threatening to overtake me at the very thought of Har—

"I want you to promise me something," Liam said, interrupting my thoughts.

The warmth of his touch helped calm me. Some of the anxiety that manifested itself as tightness in my chest slowly began to ease.

"Promise you what?" I asked.

"Don't go on the Internet for the next few weeks," Liam said.

I let out a choked snort. "What century are you living in?" I asked him.

"I'm not saying cut yourself off completely, but the only thing you should be worrying about is this tour. If you want us to be ready in time, you need to focus on what's important... like me," he said with a cheeky grin.

"You think you're the most important thing I should be paying attention to? You really do have an overactive ego."

I knew Liam was just trying to distract me and keep the rumor off of my mind. As annoyed and upset as I had been with him before, and as much as I had pushed him away, I had to be grateful that he had found a way to calm me down. My tensed muscles had begun to wind down, and my nails were no longer biting into my skin.

"Thanks," I murmured quietly.

Liam gave me one last pat on my back before standing.

"Why don't we continue practice?" Liam said.

"Sounds good to me," Nathan said. He was eyeing Liam and I curiously.

I hated that I'd gotten so upset, but it was almost worse that the guys had watched Liam soothe me like an upset child. I'd been so resolved to keep it together around him, especially when we were in front of the others. At least I could reassure myself that I hadn't been swooning over Liam like some fourteen-year-old girl. It was a small favor, but I would take it. The last thing I needed was for my band members to know I had this stupid, silly crush on my new guitarist.

I'd worked so hard to prove myself in the music industry. Being a girl in a rock band was never going to be easy. I had to show I could hack it. I had to be a professional. I didn't want to risk losing all of the respect I'd built up.

Liam slung his guitar strap over his shoulder and nodded his head to me.

"You ready to start?" he asked.

I stood up from the sofa and grabbed my microphone.

"I'm ready," I said. "I'm not going to let stuff like this keep on bothering me."

Even if that wasn't quite true, at least I could pretend.

I didn't know if I'd be able to keep myself from reading trashy blog rumors, but the memory of Liam's palm on my bare skin — the memory of his hands, of his fingers, entwined with mine — made me want to keep my promise.

# 10

Five o'clock rolled around and we put our instruments away for the day.

"I might stay a while longer to try and catch up," Liam said. "If that's cool with you guys."

The others looked impressed at his dedication. I was impressed, too, until I gathered my stuff and started to follow the others out the door. That's when Liam reached out and took my arm gently in his hand.

"Would you mind staying a bit longer to help me out?" he asked.

My suspicions immediately arose. This could have been just another one of his excuses to get me alone.

"I'm having a little trouble with the second chorus on that one song," he said.

I knew which one he meant, because I'd noticed him struggling a bit during rehearsal.

"Sure," I said. "I can stay a little while longer."

True to his word, we did work on the song for the next half hour or so.

I showed him the correct positioning I used on the strings with my fingers. He was a quick learner, just as he'd said. As soon as I showed him how I played the song, he imitated me and picked it up within minutes. Once we'd practiced a handful of times, he seemed satisfied with himself.

"That was the only one I really had trouble with," Liam said. "Thanks for staying."

"No problem," I told him. "If that's all..." I said as I got ready to leave.

"There's just one more thing," Liam said. "Can we talk about what happened earlier?"

I didn't bother playing dumb. "Thank you for helping calm me down."

The memory of that rumor about me sleeping my way to the top...

Just thinking about it made the fury rise in my chest.

"Trust me, I understand how shitty those rumors can be," he said.

"I doubt the things people said about you could be any worse than the things they say about me," I told Liam. "Do you know how hard it is to be a girl in the rock music industry? Do you know the awful things they say about me?"

"I can guess," he said. "I'm not trying to compare or one up you about who had it worse. I'm just saying I get it."

I had to wonder what exactly people had been saying about Liam's old band.

"Do you mind if I ask—" I began hesitantly. "They said shit about you, too?"

Liam shifted his gaze away. He stared out the window, avoiding my eyes.

"They said we'd stolen songs from another band. They said we were all fighting and secretly hated each other. They said we were a fake band put together by our label. They said my guitarist stole my fiancée."

I let out a sharp exhale. "Did he really... ?"

He gave me a crooked smile. "I never had a fiancée."

His voice was tight as he denied it. I had to wonder how close to the truth some of those rumors were.

I didn't want to pry. At least the media had yet to find out about my past or about Harper. That would have been another one for the rumor mill for sure.

Everyone always tried to read angst and pain into my lyrics. Writing songs was cathartic but I didn't need anyone knowing the sordid details behind them. I would have felt too exposed, as if people had access to my inner most secrets.

I was willing to write my feelings out through the music, but I wasn't about to let anyone get closer than that.

Especially Liam Knight.

"I'll try to ignore those rumors," I promised him.

The look in his eyes was soft. Understanding. He placed his hand on my shoulder. His thumb rubbed back and forth along the curve of my neck. My insides tumbled over on themselves.

"If you ever need a distraction..." Liam said with a smirk.

My stomach muscles tensed at that look. I knew exactly what kind of distraction Liam was hinting at. The heat of his palm burned into my skin, warming me from the outside in. A shivery feeling took hold of me.

His bright green eyes stared into mine, a question in his gaze. I parted my lips to speak, not quite sure what I was going to say yet, just knowing that I had to say something or else I would end up giving in to him.

Now that I wasn't so defensive, now that my guard was down, I could see that his song selection idea wasn't that bad of an idea. I shouldn't have shot him down so quickly. I had just been feeling vulnerable.

Too vulnerable.

Exactly like I was feeling right now.

"I don't think that's the kind of distraction I need." I quickly gathered my things and headed to the door, making a hasty exit. "I'll see you at practice tomorrow," I said. As I walked out the door, I turned my head just enough to see the amused look on Liam's face.

I was running again. He knew it. I knew it.

But I couldn't stop my feet from fleeing.

# 11

---

"How did you score this interview again?" Nathan asked Gael.

"I know a guy who knows a guy," my brother replied.

Nathan smacked him in the chest. Gael made an oomph sound.

"No, seriously," Gael said. "Cerise's friend Morris? His bandmate is dating some girl who writes for a magazine. She's offered to interview us before, so I figured now would be a great time to reach out."

The group of us were hanging out in the music studio, waiting for the journalist. We'd tried to rehearse while we waited, but most of us had been too nervous to concentrate.

Well, that wasn't quite true. The others didn't seem fazed at all. I was the one full of nervous energy, jiggling my crossed legs as I sat on the sofa and tapping my nails against the cushions in a staccato rhythm.

This wasn't our first interview, but it was the first since we'd signed on to our label. Small-time music blogs doing a Q and A with some local band after a show was one thing. This was another. This was legit. We were going to talk to an actual journalist who wrote for a real magazine.

"What if she brings up that trash talk?" I spoke up. "That stuff about —" I grimaced, "—about me sleeping my way to the top?"

"I'm sure she won't," Gael reassured me. "She's a professional."

I hoped my brother was right.

It was only a few minutes later when a young woman rapped her knuckles on the door and poked her head in. I instantly recognized her. I'd met Emily once before, earlier in her journalism career. She was smartly dressed in a blouse and knee-length pencil skirt. She held a notebook in one hand and what looked to be a small digital recorder in the other.

Emily scanned the room. When her eyes landed on me she gave me a bright smile.

"Cerise," she said, cheerfully. "It's great to see you again."

I returned her smile, although the corners of my lips twitched nervously. Just because she looked friendly didn't mean she wouldn't ask hard-hitting questions.

Emily did the rounds, shaking hands with the other guys and introducing herself. When she got to Nathan, he flashed her his most winning smile, and opened his mouth, ready to spout some clichéd come on, but she easily side-stepped him to greet Seth and Julian.

When she got to Liam, she blinked in surprise.

"Are you a new member of the band?" she asked. "I thought there were only five of you."

She must have done her homework on Cherry Lips. We hadn't made a formal announcement to the public about Liam's addition to the band for the tour.

"I'm Liam Knight," he said, shaking her hand firmly. "I'm going to be helping out the band as a session guitarist for their upcoming tour."

Emily immediately took out her notebook and scribbled something down.

"Do you want this interview to only be about the original five or will Liam be joining us as well?" she asked.

I looked to my brother. We hadn't discussed whether or not Liam would take part in the interview. It hadn't occurred to me that he wouldn't. Although he'd only just been brought onboard, it somehow felt like he'd been with us forever. Liam fit in so well even after such a short amount of time.

The more I thought about it, the more disconcerting the thought became.

Liam had already wormed himself into my every thought. I didn't know if I was comfortable with him also inserting himself into the band like this, too.

My brother shot me a look and shrugged.

"I'm okay with it," Gael said. "Our fans are going to notice there's a new guy onstage when we start touring. We might as well introduce them to Liam beforehand."

"It'll help us, too," Nathan said. "Liam has his own flock of fans from his old days with *Forever Night*. If we can poach a few of them over to our side, I say we go for it."

"So you're using me for my fame and not my talent, is that it?" Liam asked.

Nathan and Liam grinned at each other — another sign of the easy camaraderie that had developed between him and the guys. I was the only one who acted out of sorts whenever Liam was around.

"As long as you're cool with it?" Liam asked me.

"It's fine."

Like almost everything else when it came to Liam, I didn't really have a reason to say no, aside from the fact that being around him perpetually knocked me off balance.

Emily perched on the arm of a sofa and crossed her legs with a straight back. Her expression turned serious as she flicked on the tape recorder.

"First," she said, "Can we talk about some of your musical influences?"

"I've always been a big fan of the band *I'll Never Say*," I said. "I've always looked up to their female lead singer."

"I've never heard of them," Emily said.

"They're a bit more obscure," I told her. "And they broke up a few years ago. When I heard that they were going their separate ways, I think I moped in my bedroom for a week straight."

"And what about you?" Emily asked the others. "What bands do you guys look up to?"

"You can never go wrong with the big names," Gael said. "Metallica, AC/DC, The Stones."

"Us too," Seth nodded. "Julian's the one who introduced me to rock music, and he's a big fan of the classics."

Emily nodded and jotted down some notes.

"Next question. Can one of you explain the meaning behind the name Cherry Lips?"

I tensed up. I'd been asked this before, and I had a lie ready to go, but this time was different. Liam was in the room. He would know immediately I was making it up. Would he call me on it?

The guys looked at me expectantly. I was always the one who answered this question. I felt Liam's eyes on burning into me.

"My name means cherry in French," I said. "And, as the lead singer, I thought using the word lips was an appropriate choice."

That was the easy answer of course, but Emily just nodded and made another mark on her paper. Liam shifted in his seat with an amused smile but he didn't say anything out loud. He was happy to let the fib go unchallenged. I continued with my explanation.

"Maybe it's kind of a narcissistic thing to do, naming your band after yourself. But I'm not the first artist to do it. I'm sure you can tell I sort of have a theme going." I gestured to my hair with fingers tipped in cherry-red nail polish.

"I had noticed you seem to like that color," Emily laughed. With her curiosity satisfied, she turned the conversation to another topic.

"Cerise," Emily said, turning to me with a determined look. "I want to ask you about something more serious."

My shoulders hunched up to my ears before I forced them to relax. I didn't want to seem on edge. I just had to hope she wasn't going to bring up those awful rumors. If she did, I didn't know if I'd be able to keep calm enough not to embarrass myself.

"Go ahead," I told her.

She leaned forward, as if getting closer to me physically would help her get closer to me in a more personal way.

"Can we touch on what it's like to be a woman in the music industry?" she asked. "I'm sure there are challenges you face that your band members don't, especially considering you're in the rock genre."

That wasn't a bad question to ask. She wasn't bringing up the gossip directly, but she was giving me a way to address the hardships that came with my career choice.

"It's tough," I said. "Truthfully, you're right when you say I have to deal with a lot of stuff my brother and the other guys don't. It's hard to be taken seriously. People always underestimate you, patronize you. You have to work twice as hard at everything. The industry is still male dominated, and it can be really tough as a woman to break into it. That being said," I continued, "there are a lot of female musicians who have come before me who have broken through that glass ceiling. They've paved the way for other girls like me to follow in their footsteps, and I'm eternally grateful for that."

Emily smiled at me and nodded emphatically. "I totally get what you mean," she said. "I experienced something similar as an independent journalist."

The interview continued as Emily quizzed us on the meanings behind our lyrics, the process we went through to write songs, and other questions that had to do with the techniques and nitty-gritty details of our work. There were no mentions of gossip or rumors. She was completely professional, just as Gael had promised me she would be.

And then she said something that made my stomach drop.

"Can you tell me a bit about your love lives?"

# 12

My stomach roiled at Emily's words. Disappointment and not a bit of disgust swept through me. Is that all anyone cared about? Who everyone was sleeping with? It was supposed to be about the music, not about sleazy gossip.

Liam shifted on the sofa and eyed me carefully. I bit my tongue to keep my fit of pique under control. I didn't want to cause an outburst.

But then Emily followed up with a second question and my raised hackles began to lower.

"It must be hard for your loved ones," she said. "Everything is changing so fast. You're getting media attention, you're going to be on tour."

My tensed muscles eased. So it wasn't about tawdry rumors. It was about something deeper. I could understand where she was coming from with a question like that.

"I can jump in and answer," Gael said. "I'm in a serious, committed relationship. And I have to admit it's hard sometimes. But my girlfriend knew what I was from the start."

"And what would that be?" Emily asked with a teasing tone, as if she knew exactly what answer she was going to get.

"A rock star god, that's what." My brother gave a cheeky grin. "And Jessie wasn't impressed by that one bit, let me tell you."

Emily looked to Nathan expectantly. "And you?"

A slow, lazy smile crept across his lips. "I'm still just looking for that one special girl," he drawled.

I nearly snorted. If by *looking*, Nate meant sleeping his way across the city, then he sure was.

"Liam, as the newest member of the group, you've been pretty quiet," Emily said. "Can I ask why you've joined as a session guitarist? I'm sure your fans would love to see you form another band."

Liam's lips pressed together. "I'm just looking for something temporary right now."

"Any thoughts about starting your own after this? Or maybe even joining Cherry Lips full time?"

Liam's face turned pained. "No," he said shortly. "No plans for that."

Emily blinked, taken aback at his curt tone. I was a bit taken aback as well. Liam hadn't shown any interest in joining the band, but I hadn't thought he'd be so completely against the idea.

She changed tracks. "And do you have a special someone waiting at home for you?"

"Not in that sense," Liam replied, leaning back into his chair. "But there's this girl I've been pursuing. I think she's pretty amazing but she keep shutting me down."

My previously relaxed shoulders bunched up.

"That must be different for you," Emily laughed. "I'm sure it's usually the opposite, right?"

"I'm not used to being shot down so quickly and with such force," Liam said. "But she's in the music industry, so I hope we can continue working together closely."

It was like he wanted people to realize he was talking about me. I narrowed my eyes at Liam but he didn't glance my way.

"She sounds feisty," Emily said.

I fought the urge to recoil. Liam just laughed.

"That's a good word to describe her. But she's also beyond talented. Hard working. She's extraordinary, really." His grin faded into a smile as his gaze went soft. "I actually ran into her a couple of times but I suppose the timing wasn't right. We just recently reconnected. I'm hoping this time both of us stick around longer. Or at least long enough to convince her to give me a shot."

"I'm sure there are plenty of girls out there who wouldn't mind giving Liam Knight a chance to woo her," Emily said.

"None of them are her," he said.

If Emily were any less professional, I would have thought she'd faint into a swoon at Liam's declaration.

If I were any less professional, I might have done the same. Liam Knight knew how to lay on the charm.

But the irritation rising in my chest shoved away any thoughts of swooning or wooing. Instead, all I felt was the urge to be sick.

I couldn't understand what the hell Liam was thinking. Couldn't he see how people might put two and two together and figure out he was talking about me? There was no way he could think I'd be okay with that.

"Thanks guys, I think that's all I need." Emily got up and did the rounds again, shaking everyone's hand. When she got to me, she cracked a small smile.

"Thank you for your candid responses," she said. "Would you like me to send you the final draft before it's published? Just to make sure I represent your words correctly?"

"I'd like that, thank you." She probably wouldn't let me veto anything, but at least I'd get a heads up if she were going to release something that would give me heart palpitations.

The minute she left, I followed, intending to get a drink. I needed to get away from Liam before I said something I'd regret.

But of course, I soon heard the footsteps of him following me out the door. I tried to ignore him, but the steps got closer and closer, until I knew he was right behind me. I could practically feel the heat radiating off him.

I whirled around. We were nose to nose. I almost stepped to the side, but something inside me refused to back down. "I'm sorry, did you need something?"

"You running again?" he asked.

"I'm getting a bottle of water."

"Why are you upset?"

"Why do you think?"

He tilted his head at me. "Nothing I said was untrue."

"That's the point." I inhaled deeply, ready to rail at him. I slowly let it out, forcing myself to relax. I was going to have this conversation, calm and collected. "I don't want you insinuating there's something between us."

"I didn't." He quirked a smile. "I insinuated there's nothing between me and the girl I'm pursuing because she keeps rejecting me."

"And why do you think that is?" I asked. "Could it be because the last thing I need is for people to start speculating about who I'm dating? Could it be because the last thing I want is for people to shove me into that shallow celebrity box that makes everyone forget about the music and instead turns me into some sort of sex symbol as if the only thing that matters is how many guys I'm fucking?"

I had to pause as I ran out of breath. So much for calm.

"Is that really what you think is going to happen?" he asked.

"Yes," I said firmly. "And you know exactly what I'm talking about. It's the Taylor Swift effect. She's in the news all the time not because of her latest album, but because she's broken another guy's heart. No one cares about the true meaning of her lyrics; they just try to decipher which ex-boyfriend she's singing about. You think I want that for myself?"

Liam's eyebrows drew down into a frown. "I'm sorry," he said. "I didn't think of it like that."

"Of course you didn't. You're a guy. You don't have to think about these things."

"I was just playing around in the interview. I didn't mean to make things harder on you. I'm sorry," he said again.

The irritation tingling through me began to fade. "Apology accepted."

"But I meant what I said," he continued. "I really do think you're extraordinary. And talented. And hard working."

He had said all that, hadn't he? I'd been so upset at the rest of it, I'd almost forgotten he'd said those words. A faint glow began to take hold in my chest.

"You're amazing," he repeated quietly. "There's something different about you. You've got this fire inside you. This drive. You're going to achieve incredible things."

Liam put a finger on the tip of my chin, tilting my head up. I met his eyes.

"You wonder why I keep pursuing you even though you always shut me down?" he asked. "It's because of that fire. That radiance. You're going to burn like the sun. And I want to catch one of those rays. I want to feel that warmth, even if it's just for a minute."

My breath hitched in my throat.

"You're going to explode like a supernova, Cerise," he said. "And I want to be there to see it."

# 13

I stared at Liam, unblinking, disbelieving. I searched his eyes for any hint of mockery or teasing.

But they were open, sincere.

A sense of wonder ballooned in my chest. Liam really did think all those things about me.

My fingers began to tremble ever so slightly. I pressed my palms against the sides of my hips.

"That's some impressive symbolism," I said, pretending to smooth down my skirt.

Liam raised an eyebrow, as if confused by my statement.

"Sun. Supernova. Rock *star*." I said the words slowly.

"I wasn't trying to make a pun." He cracked a smile. "You're amazing, and soon the whole world is going to know it."

"You're the one who's amazing." The words slipped out of my mouth before I could stop them. A flush crept up my neck and onto my cheeks. "I mean, you're an amazing guitar player, and a great singer. Of course, you know that already."

"I do know that." He examined me closely. "But that's not what you meant, is it?"

Flustered, I looked away.

Liam couldn't have known how much he had motivated me. He couldn't have known how much I'd needed to hear his words back then.

He couldn't have known how important he was to me.

"Why don't you tell me what you really meant?" he asked softly.

"I didn't mean anything," I said quickly. "Just what I said. You're good at what you do."

"I think there's more to it than that." His probing eyes pinned me down, like he was trying to dissect me. Like he was trying to figure me out.

"What you said before. In that interview. About the name of your band."

My heartbeat spiked. "What about it?"

"You lied to that journalist when she asked you how you came up with Cherry Lips."

"No I didn't," I said immediately. "I named the band after myself."

"You named the band after my nickname for you."

Pulse racing, I deflected. "So what if I did? It's catchy."

"Why did you lie about it in the interview?" he persisted.

"Because—"

*Because you moved me.*

*Because you inspired me.*

"Tell me why," he asked again.

"Because you saved me."

The words came out quiet. Quiet, but not weak. Not timid. I forced myself to meet his gaze head on. His eyes were wide, perplexed. I don't know what he had been expecting me to say, but it wasn't that.

"I had almost given up on singing," I said honestly. "I had almost given up on music altogether. But what you said..." I trailed off, trying to remember his exact words. "You asked when I felt the most powerful, like I could take on anything."

"You said it was when you sang." Liam's eyes went soft and unfocused, as if searching his own distant memories. "Then you laughed and said life wasn't a musical."

I placed my hand over my heart. It was beating at a wild pace. "You told me to always be singing in here."

Liam placed his hand over mine. His large palm pressed into the back of my hand. The tips of his fingers brushed the skin of my collarbone. The speed of my pounding heart was alarming.

"Why were you about to give up on music?" he asked. "If you loved singing so much, why stop?"

My heart froze, stuttering in my chest. That lump in my gut, that ever-present swirling dark mass, began to snake its way out of the cage where I kept it locked down.

"I couldn't—" my voice cracked. "I couldn't keep singing after—"

Dark tendrils crawled along my ribcage, slowly inching their way to the very center of my chest.

"I couldn't handle it. I fell apart. I didn't want the reminder of—"

Liam closed his fingers, lacing ours together. "You don't have to talk about it."

I nodded silently. He lowered his head and, bringing our clasped hands to his lips, pecked a soft kiss against my knuckles. I stared at our entwined hands. My nerve endings tingled where our skin touched.

Liam straightened and let go.

"It would be cool if I could take credit for the band's name." His tone was light, breezy. "But if you're okay with people thinking you're just a narcissist, it's fine by me."

A teasing smile played on his lips. I let out a soft snort, relieved that he had changed the subject. Relieved that he wasn't going to push the issue.

I'd only ever told a handful of people about Harper before. Most of the ones who knew what happened were the ones who had been there. Gael. Morris. I'd rarely had to tell the story to anyone. Rarely had to say the words out loud.

I didn't know if I even could without breaking again.

"Lots of musicians name their bands after themselves." I took a few steps back, needing space. Being so close to Liam like this was dangerous. I'd already said more than I should have. More than I'd meant to. I was supposed to be turning him away, not pulling him closer. "Thank you for agreeing to keep the real reason to yourself."

"It's not my place to tell anyone any different."

"So if the subject comes up in an interview again, now you know what to say."

"You want me to take part in more interviews?" he asked. "I thought you'd never let me near another journalist again after today."

"As long as you keep it strictly about the music."

"Hm," he mused playfully. "I don't know if I can do that."

"Liam..." I said with a warning tone.

"I'm serious." He looked determined. "I told you before. I think you're amazing. I want to be a part of that."

"You are," I said firmly. "You're helping out my band."

Liam brushed a strand of hair behind my ear. "That's not what I mean."

He trailed his fingers along my face before cupping my cheek. I exhaled a shaky breath. His gaze flicked to my mouth, eyes turning dark. He drew me closer to him. I found myself leaning forward into his touch.

"You're a star, Cerise," he said. Our lips were a hairsbreadth apart. My chin tipped up unconsciously. "We both are. And we can only burn brighter together."

Liam closed the gap between us and pressed his lips to mine.

I'd thought about kissing Liam. Dreamed of it, even. But now all those steamy fantasies seemed tepid and dull in comparison. As I breathed him in, a rush of heat surged through my body.

When his tongue swiped for entrance my knees nearly fell from under me. I clutched at his shoulders for support. The softness of his lips was a delicious contrast to the firmness of his muscles.

He wrapped an arm around my waist and tugged me closer, shifting until our hips fit neatly together. I melted against him, giving in, opening up, allowing his desire to consume me.

"Been thinking of kissing you for-fucking-ever," he murmured into my mouth.

In response, I fisted a handful of his hair and crushed my lips to his.

He tried to take control of the kiss, cupping the back of my head, tilting my face to the side for a better angle. Our lips worked together, dancing and battling, our breaths combining with pants and gasps. For all that I had been trying to keep away from Liam, I was now just as eager to have him as he was to have me. The entire world fell away until it was only the two of us, lips pressed to lips, chest pressed to chest.

The slam of a door interrupted our dream-like state. My hands stilled from where they were buried in his hair. His arm around my waist jolted in surprise. We were frozen together, tensed and ready to jump apart. When nothing further happened, we slowly relaxed.

But reality had already started settling back in. The moment was over.

I hurriedly put space between us.

Liam cursed quietly under his breath.

I ran my hands over my face.

He rubbed his stubbled jaw.

We shared a regretful sigh as Liam regarded me intently. Those green eyes of his made it hard to think.

"You're right," I agreed, still slightly breathless. "We are both stars. And maybe we would burn brighter together."

We could both hear voices coming from down the hall. The sound of my brother's laughter was like a foghorn blasting through my still dazed and fogged over mind.

"Or maybe," I continued, "we'd only end up burning ourselves out."

He opened his mouth, maybe to argue or cajole. I held up my hand to stop him.

"No," I said. "I'm sorry, but no."

"Cerise..." His tone was overlaid with disappointment and frustration and heartache. I hated that I'd made him feel that way. But I knew giving in could never lead to anything good.

"You know what sometimes happens after a star burns out?" I asked.

He frowned. "No. What?"

I gave him a sad smile.

"It collapses into a black hole, consuming everything in its path."

# 14

"Shotgun."

"I already called shotgun last night."

"You can't call shotgun until you're within sight of the car."

"Says who?"

"Says the rules of shotgun."

"Guys," Seth interrupted, stopping Gael and Nathan in the middle of their squabbling. "Julian gets shotgun."

"But Julian almost always gets shotgun," Nathan said.

"Driver gets final say," Seth cut them off. "And since you guys always force me to drive, I say Julian sits up front." Seth made a face. "The last time Gael got shotgun, I was forced to listen to stories of his, quote, *sexual prowess* for two hours."

"I've got a girlfriend now," Gael protested.

"And I don't need to hear stories of all the public places you've done it, either," Seth said.

Gael and Nathan grumbled, but climbed into the minivan the label rented for our tour, taking their places in the middle seats. Julian shot Seth a grateful look as he took his place in the passenger's seat.

The minivan wasn't a fancy, high-tech, double-decker tour bus, that was for sure, but I wasn't going to complain. We had a label who actually paid for it. We didn't have to front the cost ourselves like when we were indie.

Besides, we were still the new guys on the music scene. I knew we'd get there eventually. And this was a local tour, only cities within a days drive. It wasn't like we had to be sleeping on a bus overnight.

"So that leaves me and you in the back?" Liam asked.

Damn. I hadn't thought of that. Me and Liam, crammed next to each other for hours on end.

I grabbed the door handle and pulled it open. "Guess we'll have to entertain each other."

The words popped out of my mouth without thinking of the double meaning.

"I'm sure we'll find something to pass the time," Liam said.

I expected him to follow up with some sort of innuendo or come-on, but he didn't. Instead, his voice was tired, near fatigued.

He wasn't the only one. As Seth took his place in the driver's seat, I could see the dark bruises under his eyes. They no doubt matched my own. Julian's dark hair hung limp around his pale cheeks. Even Gael and Nathan's playful antics were half-hearted, as if they couldn't summon the energy to properly tease each other.

The last few weeks had been rough. We'd practiced nearly day and night, and then some, as the final days before the tour approached. Our muscles were sore. Our heads pounded.

We probably shouldn't have pushed ourselves as hard as we had, but each of us knew how important this was. We couldn't just be good on stage. We had to be amazing. We had to be flawless.

We had to be rock star gods.

"Cerise?" Liam prompted.

I shifted my attention away from the other band members. As much as they worried about me, as the leader of the band, it was my job to worry about them.

Liam gestured for me to climb into the van first. "After you."

The vehicle was raised and I had to step up and crawl in. I was acutely aware of my backside right in Liam's face as he climbed in behind me. Luckily the hem of my skirt fell lower than I usually wore, or I might have given him an entirely too private view.

I had to wonder though. If I had flashed Liam, would he have even reacted?

Liam and I had kissed and it had been amazing. Breathtaking.

It had also been a terrible idea. So I'd pushed him away.

Liam had respected my wishes and kept his distance.

It could have been because of what I'd said to him. Maybe my last rejection had finally sunk in this time.

It also could have been because we'd simply been too busy, too exhausted, to have any sort of flirtatious tension between us.

"Anyone need anything before we take off?" Seth asked. "One last coffee run?"

A chorus of weary *no's* followed his question.

I settled into my seat, leaning my head back against the soft leather headrest. Closing my eyes, I heard the rustle of Liam plunking himself down beside me. The back of the minivan was bench style, not bucket seats. I wondered if he would scoot closer, until he was right up beside me. But no, he kept to his side of the van, pressed against the right window, leaving the middle seat empty between us.

"I've barely spent any time with Jessie in the last few weeks," Gael was complaining from the middle seat.

"You sleep over at her place every night," Nathan pointed out.

"Yeah, and that's all we do. *Sleep.*" With the way he said the word sleep, Gael's displeasure was clear. "After the tour I'm locking us together in her bedroom and not coming out for three days."

"What did I say about discussing your sex life?" Seth called out from the front seat.

"You wanted to know all about it so you can get tips, right?" Gael called back.

"I don't need to take advice on women from the likes of you."

Gael looked affronted. "My advice is solid gold."

Seth just laughed.

The guys continued to joke and banter. Liam joined in once in a while, but mostly seemed content to keep to himself. I tuned them out, listening to music with my earphones on, trying to get my head into the right space for our upcoming concert.

After an hour my knees began to ache. I might have stretched them out on the seats, taking up the whole back, but I couldn't do that with Liam there.

After shifting and squirming for what felt like the dozenth time, crossing and uncrossing my legs, Liam tapped my shoulder. I took out my earphones and raised an eyebrow in question.

"You okay?" he asked.

"Just feeling a little cramped."

"Would it help to stretch out?" Liam asked. "You could put your feet in my lap."

That was an unusually intimate offer. Or perhaps he was simply being nice, like a friend would be.

Giving my knees a break sounded like a great idea, especially if I wanted to be in top shape for the concert. But putting my feet up in Liam's lap? The thought sent butterflies flapping madly in my stomach. It might just encourage him. Might end up canceling out all my previous rebuffs.

Liam watched patiently as I debated the idea internally, expression placid, as if he would be content with my response either way.

"Sure," I finally said. "Thanks."

I unlaced my knee-high boots and toed them off. I scooted around until my back was against the door. I hesitated, just for a moment, before lifting my feet and resting them gingerly on Liam's thighs.

"Aw," he said, feigning disappointment. "I was hoping you'd have some sort of cute or embarrassing pattern on your socks so I could tease you about it."

"Sorry," I said. "Solid black is what you're stuck with."

I nestled deeper into my seat and extended my legs. I couldn't straighten them all the way — my legs were too long for that — but it was enough.

"Better?" Liam asked.

"Yeah, thanks," I murmured.

He flashed me a smile and rested his hands on my shins. My stomach tightened and tumbled over. I was fixated on that smile, his green eyes crinkling at the corners. His hands were warm, even through my socks. This was the closest we'd been, physically, in weeks. My toes curled and uncurled unconsciously. His smile widened. He ran one hand up and down my shin soothingly. I caught myself before I let out a shuddering breath.

Liam turned his head forward. "Hey Seth, about how far away are we?" he asked.

I blinked to clear my head, set free from that gaze.

"A bit more than an hour," Seth replied, looking in the rearview mirror. "Maybe less if traffic lets up."

Liam nodded. I focused on my knees, refusing to check if that smile was back on his lips.

No wonder he kept pursuing me. I'd never given out so many mixed signals in my life. One smile and I reacted like a lovesick schoolgirl.

I couldn't deny my attraction to him, not even to myself.

And from the amused look in his eyes, I wasn't keeping it from Liam, either.

# 15

"Wow," Gael said. "This is..."

"Yeah," Nathan responded numbly. "It sure is."

"Is this right?" Seth asked nervously. "I mean, the label didn't make a mistake, did they?"

I double checked the details on my phone. "This is the right one." I glanced up and scanned the concert venue we'd just pulled up in front of. The building was massive and towered over us. Dozens, maybe even hundreds, of people were already lined up around the venue and down the street. "This is where we're playing."

"Holy shit," Julian murmured.

" Don't freak out," Liam said encouragingly. "So what if it's bigger than you thought?"

"We've never played for an audience this size as headliners before," I said. "Ever."

"And by the end of the night, you can say you have," he said.

"I'm driving around back," Seth said. "We're not walking through the front entrance, that's for sure."

I made a call to our contact person at the venue as we approached the back entrance. A young skinny guy came out of a nondescript door followed by a couple beefy looking guys. Skinny kid unlocked a gate to the parking lot, and waved us through. Once we were parked, the buff guys came around to the back of the van and started unloading our equipment, lugging it into the building for us. With the back hatch open, we could hear chatter and cheering, the chanting of fans singing our songs at the top of their lungs as they waited.

"This is insane," Nathan said, shaking his head.

The guys started climbing out of the van. Liam unbuckled his seat-belt and hopped out. He held his hand out as I followed, helping me down.

I didn't have time to savor his warm hand encasing mine. My head was already whirling with excitement and dread and nerves. I'd known signing with a label was a big deal, but this was a significant level up from the bars and clubs we used to play at.

"We're doing final set up now," Skinny Guy said as he lead us into the building and through the maze of hallways. "We should be able to do sound checks soon. You can wait in the artist lounge." He nodded and pointed to a door, then left us.

We walked in. The six of us stood in the middle of the room, staring at each other. I took in the wide eyes and pale faces. Even my brother, usually so self-assured to the point of egomania, looked unsure of himself.

I pushed down my own worries and threw back my shoulders, standing tall.

"Okay, guys. This is it," I said. "All our hard work, all those sleepless nights and sore muscles and blistered fingers? This is where it got us. We're playing a massive concert hall with hundreds, *thousands*, of people dying to see us. No more playing for free drinks. No more dragging around our own equipment. We've made it. We're goddamn rock stars. And we're going to have the time of our lives out there."

Slowly, the uncertainty and fear faded from their expressions, replaced with excitement, triumph. I let a grin spread across my face, heart pounding in my chest.

"We made it," I repeated slowly, quietly, to myself.

"I could get used to having roadies carry my shit," Gael said.

"Where are the groupies waiting to give us blowjobs before the concert?" Nathan joked.

"Oh awesome, snacks!" Seth bounced to the nearest table and snatched up a couple bags of chips and chocolate bars. The others followed him, chowing down. The last thing those boys needed were sugar rushes, but I wasn't going to deny them the pleasure.

Liam was still standing near the door, his hands in his pockets. He looked at ease, expression calm, but there was a stiffness in the way he held himself.

"You're not going to eat?" I asked him.

"Not junk like that." He flicked his gaze from the guys to me. "That was a good pep talk. They really listen to you."

"Only sometimes," I said. Liam's shoulders were tense, hunched near his ears. "You okay?"

"Yeah," he said shortly.

I studied him. Thinking back to what I knew of Liam's old band, I had to wonder...

"You've never played a venue this big, either, have you?" I guessed. He pressed his lips together firmly, confirming my suspicions. "It's okay to be nervous," I continued.

"It's not nerves," he said. "There's just a lot of pressure, you know? I'm the new guy. Everyone's going to be judging me. Plus, it's been so long since I've been on stage. And even though we've practiced until our fingers bled, these songs are still new to me." Liam let out a heavy breath through his nose. "I guess it is nerves," he said reluctantly.

"You're going to be fantastic out there," I said. "You're going to fucking rock."

He gave me a weak smile. "Thanks, Cerise."

I placed a reassuring hand on his upper arm. His darkly inked skin was a tempting contrast against my own bare fingers, the hard muscles too firm to ignore. My fingertips tingled.

Even when I told myself I had to keep my distance, I found myself gravitating toward Liam. There was something about him. Whether he was being cocky or playful or vulnerable — something called to me. I wanted to ease his worries. Share in his antics. Bask in his confidence.

Shit. I was in so much trouble.

"You don't seem nervous at all," Liam noted.

I lowered my hand and took a step back. "I don't get nervous before performing."

Or, at least, I didn't usually. I loved being on stage. It felt like the one place where I could finally let go and be the person I wanted to be. The person I was supposed to be.

But Liam was right. This was a whole different dynamic, completely new circumstances.

It didn't matter. I couldn't let any of that show. My bandmates would take their cues from me.

Besides, when I'd given them that pep talk, I'd only been speaking the truth. We'd worked so hard for this. And we'd finally, *finally*, made it. I was going to enjoy the hell out of myself out there on that stage.

The door to the artist lounge opened. I heard the distant shouts of fans crying out for Cherry Lips. I expected to see one of the event staff coming in to let us know how much longer we had before going on.

But someone else was striding in. Someone I hadn't seen in a while.

Someone from my past. Someone from Harper's past.

Morris Edwards, drummer of hit rock band Feral Silence. My childhood friend. The man I'd relied on for half my life.

The man partly responsible for my fiancé's death.

## 16

To my ears, the room fell eerily silent. The sound of the guys talking and eating became muted. The only thing I heard was the rapid pounding of my heartbeat.

It had been many months since I'd last seen Morris. We'd first reconnected, after being estranged for years, because of his girlfriend. She'd found the emotional wounds still festering from Harper's death and helped him through it. She'd tracked me down and encouraged a reunion.

Seeing Morris was confusing, painful, but I didn't begrudge her for it. I had missed him over the years. I didn't regret having him back in my life.

That didn't mean I wasn't conflicted over having him show up out of the blue like this.

With his short hair cut close to his scalp and his broad shoulders taking up most of the doorframe, Morris looked more bodyguard than rock star, but anyone who saw him behind a drum set would never doubt his true calling.

"Hey." The corner of Morris's lips tilted up an inch, as close to a grin as I'd ever seen on the stoic man.

"Hey." I returned his smile with a small one of my own.

I didn't really blame Morris for Harper's death. I knew it wasn't his fault. But seeing Morris again ripped open those still barely healed scars. It reminded me of everything I'd tried to put behind me. Everything I'd tried to forget.

Everything that had resurfaced since meeting Liam.

"What are you doing here?" I asked, not unkindly.

"Came to see your show." That tilt of his lips curved a fraction higher. His brown eyes held a note of pride.

"Thanks for coming, man," my brother said. "But you gotta know we're gonna make your band look like shit compared to us." He smirked, but his eyes flicked to me.

Gael knew what had happened. He'd been there. He'd seen the fallout. He knew how difficult this was for me.

"That's a long drive, just to come out for one show," I said.

"Wouldn't miss it," Morris said simply. He regarded me silently, then held out his arms.

With a moment of hesitation, I stepped forward, letting him embrace me with a squeeze. I wrapped my own arms around him. I was taller than average, especially with my heeled boots, but Morris was even more so. The top of my head didn't even reach his chin.

His hand on my back was as comforting as it was heart wrenching. Old memories flashed through my mind. There was something missing. A second hand was supposed to be on my back next to his.

The double embrace of the two men who meant so much to me. Harper, the love of my life, and Morris, the brother of my heart.

Tears pricked the back of my eyes. A vast emptiness in my chest gaped open. The void where Harper's hand was supposed to be both burned with regret and chilled with mourning.

I let go of Morris and stepped back. I hoped my glistening eyes didn't give me away. Despite his impassive expression, from the shine in Morris's own eyes, I knew he was just as affected.

"Who's this?" Liam asked from behind me.

Blinking back tears and clearing my throat, I made introductions. "Liam, this is Morris, an old friend."

Morris held out his hand to Liam, who eyed it suspiciously.

"Morris Edwards," the drummer said.

Recognition lit up in Liam's eyes. "Feral Silence?" he asked.

Morris nodded.

"And you know Cerise?" Liam asked.

"We go way back," he said.

Liam looked between me and Morris. The frown on his lips didn't ease. If anything, it deepened.

"You two are close," he said.

I examined Liam with a careful eye. The statement was almost accusing.

"Morris is a childhood friend," I explained. "We've known each other for more than half our lives."

Despite being a little annoyed at Liam's unfriendly demeanor, that small, insecure part inside me felt just a bit delighted at his posses-siveness.

Liam Knight could have any girl he wanted, but he wanted me. And he couldn't hide his annoyance at seeing me hug another man.

That really shouldn't have pleased me as much as it did.

"You're new," Morris noted with a questioning tone, seemingly not noticing Liam's frown, or simply choosing to ignore it.

"I'm Cerise's new guitarist," Liam replied.

"He's filling in for me," I said. "Singing and playing at the same time was getting to be a bit much. We decided a temporary session guitarist would be a good idea for the tour."

Morris nodded. Way back with our old band, I hadn't played guitar while singing, either. "How've you been?"

"Working our asses off," I said. "I don't think we've ever rehearsed for a show as much as this one."

"It'll pay off," he reassured us. "It's hard work, but worth it."

"How's the band?"

"Doing great. Working on a new album. Kell's his usual annoying self. Insists on making half the album his solo songs." Morris's lips twitched upward. As much as he complained, I knew he had a soft spot for his obnoxious yet oddly charming lead singer.

"And Natalie?" I asked, referring to his girlfriend. "You two are good?"

Morris's eyes went soft, tender. "More than good." He pulled out his phone and tapped the screen before turning to show me. It was the sales page of a high end jewelry retailer, displaying a silver ring with an enormous rock.

My mouth widened into an O. "Things are that serious?"

He nodded. "Just waiting for the right time."

"Good for you," I said, even as my heart broke a little. Morris deserved to find happiness, but it didn't make the situation hurt any less.

Morris was getting the chance to marry the love of his life. A chance I never got.

There was a knock on the door before it opened. Through the open door we could now hear the screaming of the audience, loud and frenzied.

"Five minutes," the skinny kid popped his head in to say.

"Fans are going crazy," Morris said to the others. "You ready?"

"More than ready," Gael boasted. "We're going to blow the roof off."

The rest of the band joined in with nods of affirmation.

"We've got this," I said, aiming for bold and self-assured. The shaky note in my voice was so slight, I didn't think anyone noticed.

"You'll be great out there," Morris said quietly. "I know it."

His words calmed me. Filled me with determination.

"Of course we will," I replied with a smirk. "We're Cherry Lips. We're going to take the world by storm."

"Better get going, then," he said.

"Going to wish me good luck?" I asked.

Morris smiled. "You don't need it."

The band made our way to the curtain backstage. We barely had enough time to grab our instruments from the crew before the lights went down and we were given our cue. We made a circle and, with clenched hands, did a six-way fist bump, our usual ritual.

"Alright, guys," I said. I looked at each of them in turn. No hint of nerves. Just fiery resolve, an eagerness, a familiar hunger burning in their eyes. "Let's put on the show of our lives."

We took our places. I was center stage. Gael and Julian were on my left. Liam and Nathan were on my right. Seth was positioned behind us. The lights were still down. I ran through our set list in my head, preparing myself.

I had caved when it came to the set list. Liam had been on to something when he talked about switching opening and closing songs. Starting with *Nineteen* set the tone of the concert.

It wasn't just a rock show. We weren't just playing music. We were wringing emotions from the audience. We were enchanting them, seducing them.

In those moments on stage, the audience was our lover. We gave ourselves to them and asked them to give themselves to us in return.

It wasn't just a rock show.

It was a torrid love affair.

How fitting, then, our choice of opening song.

It was one of the earliest Cherry Lips song I'd ever written about my first, and only, true love.

The lights went up, blinding me. The crowd roared. Seth hit his drumsticks. Julian smashed his fingers down on the keys with a thundering crash. Nathan and Liam shredded their fingers across their fret boards. Gael joined in with bass, a familiar heavy beat thrumming through my body.

My hand squeezed around the microphone.

Ending the concert with *Nineteen* was easy. I was hyped up, running on adrenaline, basking in the glory of an enraptured audience — the past was a distant memory. It had no power to hurt me. I lived fully in the present.

But Morris had just walked back into my life and stirred up unwanted thoughts, unwanted feelings. All my old grief hit me with full force.

My throat closed up. My mouth went dry. My hands trembled.

I couldn't do this.

The concert had already started and I was so close to crying, tears were already stinging my eyes.

Shit. I had to pull myself together or I was going to blow this whole thing.

The song had a long intro. I kept my head bowed, long hair covering my face, gripping the microphone with both hands. It was a typical lead singer pose, as if I was a tiger lying in wait, waiting for the right moment to let loose with my claws and jump on my prey.

I caught movement through the curtain of my hair. Liam was sidling up next to me. It seemed as if his fingers both lovingly stroked and frantically tore at the strings of his guitar.

I lifted my head a fraction, meeting his eyes. The spotlights hit them, making them glow. Despite the cocky smirk on his face, his eyes glimmering with concern. Concern, but also reassurance.

He mouthed five words.

*You're a fucking rock star.*

A slow smile crossed my face.

I often felt vulnerable around Liam. He knocked me off balance. I had shown him too much of myself. I'd revealed more than I'd cared to.

But there were these other times. Times like this when he looked at me, so sure in my talent, so confident. He looked at me like he had complete faith in me. Like he was in awe of me.

I didn't feel vulnerable in these moments. I felt strong. Powerful.

Liam tilted his chin smugly and jerked it toward the audience, as if to say, *what are you waiting for?*

He was right. What the hell was I waiting for?

I shoved aside thoughts of grief and pain and heartbreak. I lifted my head high and looked out at the cheering crowd.

I inhaled deeply, getting ready to let loose with familiar lyrics, passionate and full of fervor.

*I'm not going to let grief stop me,* I thought to myself. *This is my moment.*

*I'm going to burn like the sun.*

# 17

Adrenaline pumped through my veins. My skin buzzed with frantic energy. My heartbeat jackhammered against my ribcage.

The concert was in full swing and Cherry Lips was bringing the house down.

Every note, every beat, had our fans jumping and stomping. Every word that left my lips elicited an explosive response from the audience.

My band members and I were in a state of pure ecstasy. There was nothing better than this.

Nothing, except for Liam's piercing eyes tracking my every movement on stage. Nothing, except for his lips nearly touching mine as he leaned into the microphone for a brief duet.

There was nothing better than being on stage with my band — except for having Liam up there with me.

I had wondered what our chemistry would look like, would feel like, during a live performance. But all my worries were set to rest.

When Liam leaned his back against mine, when he arched against me as he wailed on his guitar, when his heat seared through thin layers of clothing and sent flames licking across my skin—

The flush on my cheeks wasn't just from the hot spotlights. The clench of my stomach wasn't solely from exertion. The ache between my legs wasn't some sort of egotistical arousal from having enraptured the audience, as sometimes happened.

It was his fingers, moving so adeptly across the strings of his guitar. It was his eyes, narrowed with a single-minded resolve. It was his body, vibrating against mine from the same adrenaline high I was so familiar with.

And it was the crowd below us, waving their arms frantically, screaming their hearts out, singing along with every lyric, tears pouring down their faces.

We'd never experienced a concert like this.

And I knew it was because of Liam.

I'd been roused by his presence before. I'd experienced thrills and heat and lust.

But right then, up on stage with him?

I'd never felt so strong. So alive.

This was why I did what I did. This was why I sang. Why I performed.

I was unstoppable. I was fearless.

It really did feel like I could take on the world.

And I was just now realizing I wanted Liam by my side as I did exactly that.

As the concert wound down, as we played our final encore song, Liam drifted closer and closer, until he was right next to me, hips cantered forward. As he played, he rocked back and forth, rubbing his guitar against his body, bringing attention to his abdomen... and lower.

The suggestive pose set my body aflame. All I could think about was rushing off the stage, pulling Liam into the closest dark corner and—

And what?

My mind, body, and heart were caught in a three-way war.

My body told me I needed that man's lips on mine. I needed his hands on my skin. I needed his hips between my thighs.

My heart told me I needed his arms wrapped around me. I needed his heart beating next to mine. I needed him to hold me close and never let me go.

My mind told me either of those two options was a bad idea. The worst idea.

Jumping into bed with Liam would ruin any sense of profession-alism I'd been trying to achieve between us. Giving my heart to him would only lead to heartbreak and regrets.

In the final few moments of the song, our eyes met.

I saw the same hunger reflected back at me.

My body sucker-punched my heart and mind, sending the two of them reeling with wicked glee, leaving it in sole control.

The song ended. The concert was over. We threw guitar picks, drum sticks, water bottles and towels at the audience, giving a few lucky fans a literal piece of the band.

As we left the stage to a cheering crowd still shouting for another encore, Liam put his lips to my ear.

"I don't care what the others are doing after this concert," he murmured. "But you and I need to talk."

Talk? My body whined and squirmed inwardly. The last thing it wanted to do was talk. It wanted arms and legs tangled together. It wanted hands roaming my body. Liam's hands.

Nevertheless, the six of us headed back to the artist lounge. I wondered how in the hell I'd get Liam alone.

"Hey," Gael said to me. "Nate wants to go clubbing."

"Morris said there's an awesome place a few blocks from here," Nathan added.

I saw an opening. I seized it.

"You go ahead," I said. "I need to talk to the venue manager. Business stuff."

That wasn't unusual. Sometimes there really was stuff to discuss. Like handing over the money they owed us. There was no worry of being stiffed now that we had a label, but Gael wouldn't think to connect the two.

"I need to make a few phone calls first," Liam said.

It was a pathetic excuse. What was so urgent that he had to make a phone call after midnight on a Saturday?

None of them questioned it.

"Cool, see you there," Gael said, just like I knew he would.

They gathered their things and soon left.

We were alone.

I stared at Liam. His skin still glistened with sweat from the stage lights. His t-shirt clung to his chest, every peak and valley on display. His dark denim hung low, exposing a bare stripe of slim toned torso.

"Cerise..." he said, still slightly out of breath. He stopped there, as if he didn't know how to continue. He swiped his hand down his face and rubbed at the stubble on his jaw. When his eyes met mine again, my heart clenched in my chest.

I'd been so adamant in my resolve. So sure that turning Liam away was the right thing to do.

The way those green eyes were gazing into mine, so full of hunger... but also something else. Patience. Awe.

My body had shoved aside my mind and my heart, but now those two forces were pushing their way to the forefront.

I'd been so worried what people would think. So worried how this would affect the band.

But if I was being honest with myself, I knew those were just excuses.

"Cerise, you keep on saying this is a bad idea, but—" Liam started.

I stepped forward. He cut himself off.

So what if gossip mongers speculated about my personal life? They talked trash about every celebrity. Their opinions didn't matter. All that mattered were our fans — and deep inside I knew that.

I pressed myself against him. Liam's eyes narrowed.

So what if he was on tour with us? Like he kept saying, it was temporary. We wouldn't be working together forever.

I ran both hands through the hair at the back of Liam's head, thick and damp. He made a sound, low in his throat.

All my excuses for pushing him away were just that — excuses. There was another reason I'd pushed him away. A reason I hadn't wanted to admit to myself.

I leaned into Liam. He brought his hands to my hips.

I'd been afraid of opening up. Of letting someone in. I'd been afraid of being hurt again. Afraid of experiencing the loss, the utter devastation I'd felt when Harper died. I'd been weak. I'd fallen apart. I'd barely managed to pull myself together afterward. I'd never wanted to feel that way again. And the easiest way to make sure that happened was to never open myself up. Ever. To anyone. But with Liam—

I lifted my chin. He lowered his head. Our lips were a hairsbreadth away from each other.

I didn't feel weak around Liam. I felt strong. He turned me inside out and muddled my head, but I never felt lesser when I was around him. I never felt like I was anything other than myself. Vulnerable but with a strong will. Unsure and yet still capable of being bold. I was myself around Liam. I was Cerise.

The real Cerise.

"What happened on that stage—" Liam tried to say. I cut him off.

"Do you really want to talk?" I asked.

"I know you felt what I felt up there."

"Or do you want to kiss me?"

His gaze flicked to my mouth, pupils dilating, fixated. "I've been thinking of those lips of yours for weeks."

"Still talking," I murmured, inching closer.

"Fuck it," he growled.

Liam closed the distance and captured my mouth with his.

# 18

The first touch of skin to skin was exhilarating. Although it had only been a few weeks, it felt like I'd been waiting for this forever. Yet somehow it also felt like we'd been doing this for years. I inhaled deeply, taking in his scent as I took in air. The sensations, the taste, the smell — all of it was so foreign, but so familiar.

His tongue swiped for entrance. Clenching his hair in my fist, I opened up to him. Our tongues battled, hot and slick. He gripped me tighter, clutching me to him as if afraid I would float away with the slightest nudge.

I couldn't say I blamed him. Our entire relationship up until now had been all push and pull, all hot and cold. No wonder he was afraid I'd back out.

But that wasn't going to happen this time. I was all in.

The only problem was, Liam didn't know that.

He pulled back with a huff of air. I whined, following him. He held me at arms length and shook his head.

"I was serious when I said we needed to talk." His lips were shiny and wet, his eyes dark with lust. And yet, he had stopped.

"What's wrong?" I asked.

"Doesn't this seem a little familiar?" he asked.

My heart, that little part of me that wanted to open myself up and let Liam in, wriggled with glee. Liam felt the same way I did. It felt like we'd done this so many times before. Like we'd kissed a dozen, a thousand times. Like we were meant to be—

"The last time this happened," he said, "you compared our relationship to a black hole."

The words weren't accusing, or upset. He said them matter-of-factly.

Now it was my turn to pull away. I left the circle of his arms completely.

"Why does that matter?" I asked.

"I don't want this to just be a moment of lust," he said. "I don't want you regretting this."

"I won't—" I said, before quieting.

How could I explain to Liam my change of heart? That I was worried being with him would make me weak? It had done anything but that. It had made me strong. How could I explain to him that I wasn't scared anymore?

"I told you before," he said to break the silence. "You're a star. You're a supernova. You're going to do amazing things, and I want to be by your side when that happens." Liam shook his head. "But we're not going to do something you'll regret."

"Do you know," I began, slowing making my way back to him, "what happens when stars collide?"

"No... What?" he asked carefully, as if he were defusing a bomb.

"When two stars collide, the force of it is powerful enough to forge gold and platinum." I bought my lips to his, just barely brushing them with mine. His pupils dilated, going dark and heated. "The force of it is so powerful it warps time and space."

Heat flashed in those green eyes.

"When two stars collide," I whispered into his mouth, "they burn with the fire of a billion suns."

His jaw tensed. His nostrils flared. With a deep growl, his lips came crashing down on mine.

The kiss was hungry. It was greedy. It was possessive.

It scorched me from the inside out.

I moaned into Liam's mouth and grasped at his firm, inked arms for balance. He pulled me closer with one hand and buried the other in my hair. He tugged on the strands almost roughly, tilting my head back. With this better angle, he thoroughly devoured my mouth, leaving me panting and gasping for air.

He nipped at my lips with his teeth before soothing the sting with his tongue. I whimpered and sighed at both the hint of pain and the rush of pleasure that followed. A pulsing heat settled between my thighs. It was similar to what I'd felt on stage, leaving a sweetly throbbing ache.

I felt Liam hardening in his jeans and I knew he was feeling it, too. I ground my hips against his, seeking friction, trying to relieve that ache. He let out a grunt.

"You better stop squirming," he murmured into my lips.

"Or what?" I challenged him, breathless.

"Or I'm going to fuck you right here and now."

I whimpered at the thought and rubbed against him even harder.

Liam's eyes flashed. "You trying to call my bluff?"

"I thought it was a promise."

He growled. "You're going to be the fucking death of me."

"You want to keep talking again?" I asked. "Or do you want to throw me down on that sofa and make good on that promise?"

That was all the teasing he could take. His fingers dug into my hips as he did just that, hauling me halfway across the room and tossing me onto the cushions on my back. I propped myself on my elbows and watched him follow. He crawled up my body, spreading my thighs open so he could settle his hips between them.

The heavy weight of him between my legs sent another throb shooting through me. My inner muscles were clenching and pulsing. I was swollen and wet with desire.

I couldn't wait any longer. I attacked his studded belt, unbuckling it with haste. He went straight for my panties, pushing my leather skirt up and out of the way. He hooked his fingers underneath the elastic and tugged, nearly ripping them with the force of it. He untangled the black fabric from around my ankles and threw them to the floor.

I pulled down the zipper and pushed his jeans down around his thighs, just low enough for his hard cock to spring out. I marveled at it, taking in the girth, the slight curve, the weeping tip.

His hands slid up my legs, his fingertips leaving a blistering hot trail along my skin, spreading me wider. His eyes were fixated as I was revealed to him.

He pressed two fingers inside me just as I took him in my hand.

We groaned in unison, bodies tensing, then relaxing. I ran my hand up and down, exploring the shape of him, the texture. He pumped his fingers in and out, the rough callouses of his fingers a delicious friction against my inner walls.

I guided his length until the head was nestled between my lower lips. His whole body jerked. He fumbled in his jeans pocket, pulling out a foil wrapper and quickly rolling on protection. I tilted my hips to get the right angle.

Our eyes locked.

"You sure?" he breathed.

"Fuck me," I demanded.

With one slow thrust, he entered me. We trembled together, both of us overwhelmed with pleasure, overwhelmed by need. Overwhelmed by the intimate moment we were sharing.

He pulled out. I whimpered. He pushed in. I moaned.

His hands went to my hips, digging into skin. My legs wrapped around his waist, clinging to him. I was still wearing my leather corset. He was still wearing his t-shirt.

We found the perfect rhythm, rocking back and forth, until we finally found our peaks. I cried out, my inner walls clamped down around him, squeezing. He let out a choked grunt, his cock twitching and pulsing inside me.

We didn't break eye contact the entire time.

His hips stilled. My now weak legs fell to the cushions, splayed on either side of him. We panted together with shuddering gasps of air, until our breathing evened out.

We were still staring at each other. A slow, satisfied smile crossed Liam's face

"Fuck," he said with a shaky laugh. "I can't believe we just fucking did that."

"I'm not usually one for public sex, but—" My mouth spread wide with a no doubt besotted smile.

We stayed on the sofa with our limbs locked together, not making any movements to get up, just enjoying the afterglow.

My gaze focused on his face. I ran a thumb across his bottom lip. It came away red. "My lipstick is all over you."

His face fell. "Shit, really?"

"You look like a clown."

He grimaced. I laughed.

"I've got some makeup remover cloths," I told him.

We finally got off the sofa and took a moment to clean up. I scrubbed at Liam's face with the dampened cloth.

"Maybe you should wear makeup after all," I teased. "Really go all out with that glam-rock look."

He whisked me into his arms and swung me around. I shrieked, enjoying myself like I hadn't in ages.

"I thought you didn't have a thing for guys in eyeliner?" he asked.

"I don't." I swatted at his shoulder until he put me down. He did, but kept his arms around my waist. "Gael's going to wonder what's keeping us."

"Maybe I should make up some excuse," Liam said. "There was a dire emergency."

"Like what?"

"Your life was in danger."

I raised an eyebrow. "Was it?"

"Yeah. You were dying for my cock."

I made a face at him. "Don't you dare say that or I really will kick you in the nuts with my boots. I don't care how great the sex was."

Liam laughed and squeezed me. "Come on, Cherry Lips. Let's go clubbing with your boys."

# 19

"So how exactly does this work?" Liam asked.

We'd arrived at the club to find a drinking game already in full swing. The guys, minus Nathan, had secured a private room. Gael and Julian were halfway to being trashed, but Seth was driving us home after this so he was still sober.

Liam and I were in agreement about not telling the guys right away. This was still new to us. We were supposed to be concentrating on the tour. Gael was overprotective and might beat the shit out of Liam for touching his little sister. All were good reasons to keep it to ourselves, at least for now.

As we joined the others sitting around the table in the middle of the lounge, Liam questioned them when they told him what game they were playing.

"I've never heard of a game called Poker Face," he said. "Only the song."

"Don't worry, we're not going to make you sing it," Seth said. "The point of the game is to keep your face as expressionless as possible while each person takes their turn saying something to make you react. Anyone who so much as twitches a muscle has to take a shot."

"That's not too hard," Liam said.

"You think?" I asked, amused. "The drunker you get, the harder it is to keep a straight face."

"And we like to up the ante," Seth continued. "It's too easy if you're just taking a shot of vodka or rum. I like to create my own concoctions."

"Sounds interesting," Liam said.

"You have no idea what kind of shots Seth comes up with," I warned. "It's enough to sear the flesh from your tongue and make you puke all over the floor."

"Are you game?" Gael asked.

"I'm game," Liam replied. "I'm sure I can take whatever Seth throws at me."

"You say that now," I muttered.

"Wait," Gael said. "We can't start without Nate."

"He's probably busy dry-humping some chick on the dance floor," Seth said.

"And miss a chance to see the new guy keel over?" Nathan said as he walked up to us. "Wouldn't miss it for the world."

"So what you mean is, you already got your rocks off in a dark corner somewhere?" Gael asked.

A self-satisfied smirk crept across Nathan's face.

We took our places sitting around the table in a circle. Seth finished setting up dozens of shot glasses filled with whatever disgusting mix he'd instructed the bartenders to come up with this time, along with some non-alcoholic ones for himself since he was DD.

"Alright, let's start," Seth said once everything was ready. "Liam can go last so he can see how the game goes for the first round." He nodded to me. "That means you start and we go in a circle."

I didn't have to think for long. Last time we'd played this game, I'd been completely demolished. I'd spent the last several weeks coming up with some good ones I could use next time. I was determined to stay sober tonight.

"It was kind of hard concentrating on tonight's concert, since I'm on my period and bleeding out of my snatch—"

"Stop!" Nathan cut in as all the guys blanched. "Fuck, why do you always go for the gross female stuff?"

"Take your shot," was all I said in response.

The guys grumbled but each took up a shot glass.

"Here goes," Julian murmured.

They all knocked them back at the same time. Liam immediately started gagging.

"Shit," he choked out. "And you guys play this voluntarily?"

"This isn't even my worst," Seth said. "I'm going easy on you because it's your first time."

"What's in here?" Liam coughed.

"Alcohol," Seth said.

"I mean, aside from that?" Liam made a face. "It's like... raw eggs. And pickle juice. And what's that crunchy bit?" He shuddered. "This is godawful."

"Good," Seth said. "That's your incentive to win." He turned to Julian. "Your turn."

"Pineapples," Julian said flatly.

My eyebrow almost twitched, but I suppressed the urge. Liam's face was blank, although there was a hint of confusion in his eyes. He didn't know what Julian was talking about.

Seth, Gael and Nathan, however, all made various sounds of laughter, from a quick exhale through the nose, to a snorted chuckle at the back of the throat.

"You've been saving this one, haven't you?" Nathan accused as they knocked back their shots. "You knew it would get us and you want to make us look weak in front of the new guy."

"How long are you going to keep calling me new guy?" Liam asked.

"Until I come up with a better nickname," Nathan drawled. He took his time glancing at each one of us.

"I was hitting on this one groupie out on the dance floor," he started to say. "She was totally into me, but she was also one of those fangirls, you know?"

I wondered where Nate was going with this, knowing it couldn't be good.

He continued. "As much as she wanted to jump my bones, she also wanted to know more about the band. When I mentioned the new guy she said, *Oh yeah, from that old band Forever Night? Isn't he some kind of washed up loser now?*"

Liam's eyebrows immediately drew down into a frown with a grunt. Nathan snickered. Liam groaned.

"No fair," he said. "You targeted me on purpose."

"You need thicker skin," Nathan said as he handed Liam another shot glass.

Liam grimaced, but didn't choke or sputter.

"It goes down smoother the second time," he croaked.

"I'll need to make the next round even worse," Seth said.

"Great," Gael said. "You had to go and challenge him."

Seth rubbed his hands together with wicked glee, contemplating what he would come up with next. I didn't like the evil glint in his eyes. Thank god we still had another handful of shots to go with the current batch.

"My turn," Seth said. "I was just thinking yesterday that we should rename the band *Hairy Tits*."

None of us reacted. His face fell.

"Aw, come on," he said. "Nothing? Not even a single twitch?"

"Sorry kid," Gael said. "You'll have to try better next time." Gael looked to Liam. "He's great at coming up with drinks, but he's absolute shit when it comes to playing the game."

"Hey!" Seth protested.

Gael grinned. "You reacted. Take a shot."

"You didn't announce it was your turn yet," Seth retorted.

"Fine," Gael shrugged. "Now it's my turn and I think Seth's going to die a virgin."

Seth squawked. "I'm not a fucking virgin!"

Gael handed him a non-alcoholic shot glass. Seth continued glaring as he took his own shot. He sputtered, sending liquid splashing from his lips.

"He's also complete shit at taking his own medicine," Gael added.

"You guys suck," Seth complained as he wiped his chin with his hand.

"Liam's turn now," Nathan said. "Let's see what you got."

Liam went silent. He seemed to be studying the shot glasses intently. Without lifting his eyes, he spoke the next words in a hushed voice.

"Do you guys know what happens when two stars collide?"

I couldn't stop the sappy smile from sneaking across my face. The others looked confused. Liam shot me a look, an equally warm smile playing on his lips. That had been meant for me alone.

"I don't get it," Gael said, looking between the two of us.

"Inside joke," I said.

"You two already have inside jokes?" Nathan raised an eyebrow.

I mumbled something indistinct, not trying to explain. I took the shot glass, ready to toss it back.

Liam put a hand on mine, stopping me.

"What do you say we skip out?" he asked.

"And do what?"

"Let's dance," he suggested. "I'm still pumped up from the concert, aren't you? Let's work off some of that energy."

I shot a glance at the guys. Gael eyed us for a moment, but returned his attention back to the game, seemingly not thinking anything was unusual about the offer.

I took Liam's hand and let him lead me through the crowded club.

He kept us to the edge of the the dance floor, away from the press of bodies.

"Don't want your legions of fans to see us and end up getting mobbed," he explained.

"You just want to feel me up in a dark corner," I said.

"That's a perk," he acknowledged with a wicked grin.

I wrapped my arms around his broad shoulders. He put one hand on my hip, his thumb rubbing small circles in the hollow. He put the other on the small of my back, pressing us close. I shivered, remembering what it had felt like to have those hands under my clothes, on my bare skin.

"What was with that pineapple comment?" Liam asked as we swayed together.

"Let's just say it involves a drunken party, a terrible dare, and a sore ass the next morning."

Liam raised an eyebrow.

"Trust me," I said. "You don't want to know more."

"That's a weird game," he replied. "Is it all supposed to be truthful statements?"

"You have first hand experience I'm not on my period," I chuckled. "Are you worried about what Nate said?"

Liam's lips pursed.

"You know you're not washed up," I scolded him. "You're supposed to have an ego to rival my own."

"Even egomaniacs sometimes have moments of self-doubt," he said.

"I've often thought the exact same thing."

"Whenever one of us gets down on ourselves, we'll have to remind each other how kick ass we are."

We smiled at each other. The room seemed to tilt, the floor turning wobbly beneath my feet — that familiar disorientation I always felt around Liam. This time, it didn't make me feel anxious or overwhelmed. It didn't make me feel like running away.

It made me want to stay wrapped in his arms, staring into those green eyes forever, until the stars went dark and the universe met its end.

We had stopped swaying. We stood in the middle of the club, dreamy expressions on both our faces. How embarrassing.

For once I didn't care.

We couldn't gaze into each other's eyes forever though. Eventually the real world intruded.

"I'm really thirsty," I told him. "I worked up a sweat on stage. Want me to grab you something from the bar while I'm there?"

"A beer is fine," Liam said.

With one last lingering look, I pushed my way to the bar. I leaned over the counter and waved to catch the bartender's attention. His eyes caught mine. His gaze immediately fell to my chest. He came over. I almost rolled my eyes. Of course my corset got his attention.

"One beer, one whiskey sour," I told him.

The bartender was at least professional enough to look me in the eyes while I ordered. He left to grab the drinks. I rested my back against the bar, waiting patiently. I was glad Liam had only wanted a beer. I certainly wouldn't have ordered him that twelve year high-class stuff he'd gotten last time, that was for damn sure.

I felt a nudge on my shoulder. I shifted away before a voice said my name.

"Hey, Cerise."

Morris appeared beside me, his wide frame casting a shadow and blocking the club's strobe lights from my eyes.

"Hey," I returned. My chest squeezed, but it was only the barest hint of an ache. Seeing the proud look in Morris's eyes made my heart swell. "Did we fucking rock out there or what?"

His lips tilted upward. "You fucking rocked," he agreed. "I knew you would."

"You want a drink?" I gestured to the bar.

He shook his head. "I don't drink."

"Since when?" Morris had always been, if not a heavy drinker, at least more than happy to chug back any beer that came his way.

"A while," was all he said. "You guys were really great out there."

"I heard our fans compare us to Feral Silence," I lied, hiding a smile. "Some even said we were better."

"Don't let Kell hear that," Morris chuckled lightly.

"I can handle that raging narcissist," I said. "After all, I've been putting up with my brother my whole life."

"How is Gael?" Morris asked.

"He's good," I said. "Surprisingly good, actually. I didn't think he'd ever settle down, but..." I shrugged and cast my eyes up to the second floor VIP room. I could see Gael and the guys through the glass walls. "Being in love suits him. He's been acting out a lot less."

"Not like he could have acted out worse," Morris said dryly.

"Gael did go a bit too wild once the band got popular," I said. "I was getting sick of bailing him and Nate out of jail or finding them in the middle of a trashed hotel room."

"And what about you?" Morris asked quietly. "How have you been dealing with Gael's new relationship?"

"I'm cool with it. I'm grateful to Jessie, actually. She's keeping Gael out of trouble."

"I'm glad."

I studied Morris. "Were you worried I would feel left out or something?"

"I know how much you rely on Gael," Morris said. "He's part of your support system."

Gael was my only support system. I didn't have anyone else. I loved the guys in my band like they were my own brothers, but I had to be strong around them. Had to be a leader. I couldn't afford to fall apart in front of them.

Morris must have sensed my thoughts, because he gave me a sympathetic look. He patted my upper arm with a large palm and left it resting on my shoulder.

"If you ever need anyone..." he trailed off, leaving the rest unsaid.

I appreciated the offer. Morris was one of the very few people who knew what happened, who would understand.

I took his other hand in mine. "Thank you," I said.

"What's going on?"

I turned my head to find Liam behind us.

"Hey," I said. "Sorry, I ran into Morris and totally forgot about the drinks."

There was a scowl on Liam's face. He pinned Morris down with a stare. "Hey. What are you still doing here?" he said bluntly.

"Decided to stick around after the concert." Morris eyed him carefully. "It was a good one," he added.

"Thanks," Liam said shortly. He put his arm around my waist and tugged me to his side. "You and Cerise talking about work?"

"Talking about a lot of things." Morris turned his attention from Liam to me. He patted my shoulder again. "I'm here if you need me."

I rested my hand on his briefly. "Thanks."

With a nod at Liam, Morris took off. Liam tracked him with a shrewd eye as he disappeared into the crowd. His frown hadn't eased. I narrowed my eyes at him.

"Okay," I started, pulling away. "What the hell was that?"

He shifted his gaze to me. "What?"

"That *macho-caveman-possessive* act," I said.

"You and Morris are close." He echoed his words from before.

"Yes," I said. "We're friends."

"Were you always just friends?" Liam asked. Now I was sure there was a hint of accusation in his tone.

"There's nothing between me and Morris," I said. "We're friends. That's it." I looked Liam over and folded my arms over my chest. "Look, I don't do the jealousy thing," I told him. "If you've got trust issues, that's on you."

We stared at each other, both unwavering.

"I'm sorry," he finally conceded, although it sounded as if he were forcing the words out. "I guess I overreacted. I just saw you and him and—" Liam's shoulders slumped. "We just had this amazing moment between us. I guess I'm still sort of in that clingy mindset. Kind of pathetic, right?"

I considered his explanation. "It's not pathetic," I told him. "I get it. I suppose I'd be pretty pissed if I saw some girl all up on you."

He threw me a relieved smile. "I'd hate to see a pissed off Cerise."

"You sure would," I agreed. "Just ask my brother."

The tense moment between us was over. We were back to our sappy smiles and easy laughs. Some guys were just overprotective like that, weren't they?

There wasn't really anything to worry about, after all.

## 20

"Ughh..." Gael groaned, rubbing his temples with his fingers. "My fucking head."

"That's what you get," Nathan chuckled, then let out of moan of his own. "Shit. I'm gonna puke."

"Not in the rented van," Seth called back. "If you really need to, let me pull over first."

"You're a monster," Julian told Seth. "I hate you."

"No, you don't," Seth grinned at his friend. "You love me."

Julian grumbled.

The drinking game had continued while Liam and I were on the dance floor and my poor boys were in a world of pain. Of course, they didn't deserve me feeling sorry for them.

"You brought it on yourselves," I told them. "You're just lucky we don't have a concert tomorrow."

They continued to whine and complain as Seth dropped each of them off at home. Liam and I were the last ones left.

I glanced at Liam. I wanted to invite him to come home with me, but I didn't want Seth to know.

Liam squeezed my hand discreetly and called out to Seth from the backseat.

"I bet you're tired after driving all night," he said. "Why don't we drop you off next and I'll take the van back tomorrow morning?"

My heart beat a little thrill.

"Thanks man, appreciate it," Seth replied. He drove a few more minutes then pulled up to an apartment building and put on the brakes.

"You really rocked tonight," he told Liam as he grabbed the handle and swung the car door open. "I'm glad you showed up at our audition. Maybe we should bring you on full time," he half-joked.

Liam's expression went blank, even as his fists clenched into a ball. From his odd reaction, I had to assume joining the band was the last thing he wanted to do.

We watched Seth enter his building as Liam climbed into the driver's seat.

"So," Liam said, glancing at me through the rearview mirror. "Your place or mine?"

I had to suppress a silly little smile.

With a few quick directions, Liam navigated his way to my condo. We parked and rode the elevator to my floor. We were silent, but the tension between us hummed in the air. We were finally standing outside my front door. I hesitated before putting the keys in the lock.

"Are you going to warn me about the mess?" he asked. "I'm sure I've seen worse."

"No," I said, fumbling with the keys.

I hadn't had a man in my apartment since...

Since ever, really. I never invited guys home. It always felt too personal. Like an invasion of space.

Liam put his hand on mine. "You don't have to invite me in."

I met his eyes. "If you don't follow me into this apartment and immediately throw me down on the bed, I'm going to scream."

"You'll be screaming all right," Liam smirked. "I'll make sure of that."

My inner muscles clenched and throbbed.

I unlocked the door and we walked in. I wondered what Liam would think of the place. I tried to look at everything through new eyes, imagining what he might see. All my furniture was neutral colors, shades of beige and brown. Two overstuffed armchairs matched an equally squishy looking sofa. There was no TV in the living room, but there was a huge computer monitor on my desk in the corner.

"I'm surprised everything isn't red," he said, taking a look around.

"I have at least some taste, thanks very much."

My place was homey and cozy, warm and inviting. The outside word was such a harsh place, cold and painful. I wanted my home to be a safe, comforting spot.

"I thought you said your place wasn't a mess?" he teased, nodding to a bra hanging off my desk chair.

I snatched it up and quickly tossed it behind a closet door.

"If one stray bra is all that's left lying around, I don't think I have much to be embarrassed about."

"I see you wear black bras as well as panties and socks," he noted.

"Sorry there's no cute cartoon kittens or superhero themed underwear to tease me about."

He came up behind me and gripped my hips.

"I'll just have to tease you in other ways," he said.

My whole body flushed at the wicked intentions behind his words.

"Is that another promise?" I asked.

He brushed my hair aside and placed a kiss on my neck. I shivered. His hand slid down my stomach, going lower and lower, until his fingertips were a mere inch away from that tantalizing spot at the apex of my thighs. He kept his hand there, not moving any further.

"Tease," I breathed.

He only chuckled.

Reaching back, I cupped his cheek, stroking his skin as his fingers clenched the fabric of my skirt.

I took a step, forcing him to follow as I started off towards my bedroom. We were steps away from the bed when I turned around to face him. He tilted his head down and captured my mouth, lips moving hungrily over mine. Delicious sparks spread over my skin.

Liam hooked his thumbs into the waistband of my skirt as my palms slipped under his t-shirt. I let out a longing whimper into his mouth, the feeling of his toned torso under my fingers sending my heart to a flurry of wild beats. My skirt fell to the floor. I ran my hands all over his abs and chest, greedy and wanton, but he didn't let me enjoy it for long.

With a swift movement, I was tossed onto my bed. Liam pulled his t-shirt up and over his head, throwing it on the floor. My gaze roamed his body as I leaned back on my hands.

"Like what you see?" he asked, lifting his eyebrow with a knowing smirk.

"You already know you're hotter than sin, you narcissist."

His lips quirked up. "Sometimes a guy likes to be reminded."

Throbs raced between my legs as he crawled into bed. He rolled my panties down, keeping his eyes locked with mine. I felt the callouses of his fingers and the softness of his lips traveling up my legs. His fingertips circled my entrance. My very core scorched with need.

"You know how you keep on saying I'm amazing?" he asked, his voice a low murmur. I nodded without words. "Add this to your list."

With one last smirk, he dove between my thighs.

My legs clamped down around his shoulders, my moans filling my bedroom as my need was finally met. I pressed the heels of my feet into his back, drawing him in, encouraging him. I twisted my fingers through his hair, savoring his mouth, his lips, his tongue.

Liam hadn't been bragging. He was amazing at this. On and on it went, thorough and all-consuming, until my pleasure reached its peak. My hips jerked up and against him. I gripped the sheets, eyes squeezing shut as waves of a powerful orgasm rolled through me, stealing my breath.

As I slowly came down from the high, my whimpers were interrupted by the sound of his belt unbuckling and his jeans hitting the floor. He rolled on protection as he scanned my body from feet to head.

My limbs were still shaky, but when he made a movement to settle back on top of me, I grabbed him and flipped us around, climbing on top of him. Liam's lips parted in surprise but he didn't speak. His eyes just turned even hungrier, filled with a rabid lust. He liked that I was taking charge.

I took full advantage of that, running my fingers across his shoulders as I devoured his lips in another fiery kiss. He hurriedly unlaced my corset and tossed it to the floor, then palmed the undersides of my breasts. I tossed my head back, exposing more of my chest. He flicked my nipples with his thumbs, then sat up to suck and nip at them. I shuddered, my insides throbbing, as if my breasts had a direct line to my core.

One hand found my folds again. He parted me, making room for his tip to nudge against my entrance. I met his eyes. They were wild, dark and ravenous. In one swift motion I sat up then forced myself down onto his cock. His moan matched my own as my inner walls spread and clenched around him. I dug my nails into his chest, lifting my hips to take him deeper. The firm squeeze on my breasts made me bite my lower lip. I could feel every hard inch pulsing in me, pleasure spiraling higher with every swivel of my hips.

He let his fingers roam over my flesh, squeezing, grabbing and kneading. Every touch sent me closer to the edge. The heat inside me increased by the second. We moved together, him thrusting and me bucking, our bodies meeting one another in this animalistic ritual.

His fingers found my clit again as he circled his thumb around and around, pressing down. With that, another orgasm tore through my body, sending me into a tailspin of pure bliss. I cried out his name with a ragged moan, the sound resonating through the walls of the bedroom.

As I pulsed and fluttered around him, he groaned and jolted his hips upward. His cock twitched inside me and I knew he was following me into that bliss.

After long moments, my muscles relaxed and I collapsed onto him. His legs went limp, his low moan audible over mine. We lay still, gasping for breath together, trembling in the aftermath.

"Holy fuck," he groaned.

"Mmm," was all I could muster.

When I could finally move again, I rolled over next to him, snuggling my back up to his chest. I could feel his cock still half-hard against me.

His finger trailed and up down my stomach, circling my belly button, mapping out my skin. A slow trail of kisses up the back of my neck had me giggling like a besotted schoolgirl. His hand crept lower and lower.

"Stop," I half-moaned, half-laughed. "I can't go again. I'm done."

Liam hummed in amusement and crushed me to his chest. "Just want to make sure you've gotten your fill."

"I appreciate your generosity but I'm more than satisfied."

He squeezed me again. We lay there cuddling as our breathing evened out. I was just about to drop off into sleep when he spoke.

"Can I ask you something?" he said in low tones.

"Anything."

He went quiet. I could practically hear him thinking, could hear his hesitation. I was filled with a sort of dread, wondering what terrible subject he was going to ask about.

"What changed your mind?" he finally spoke up.

"Does it matter?"

"Yes.

I was glad he was pressed against my back, so he couldn't see the panic in my eyes. I didn't know how much to tell him. How much to reveal to him.

But if I was going to be in this, truly in this with him, I couldn't keep it to myself.

"I was afraid," I confessed.

"Of what?"

"Of opening up," I said. "Of being vulnerable. Of being weak."

Liam huffed out a snort. "You're one of the strongest people I know."

"Sometimes," I agreed. "But I wasn't always. And I never wanted to feel like that again." I turned in the circle of his arms. "But I realized something up there on that stage. I don't feel weak around you."

Liam's eyes went soft, understanding. He stroked my hair with a soft hand.

"It was just like you said before," I continued. "When I'm singing, I feel like I can take on the world. But I realized, I don't want to do it alone."

I laid my head on his chest and closed my eyes. I could feel his heartbeat against my cheek.

"I want to take on the world with you by my side."

## 21

I woke up to the smell of bacon and coffee. Rolling onto my back, I stretched until my joints popped. The bed was warm. I could have stayed lying in the heap of blankets forever.

But the idea of breakfast was too compelling. I rummaged around in my drawers for a pair of clean underwear, then looked around for something easy to put on. My eyes landed on Liam's t-shirt, tossed haphazardly on the floor. A flush reddened my face.

That would be way too cheesy. Wouldn't it?

I debated with myself for a few minutes.

I swiped up the shirt and tugged it on. The hem fell just low enough to cover my important bits.

It smelled like him.

With pinked cheeks, I left the bedroom and padded over to the kitchen in bare feet. Liam was standing in front of the stove in his boxers, spatula in hand. His soft hair was all messed up at the back, sticking up in all directions. He hadn't showered yet.

I came up behind him, careful to make shuffling sounds so I wasn't sneaking up. He turned his head just as I wrapped my arms around his waist and laid my cheek against his broad back.

"Good morning," he said with a smile.

"Morning," I murmured back before letting out a yawn. "Coffee?" I asked expectantly.

"Are you one of those, *can't function without caffeine* types?" he asked, amused.

"Mmm," was all I said. It was too early in the morning to communicate in full sentences.

"I've made a pot over there," he said. "Hope you don't mind I made myself at home."

My only response was to squeeze him tight and place a kiss on his inked arm.

"Do you have any plans for the day?" he asked.

I shook my head.

"I have an idea for something fun we could do," he said.

Liam kept his tone light and casual, but I was suddenly abruptly awake.

"Like... a date?" I asked carefully.

He shrugged easily, but his shoulder muscles tensed up. "Sure."

"I'd love to," I said.

"Yeah?" he asked with a hint of relief.

"Did you think I'd say no?"

"We never really talked about..." he trailed off.

"Ooh, are we having The Talk?" I teased. I turned him around to face me. "I told you. I want you by my side."

Green eyes met mine, somber. "I want to make sure we're on the same page."

"You want to make this official?" I smiled. "I, Cerise Moreau, want you, Liam Knight, to be my boyfriend."

"Isn't this supposed to be the other way around?" His lips quirked up. "Shouldn't I be getting down on one knee?"

"Hold up now," I said. "You're not supposed to skip the entire book and go straight to the last page."

"I'm a patient man," he said, a sparkle of good humor in his eyes. "I can wait."

My heartbeat thumped heavily in my chest. He'd said those words before, and he'd proven them true. I'd put Liam through a lot of shit to get to this point.

I cleared my throat and took the spatula from his hand, taking over breakfast duties.

"So where are we going?" I asked.

"It's a secret."

"And are you that type of person?" I asked.

"What type?"

"The type who likes to keep secrets?"

His expression turned oddly pained. He turned and opened the fridge door.

"No," he said, his voice tight. "I hate secrets."

I'd been joking, but Liam had reacted strongly. I had to wonder how serious he was being.

"Did somebody throw you a surprise birthday party that backfired spectacularly?" I asked, trying to lighten the mood.

He poked his head out from the fridge, looking confused.

"To hate secrets that much," I clarified.

His expression eased, until a small smile was playing on his lips.

"Nothing like that," he said. "I just don't like having things kept from me, that's all."

"Understandable," I said.

But the smallest hint of worry started to nag at me. I was keeping something from Liam. He didn't know about Harper. He didn't know what happened.

But was it really that important for Liam to know? My past was just that — the past. It had nothing to do with me and Liam right here and now.

"Bacon's ready," I announced.

We grabbed our coffee and food and perched ourselves on two bar stools at the counter.

"Sorry I don't have a proper kitchen table," I said.

"No worries." Liam looked around, taking in the rest of the apartment. "You've managed to do a lot with a small space."

"I read a lot of interior decorating magazines."

"Do you really?"

"No."

We shared a laugh.

As I sipped on my coffee, Liam nodded to one of my many book-shelves.

"Who's your favorite author?" he asked.

I had to think about it. "I guess I like Jane Austen the most."

"That's a good one."

"Yours?"

"Terry Pratchett," he replied without thinking. He jabbed his finger at the bookshelf. I looked to where he was pointing. "Is your favorite Sense and Sensibility?"

My lungs froze.

Because it was.

Harper had given me that exact book to me as a birthday present one year.

My entire body went eerily still.

Liam took it in his hand and opened the front cover. Something light and thin fell out. He picked it up between two fingers.

"You really have been friends for a long time," he said.

It was a photo. A photo of me and my friends back in high school.

It was a photo of me, Morris and Harper.

I suppressed the urge to snatch it away. I clasped my hands together in my lap.

He flicked his eyes to mine. "This is Morris, right?" he asked. "Who's the other guy?"

"H—" I faltered. My mouth went dry. I tried not to choke on the words. "That's Harper. We were all in a band together."

I waited for the gaping hole to open in my chest. Waited for ice to crystalize around my heart.

But as I waited, muscles locked and tensed, I realized something.

The gaping hole was no longer all-consuming. It was more like a small fissure. Bitingly cold darkness pricked at the edges of my ribcage, but didn't spread further.

It hurt, yes. Thinking of Harper still caused me pain.

But it was more distant now. It was like when I was on stage. I still *felt* it, but it no longer brought me to my knees. It no longer caused me unbearable anguish.

"How old are you guys here?" Liam asked.

"I don't know," I murmured. "I was maybe fifteen. The guys were a little older."

"You're cute as a brunette," he said. "You ever think of letting your hair go natural again?"

"No."

"Hm." He studied the photo. "So this is your first band?"

"Yeah."

"You were the singer and Morris played drums, right?" he asked. "Was Harper the guitarist?"

I nodded silently, not able to speak.

He glanced up at me when I didn't respond out loud.

"You okay?" he asked.

"Nostalgia," I lied.

"I don't know much about your past," Liam said, examining the photo. "But I'd like to."

I wasn't ready to tell him the whole story. But—

"Our band broke up a few years after that photo was taken."

"I'm sorry," he said. "That's always hard."

"It was." The fissure in my chest threatened to widen.

A slight frown crossed Liam's lips. "And Morris?"

"We—" I swallowed hard. "We drifted apart, actually. We grew up together, but until recently, I hadn't seen him in years. It was too hard, I think, for both of us. He left shortly after..." I stopped, not wanting to say it. "After the band separated."

Liam squeezed my hand. I squeezed back with a tight, shaky grip.

"So you lost your friend and your band at the same time," he murmured. "I get it. When my band broke up—" he shook his head. "They were my best friends. It was like losing family, you know?" Liam looked down at the photo again. "You were cute even back then. All innocent and wide-eyed, no makeup and messy hair."

"Luckily I've mastered the art of the smoky eye since then," I joked.

Liam cupped my face and swept his thumb under my eye. "I think that smoke's more of a raging forest fire."

I winced. "I probably look like a raccoon after last night, don't I?"

"A little bit," he agreed. He raised an eyebrow. "You want to go wash up together?"

"Is this an invitation for shower sex?" I asked, perking up.

He laughed. "You're so direct. You cut right through the bullshit."

"Is that bad?"

"No. I love it. It's refreshing."

"So that's a yes on the sex?"

His only response was to usher me out of the kitchen and into the bathroom with haste.

## 22

"How old are you again?" I asked Liam.

"Twenty-six. Why?"

I pointed to the sign in front of the building we were standing in front of.

"I think you missed a few words in that sign," I said.

He followed my finger and laughed.

"Just because it's a science center for kids doesn't mean adults can't enjoy it," Liam said.

"What made you think of a science center for our first real date?" I asked. "Not that I'm complaining. I'm sure it'll be fun. But I was expecting something a little more..."

"Adult?" He exaggerated a leer. "X-rated?"

"Mature."

He just grinned.

Once we'd given our tickets to the attendant Liam took a map and tugged me along eagerly.

"Come on," he said. "You're going to love this."

Our first stop was at one of those static electricity orbs that makes your hair stand up on end. Liam took the bullet and stepped up, letting me be the first one to laugh at the other. His long-ish hair stuck out in all directions. I suppressed a grin.

"You look like a lion with a straggly mane," I told him.

When it was my turn, my hair was too long for all of it to properly float in the air like his had, but it was enough to cause a tangled mess. Liam teased me as I grumbled and fought to smooth down the strands afterwards.

Out next stop was what I called The Bubble Room. It was filled with floating bubbles and foam in all manner of shapes and sizes. In the middle of the room stood a foam machine shaped like a cannon that could be let loose on unsuspecting victims. One setup was large enough for a fully grown adult to stand in the middle of a plastic ring and be encased in a bubble the size of their entire body.

We spent a good twenty minutes blowing bubbles at each other and chasing them to pop. Liam blew a handful of foam in my face and I shrieked out loud. I got him back by smacking a handful of cold, wet foam under his shirt and onto his bare skin. I enjoyed his startled jump and high pitched yelp. The two of us made more noise than the kids.

Then there was the crazy perspective room, a room with a giant robot arm you could maneuver yourself, a room with a huge sandbox and wind machine to demonstrate air currents, and more.

I was having more fun than I had in a while. I didn't have to put on a show of being cool, of being self-possessed. I didn't have to be the one to tell others to calm down and act like professional adults. I was able to let loose, to be just like a kid myself.

At one point, I stopped and watched Liam. He was playing with an old time Morse code machine, frantically tapping the buttons with glee as he pretended to send an important message.

My heart swelled in my chest. I hadn't felt this free in years.

I went to him and asked what he was doing.

"Sending Gael a message that there was another dire emergency," he said with a wicked grin.

"We are not sneaking off to have sex in a children's science center." As much as the idea of it sent a thrill down my spine.

We spent nearly three hours hopping from room to room when Liam looked at the time on his phone and slowed us down.

"This place has a lot of exhibits, but there's one in particular I think you'll love," he said. "It's the real reason I brought us here."

Intrigued, I followed as he guided me through the building. He stopped in the middle of a hallway just before we reached a set of double doors.

"Close your eyes," he urged.

"That's putting a lot of faith in someone who tried to smother me with bubbles."

"No smothering this time, I promise."

I did as he asked and closed my eyes. He took my hand and lead me with baby steps through the doors. I immediately felt a change in temperature. This new room was cooler, and quieter. There were no screaming children. The few voices I did hear were distant and echoed. The room must have been vast.

"Can I open them?" I asked.

"Not yet." Liam positioned me just so in what I expected was the middle of the room. "Now. Look up."

I opened my eyes. The room was near pitch black. I could barely make out Liam next to me. I looked up.

Stars. My vision was filled with stars, hundreds of them, thousands of them, tiny pinpricks of white, gold, blue and red, glittering against a velvety dark sky.

"What—?" I began to ask.

"We're in a planetarium," he explained.

I didn't say anything. I just stared, awed, at a replica of the heavens projected on the domed ceiling. The stars were circling around the center, not stationary, moving at an almost dizzying pace. It had to be a sped up version of their actual paths.

"This is so cool," I said in a hushed voice.

"This isn't the coolest part." He turned me around and directed my attention to the far right corner. "Wait for a second."

Moments passed. I waited patiently. The stars swirled around me. Then—

A blast of light occurred before my eyes. A flash, maybe ten times as brilliant as the brightest star, lit up the dome. I stood still, mesmerized, as a star flared up and went dark in front of my eyes, leaving behind it a cloud of colorful dust and gas.

Liam's lips touched my ear. "You just watched a star explode into a supernova."

My breath caught in my throat. I swallowed hard. The back of my eyes stung with the beginning of tears. I blinked them away rapidly, overcome with a dozen different emotions. I couldn't speak, for fear of my voice trembling.

Liam wrapped his arms around my waist from behind.

"That's going to be you," he said. "And I'm going to be right there." He pointed upward toward the rainbow of stardust.

"Where?" I asked, voice thick and wavering.

"In the heart of that nebula is a neutron star." I felt his lips curve into a smile. "Neutron stars are very magnetic, you know."

I couldn't help it. I let out a giggle that almost become a sob. Liam's arms tightened around me, not saying a word. I basked in his embrace for long minutes.

"Thank you," I told him eventually, breaking the silence. "This was a really fun date."

He placed a kiss on the top of my head. "I'm glad you enjoyed yourself."

"Now the pressure is on," I said, trying to lighten the mood. "I don't know how you're going to outdo yourself for our second date."

"Why don't you plan it?" he suggested.

"Nothing can top this."

"It doesn't have to be grand. It just has to be you."

I was already brainstorming a few ideas, but I knew nothing I came up with would ever top this.

Liam took me to see a supernova, and told me he was going to be the star right in the heart of it. He didn't know how true his words were.

Liam was already in my heart.

## 23

We continued to watch the stars long after the supernova had come and gone.

"Maybe we can go on a picnic at night and stargaze for real some time?" Liam suggested.

"I'd like that." I turned in his arms, looked around furtively to make sure we weren't being watched, and pressed a quick kiss on his lips. "What else do you have planned for the day?"

"There's still some more exhibits left to see. Or," he said, sneaking his hand down my back to cup my ass discreetly in the darkness, "we could go back to my place and I could cook you dinner?"

His place. Alone. Together.

My insides throbbed and pulsed.

"I could go for a nice home cooked meal," I said.

The hand on my ass snuck under my skirt. Calloused fingers trailed between my inner thighs. My stomach muscles clenched.

"Let's get out of here," he murmured in my ear.

I nodded eagerly.

The drive to his place wasn't long, but it seemed to take ages. I was surprised when we pulled up into a house and not an apartment or condo building. The place looked huge, three stories with a gated driveway.

"I thought your band never hit it big?" I asked.

"Hm?"

I nodded to his home. "I know it's not a mansion or anything but it's still pretty impressive."

"My parents are well off," was all he said. I was surprised at how curt he sounded. Then he flashed a small smile. "You should see the house my sister bought."

When we walked inside, I was even more impressed. This wasn't some frat-house bachelor pad. The decor was all clean lines, modern furniture, and a state-of-the art kitchen with marble countertops.

I'd noticed Liam tended to wear brand names and order expensive drinks, but his parents must have been more than well off to give their son enough money to buy a house like this one at his age.

I thought about the shitty apartment my mom had rented. I didn't want to feel intimidated, but this was the first time since I'd met Liam that I felt almost ashamed of how my brother and I had grown up.

I shook it off. It didn't matter how much money our parents made and it didn't matter how we'd grown up. The only thing that mattered was the here and now.

Liam went to the fridge and started taking out a handful of items.

"Are you really going to cook dinner?" I asked. "I thought that was just an excuse."

"I'd never let a lady go hungry," he grinned. "Is pasta okay?"

"Sure." I was even more impressed now than I knew Liam could cook. At least that meant he didn't have some sort of private chef. That would have been too much for me to handle.

I leaned against the island counter and watched him work, putting a pot of boiling water on the stove and chopping fresh vegetables like tomatoes and bell peppers.

"I like seeing this other side of you," I said. "You'd make somebody a good house-husband."

"Is that how it's going to be?" He looked up from the chopping board and smiled. "You bring home the bacon and I make sure there's dinner on the table every night?"

The thought of such an arrangement sent my heart pounding. I knew he was just teasing but the idea of me and him living together, of enjoying that kind of domestic bliss...

My stomach flipped. I didn't know whether it was from panic or excitement.

"You're pretty handy with that knife," was all I said.

"I learned to cook a long time ago," he explained. "My dad made sure of that." He sounded oddly sad as he said it. I wondered...

"Is your dad...?" I trailed off.

"He's doing good," he said. "He's a lawyer. Actually helped read through my first record contract."

"And your mom?"

He paused, the hand holding the knife hovering in mid-air.

"She's across the country. Her and my dad split when I was a kid. That's why it was dad who taught me to cook. Mom wasn't around."

"They divorced?"

"Yeah. It's fine." Liam shrugged but his pained eyes belied his casual pose. "They weren't happy together anyway."

"Lots of fighting and yelling?" I guessed.

He cast his gaze down before retuning to the cutting board.

"No. I had no idea things were bad. Until—"

Liam pressed his lips together and sliced through a bell pepper with more force than needed.

I hesitated. "Can I ask what happened?"

"She left him for another guy. Left us. Went off and started another family. Haven't heard from her in years." Liam said the words so fast I also thought I misheard.

"I'm so sorry."

"It's fine." He shrugged, but he clearly wasn't. His mother leaving him had hurt. "I have some good memories of growing up. Like my dad teaching me to cook." The tension between his brows softened. "My sister and I used to stand on a little stool and watch him in the kitchen when we were young. He never wanted us living off frozen pizzas and take out when we grew up."

A pang of jealousy shot through me, even though I knew it was petty.

"My dad bought me my first guitar," he continued. "He was sure it was just a phase and I'd never put the time in to practice, but I insisted I was serious about it. When he saw my band perform for the first time, he admitted he'd been wrong." He smiled softly. "He was so proud of me that day."

A hollow feeling ate at my stomach.

"What about your parents?" he asked. "Did they support your music?"

"Not really," I murmured. "My mom raised us alone. She was young. She tried her best, but..." I shrugged. "A young single mom working two jobs who went out partying every weekend with her friends didn't really have time to worry about nurturing her kid's hopes and dreams."

Liam's expression turned sympathetic. "It sounds like you and your brother raised yourselves."

"It seemed normal at the time," I said. "All our friends growing up had similar stories. It's like we used to say: *broken homes and broken windows.*"

"Broken windows?" Liam repeated with a furrow brow. "Did you grow up in a bad part of town?"

"I suppose," I said reluctantly. "It wasn't the sort of place you'd want to wander around at night, that's for sure."

His eyebrows now shot up. "You're saying it was unsafe? Just how bad was it? Drugs, violence?"

Unsafe. Violence.

Every muscle in my body immediately tensed. This conversation was wandering too close to all kinds of stuff I didn't want resurfacing.

"What kind of pasta are you cooking?" I came around the island counter and popped one of the cherry tomatoes into my mouth. Liam batted my hand away with a light swat.

"No sneaking bites before dinner." He was eyeing me curiously. "If you didn't have much growing up, where you'd get your first guitar?"

"Borrowed it." If he wasn't going to let up on the questions, at least the subject had taken a U-turn. "My friends and I went to this youth center after school. It kept us kids off the streets and out of trouble. They had some instruments donated. At first we were just playing around, but a few of us got serious about it."

"You and Morris?" he asked.

My throat closed. I nodded.

"Yeah. We had a great thing going on," I managed to say.

"Hm." He went back to chopping vigorously, as if just hearing Morris's name had offended him somehow. "So the two of you have always been close."

I had to wonder just how well Liam thought Morris and I knew each other. There had never been anything between us. For me, there had only ever been Harper.

The pot of water boiling hissed as it bubbled over the rim. Liam cursed and hurried to the stove. I was grateful for the interruption of his game of twenty-questions.

Even though Liam and I were together, talking about my past still hurt.

I couldn't imagine that hurt ever going away.

## 24

The dinner Liam cooked was surprisingly delicious. Even though he knew his way around a kitchen, that didn't necessarily mean he could put together something tasty. But the pasta was expertly cooked and the sauce was the perfect blend of savory spices and fresh vegetables.

We ate dinner without Liam asking any more heart wrenching questions. We kept the conversation light, mostly talking about the tour.

I offered to do the dishes since he had cooked. He insisted on helping. Liam's definition of helping was pressing up against my back, his hips nestled firmly against my ass, and his hands running up and down my sides.

"Stop distracting me," I scolded with a laugh. "You're making me get water everywhere."

He bit down lightly on my ear.

"We're going to leave this kitchen more of a mess than we left off," I warned.

His hands stroked down my hips and back up my inner thighs.

"Do you want me to drop a dish and break it?" I asked.

"I've got plenty more." His fingers skirted the edges of my panties.

My legs went weak.

"The dishes can wait," I said, giving in.

"I've got a dishwasher anyway."

I glared at him. "Then why are we doing this by hand?"

"Because I love the view of your ass from this angle."

"Asshole."

He ground his hips against mine. His cock was hardening in his jeans. My inner muscles clenched at the memory of him inside me, hot and thick.

"Why don't I give you a tour of the place?" he said.

"Only if your bedroom is stop number one."

Liam took my hand and tugged me out of the kitchen, up two flights of stairs and down a long hallway. He opened the door to a large bedroom with a king sized bed and plush carpet. There was an acoustic guitar in a stand in the far corner and a vinyl record player in the other. I supposed in a house this big he didn't have to worry about neighbors complaining about the noise.

Despite the ache between my legs, I took a moment to look around. Liam had seen where I lived. He'd gotten that peek inside my head. I couldn't help but want to do the same.

He had several tall bookshelves, but instead of books they held rows upon rows of CDs and vinyl records.

My eye caught one CD in particular, a first edition of *Forever Night*'s debut indie album, signed by all the band members. There weren't many copies of these left. I'd looked myself, but had never been able to score one.

I picked it up, examining the album cover. It was all abstract swirls with a pale moon, almost like Van Gogh's *The Starry Night*, but with black and red instead of blue and yellow.

"You're holding two hundred dollars in your hand right now," Liam said.

I whistled. "Is that how much one of these things is worth?"

"Last time I checked, that was the going rate online."

"I wonder how much one of our signed debut albums is worth."

"Five hundred."

I blinked at Liam.

"I checked that, too," he grinned.

"Damn," I murmured. "Do you mind if I...?" I gestured to the CD.

"Go ahead."

I opened the case and pulled out the liner notes. The lyrics were printed on the folded sheet, along with thanks and acknowledgements. Liam had thanked his dad and sister, along with a handful of other names I didn't recognize.

He also thanked the other band members for *"jumping on this crazy ride with me."* When I looked for the other band members, I saw they had thanked each other as well, all with sentimental messages.

There was no sign of tension or strain between them. They each sounded genuine, sincerely appreciating, and perhaps even loving each other. They seemed like a true band of brothers.

My heart ached for Liam, knowing they had broken up only a few years after these messages were written.

The first time I'd lost my band, it had been under terrible circumstances. The thought of also losing Cherry Lips was unthinkable.

I felt Liam's eyes boring a hole into my back. I put the CD back on the shelf.

"Can I ask what happened?" I asked softly. I had to know.

His eyes darted to the side. "We had a falling out."

"Creative differences?"

He smiled sadly. "That's the official story."

"What's the real story?"

"I was betrayed."

My lips parted in surprise. That was a strong choice of words. "Who — How—" I didn't know what to ask first.

He shrugged. "My guitarist took advantage of my trust in him. The details aren't important."

They were important. I wanted to know more about Liam, just as much as he wanted to know about me.

But I worried if I pressed him, he would want me to open up in return.

I wasn't ready for that.

We were just at the start of our relationship. There was no need to rehash all the awful details of my past when the day had been going so well. Liam's eyes were already downcast, an almost haunted look on his face. I didn't need to add to that.

I went up to him and wrapped my arms around his neck, pressing my chest to his.

"I'm sorry," I told him.

His hands went to my hips. I ran my fingers through his thick hair. His eyes went heavy-lidded, enjoying the sensation.

"I'm over it," he said. "What happened was shitty, but I've moved on to bigger and better things."

"Like Cherry Lips?"

"You certainly are bigger and better." He gazed down at me, green eyes bright and clear. "I'm grateful you took a chance on me."

"Wasn't really a chance," I said. "No matter who else had auditioned for us, you would have been better in the end, anyway. It made sense to go with you."

"Still. Thank you."

"Don't thank me. Thank Gael and Nate. I had about a million objections."

"And now?" he asked. "Do you still object to my presence?"

"I suppose I can tolerate you."

"Faint praise."

"That's high praise," I corrected. "I didn't want anyone else joining my band, ever. The fact that you're here says a lot about your talent."

"Better quit talking me up or I'm going to get a swelled head."

"Isn't it a bit too late for that?"

"At least I can keep my ego in check most of the time, unlike your brother."

"He's gotten better. Thank god. There's enough egomaniacs in Cherry Lips already."

"Yourself included?"

"I'm aware of my faults."

"Do you think—" Liam paused, hesitating, then started again. "How do you think Gael will react when he finds out?"

"About us?" I raised an eyebrow. "He'll try to punch you in the face."

"Why do I have the feeling you're speaking from experience?"

"There's an overprotective-brother cliché because it's true."

"So you're saying we shouldn't tell him? Or the guys?"

"Not yet," I said. "Not until the tour is over, at least. They'll all get their panties in a twist about dating within the band and what if we break up and blah blah blah." I shook my head ruefully. "We don't need that distraction."

"So when the tour is over, we come clean?"

"You make it sound like we're keeping a dirty little secret. We're keeping our relationship to ourselves to prevent unnecessary drama."

"Sounds fair," Liam said. "When the tour is over, I'll be out of the band and their objections won't matter any more."

Out of the band.

After the tour, Liam was going to leave.

He wasn't going to leave *me*, but my band made up a huge part of my life. With the time I put into recording and rehearsing and touring, how easy would it be to maintain a normal relationship? I'd never had to worry about that before.

A small part of me wondered if, maybe, Liam staying in the band wouldn't be such a bad idea.

Then I remembered how Liam reacted the two previous times the idea was brought up. He'd went cold and tensed up.

What was so wrong with the idea of him joining Cherry Lips?

"I have to admit," Liam said, "I was worried when I first started. Being thrust into an already established group is hard. But your guys are cool. I like them."

"And what about me?" I teased. "Do you like me?"

His eyes darkened. His hands squeezed my hips. "I fucking adore you."

My heart squeezed tightly, before floating up and out of my chest. It sounded like he really meant it.

"I guess you're okay, too," I said in response, a smile playing on my lips.

A wicked expression crossed his face. "Just okay? That's not what you were screaming last night."

I stood on my tiptoes and brought my lips to his, just barely brushing them.

"Maybe I need a reminder."

He closed the gap and crushed his mouth to mine. He swiped the tip of his tongue along my lower lip and I opened for him. Smoothing his hands over my ass, he pulled me close. The firm grip had me whimpering in his mouth.

He tugged my skirt down over my hips as his teeth grazed my upper lip. I loved how demanding he was, touching me in all the right places. He grabbed my ass cheeks and squeezed hard, sending waves of pleasure coursing through my body.

"Greedy," I hissed, tipping my head back.

"Can't help it," he grunted, nibbling along my neck. "You're so fucking tempting."

My belly twitched in excitement. I couldn't wait to have his hips between my legs again. I couldn't wait to feel him moving inside me.

I started off towards his bed, kicking my boots off along the way. I looked up at him over my shoulder. Liam was practically licking his lips, as if he was about to devour me. I didn't break eye contact with him as I lay down on his bed and spread my legs, my thin cotton underwear the only barrier. I trailed my fingers down my chest, along my stomach, to the apex of my thighs. I inched lower until I found that one spot. I rubbed at myself, letting out a stifled moan, keeping my eyes locked on Liam the entire time.

"That's the sexiest fucking thing I've ever seen," he murmured, sending my pulse rising.

He yanked his shirt off almost violently, his jeans soon following. I marveled at his toned, inked skin. The moment his cock was free of his underwear, my mouth almost watered. Naughty ideas about what I could do with that cock began to fill my head.

But that was for another time. Once Liam had rolled on protection, he climbed into bed. He yanked my panties down my legs, his mouth planting hot kisses on my thighs, making me squeeze my eyes shut. I gripped the sheets hard as his lips moved along my skin, going closer to my entrance and then pulling away, teasing me.

I grabbed a fistful of his hair and tried to direct him where I wanted him.

He chuckled. "Now who's being greedy?"

Before I could gasp out a reply, he flicked his tongue across my clit. I moaned out loud. He licked firm lines up and down, parting my folds. Every lick and suck and twirl of his tongue drove me crazy. He slid two fingers between my lower lips, caressing but not entering, showing me again what a tease he was.

"Fuck, you're dripping," he groaned against my skin.

I grabbed his wrist. Raising it to my mouth, I slipped his index and middle fingers through my lips, tasting myself on his skin. As he watched, his eyes burned with an inner fire, his muscles bunched as if seconds away from pouncing.

There had been enough teasing from both of us. I wanted more. I wanted him. All of him.

Once more, I tugged on his hair.

"Fuck me," I demanded breathlessly.

His eyes flashed with hunger. He sat up, parting my thighs with his knees. Our eyes met.

With one slow thrust, he entered me. His long, hard inches stretched me wide. My head thumped back onto the bed at the delicious friction against my inner walls. My whole body throbbed with need.

His muscles tensed and flexed with every thrust as he braced himself above me. I placed my palm on his chest, wanting to feel his firm skin against mine. He growled and tilted my hips up, thrusting in from another angle. I cried out as my fingernails dug into his skin.

"More," I moaned. I couldn't keep my eyes open any longer. My lids fluttered shut as pleasure began to overtake me.

Every slide of his cock, every thrust and withdrawal, made me melt, taking away the strength in my muscles. Liam returned his fingers to my clit, playing with me, coaxing me relentlessly to another orgasm.

Pulses of pleasure ripped through me. I groaned, loud and long, body squirming as my orgasm had me writhing on the bed. My inner muscles squeezed and clenched down around him. Liam's guttural grunts filled his bedroom. He held onto my thighs and his cock twitched inside me.

Eventually, he stilled his hips. The sweat on his brow told me he was just as spent as I was.

Exhausted, I used the last of my energy to pull him down to lie on his back beside me. He circled his arm around my shoulders and held me close.

I snuggled up against him as a whimper of satisfaction escaped me. I kept my mouth shut, watching his chest rise and fall. I pecked a quick kiss on his skin, running my fingers up his stomach.

Liam bent his head towards me, tightening his grip around me for a second. He buried his face into my hair, sliding his hand along my shoulder.

We shared the tender moment in total silence, enjoying a long calm. Neither of us seemed willing to talk.

The sense that I had been missing out on something for years hit me. As I felt his body heat on my skin. I recognized it for what it was...

Safety.

Security.

Peace.

With his arms around me, I was overcome with the feeling that he would stay by my side no matter what.

"I can hear you thinking," Liam murmured, sounding amused. "You want to share with the class?"

I debated whether or not to tell him. It would probably sound stupid out loud. But—

"You make me feel safe," I confessed.

Liam didn't laugh, just hummed thoughtfully. "I imagine that's something you don't have much experience with, considering the way you grew up."

I shrugged a single shoulder. "It wasn't all bad. I had my friends. We were like our own little family."

"And then you lost them," he said quietly. "How long ago was that?"

"Five years."

I'd been nineteen.

*Nineteen.*

I wondered if he was doing the math. If he would put two and two together.

"I'm sorry." The words were muffled as he spoke them into my hair.

"It's still hard," I admitted, even though he didn't know all the details. "But I've got my brother, and Julian and Seth and Nate. And now I have you."

"We both have bigger and better things." He tightened his arms around me and kissed the top of my head. "We have each other."

# 25

The next morning, I woke up to bright sunlight hitting my eyelids. I threw my arm over my eyes to shield them, but the damage was done. With a grumble I rubbed at my face and sat up in bed.

Liam was sound asleep next to me, sheets and blankets tossed to the side. I let myself thoroughly enjoy the view of his broad back and naked ass before stretching and climbing out of bed.

I made my way downstairs to get some coffee. Once I had a large mug, I wandered around the house as I sipped at the life-saving liquid. Liam had never actually given me the tour.

It was a mostly normal house, with a living room, dining room and fully furnished basement den. The thing that struck me most were the guitars in almost every room. Not all of them were in stands. Some were just lying around, as if they'd been haphazardly set down and forgotten.

One acoustic guitar in particular called to me with its shiny-smooth dark wood finish. I set my mug down, took my place on a sofa in the den and pulled the guitar into my lap.

It felt like I hadn't written a new song in ages. I'd been so focused on recording old songs for our album and getting ready for the tour.

But now I felt a trickling of music notes and the stirrings of lyrics begging to be let out.

I began strumming and humming, not fully aware of what I was doing, just letting my subconscious take over.

"Was the sex that inspiring?"

I jumped, guitar strings screeching.

"Sorry," Liam said as he finished coming down the stairs and took a seat beside me. "I didn't mean to scare you."

"You walk like a cat," I accused.

He wrapped his arm around my shoulders and kissed the side of my head. "I didn't realize you were so absorbed in the music. Do you usually get that way when you compose?"

"Sometimes. Depends on my mood, depends on the type of music."

"And what type of music are you writing now?"

"I'm not sure," I said. "It's sort of uplifting, but melancholy at the same time. I don't know. I can never really tell how my songs are going to come out until they're done. It's like my brain shuts off and my instincts take over."

"Makes sense," he said. "They say music comes from the heart, from the soul. Maybe we can write a song together sometime."

My chest twinged. Harper was the only one I'd ever written songs with. Ever since he'd died, I'd composed all my songs by myself. It had been too painful to do otherwise, even with Gael. Writing was too personal, too private, to do it with just anyone. I had to let down my barriers, had to open up and let all my thoughts and feelings rise to the surface. Harper had been the only one I'd ever felt comfortable enough to do that with.

"What do you think?" Liam asked expectantly.

"I don't know," I said, hesitating. "Writing is kind of a solitary thing for me."

"You don't co-write songs?"

"I used to." I looked down at the guitar in my lap. "It's been a while."

"Do you maybe want to try again?" Liam asked.

The thought of trying to write a song with Liam, with anyone really, sent a spike of panic shooting through me.

"I don't—" I swallowed hard. "I don't think so. Not yet." I set the guitar down and stood up in a hurry. "What are your plans for the day?" I asked. "If you're free I have an idea for our second date."

Liam studied me, disappointment almost palpable. He nodded once, as if to himself. "My day's open."

"There's this fun fair going on at that youth center I told you about. A fundraiser. It's mostly for kids and families, but after our science center date, I figure you won't have a problem with that." I flashed him a wavering smile, hoping he wouldn't press me.

"Sounds fun." He got up from the sofa, too. "When should we head over?"

I was glad he wasn't going to press me on the issue.

"Let's get showered and dressed, then go," I said.

He quirked a smile. "Care to join me?"

I returned the smile. Of course I did. In fact, I'd been planning on something like this for a while.

With a nod, I followed Liam down the hall and into the large bathroom to the left. It was huge and luxurious, but there was no bathtub. The big, wide shower was perfect for what I had in mind.

Liam turned on the water and tested the temperature until it was just right. He stepped in and shut his eyes, tipping his head back as thick drops streamed down his chest and his stomach. I rolled my panties down and off my feet and joined him in the shower.

I grabbed a bottle of bath foam. I popped the lid open and poured some over my hand, a wicked smile on my face. Liam moaned softly as I rubbed it over his chest, soaping him up. My hand slipped further down, finding his cock. I wrapped my fingers around it.

His eyes snapped closed as he hissed in pleasure. He snaked his arm around me and pulled me in. His cool lips met mine in a demanding kiss. I stroked his cock, feeling it pressed against me. The pleased hum he let out encouraged me on. The water drenched my hair, getting into my eyes, but I wasn't going to let it change my plan.

I stepped forward, his cock throbbing in my grasp, stopping only when his back was firmly pressed against the wall. I gave his shaft a good squeeze, moving my lips down to his chest. I trailed my tongue down his body, bending my knees. For once, I didn't want condoms to get in my way. I wanted to feel those inches in my mouth. I wanted to taste him, like he had tasted me, over and over again. I wanted to make him squirm, like I had the night before.

I looked up at him. His hungry eyes were locked on mine. I stroked. He moaned. I squeezed. He grunted.

"You're a fucking tease, aren't you?" he said with a whisper.

I let a wicked smile creep across my lips. "It's only a tease if I don't follow through."

Lowering myself to my knees, I shifted my gaze down to his cock. It extended beautifully from his body, brushing against my cheek. I put my free hand on his hip and swiped the tip of my tongue across the head. The shaft twitched as Liam let out a deep sound from the back of his throat.

I closed my eyes, snaking my tongue out. I swirled it around the head at first, twisting the base of his shaft. He reached down and grabbed a fistful of my hair, the taste of him warm in my mouth.

In a slow, careful move, I let him in. His long, delicious groans filled the bathroom, his body tensing. Liam's fingertips glided into my hair, before he pressed them into my scalp.

"Fuck, feels so good," he groaned, easing the pressure. I wanted to say something to him, maybe tease him some more, but I didn't. I'd have to pull him out, and that was the last thing I wanted.

I was enjoying having him inside me, edging him with my tongue. The wetness that had been gathering between my legs was proof of that. For once, I decided to keep my hands off myself. This was about him, and him alone. This was about giving him as much pleasure as he'd been giving me. I wanted him to fall apart under my hands the way I always did under his.

I started a steady rhythm, taking more than half of his cock and letting it slide out. I kept the head in my mouth, knowing how sensitive it was. My tongue ran circles around it, I sucked on it with vigor, loving his growls.

Liam rocked into me slowly, making sure he never went too deep. He let go of my head and pushed my hair back from my face. He kept his hand there, trailing his fingers down my cheek and then back up. His knees shook as he cupped my face. I could tell he was close.

I stroked him faster, my muffled moans much lower than his grunts. I stole a glance up at him. His eyes were trained on me. His chest was heaving. In my eagerness, I sucked him down even further, going deep, until he touched the back of my throat.

"Fuck!" Liam groaned, banging his palm against the wall. I retreated, holding on to his hip tighter. I grazed my fingers up his side, bobbing my head up and down on his cock.

His hand slipped up and back into my hair. He tugged on it as I sucked harder and faster. I let go of his hip, and grabbed his length.

His taste was growing stronger by the second. The pulsating of his cock screamed to me that his orgasm was just moments away. His loud cries echoed back at the walls of his bathroom as he exploded deep in my mouth. I didn't even think of pulling him out. I stayed where I was, feeling his warmth streaming along my tongue.

I whimpered my satisfaction, his gasps still lingering in the air. My throat muscles relaxed as I ran my tongue up his shaft one last time. Liam tilted his head back, giving a short laugh. I eased him out.

He pulled me up from my knees and kissed me desperately. His hands trailed down my stomach, looking for the wetness between my legs. I shook my head and pushed him away. He made a sound of disappointment.

"As much as I'd love to, we've got somewhere to be, remember?" I told him.

He almost pouted. It was adorable. I chuckled and soaped him up, washing him for real this time.

"You can make it up to me later," I promised him.

Liam always knew exactly what to do, exactly what to say, to drive me crazy, to knock me off balance. I loved that for once, I had been able to do the same for him.

We finished our shower quickly. When I stepped out and grabbed a towel to dry off, I realized I didn't have a change of clothes.

"Don't suppose you've got any girl's clothes around here?" I asked him.

"My sister probably left a few things lying around after her visits."

Liam managed to scrounge up a few sets of clothes. I had my choice between a hot pink bodycon dress, a pair of tiny running shorts and tight tank top, and a pair of black yoga pants with a loose black shirt cut off at the midriff.

I decided to pair the hot pink dress with the shirt. I could totally rock a bodycon dress with a black crop top.

While Liam got ready, I examined more of his house. The kitchen was still a bit of a mess. We'd gotten distracted before we'd finished cleaning up. I decided to be a good houseguest and put some things away.

After loading the dishwasher and wiping down the counter, I looked around for anything else that needed taking care of. There were some papers lying around, so I decided to sort them, seeing what was important mail and what was just junk to be recycled.

I had just picked up the papers when I noticed one of them was a crumpled piece of heavy folded card stock. It looked like it had been crushed, and then smoothed out again.

Curious, I unfolded it. It was a wedding invitation. Paula and Chad. I didn't recognize the girl's last name, so she probably wasn't anybody in the industry. But I did recognize the guy's name.

Chad Emmerson, the guitarist of Liam's old band.

I frowned. They'd had a falling out, hadn't they? Why would he have sent Liam an invitation to his wedding? Unless he was just being polite and inviting everyone. Maybe there weren't any hard feelings on Chad's part. Maybe it was just Liam who was still affected by it.

Maybe that was why he'd crumpled the invitation. But if that was the case, why hadn't he thrown it out? Why had he smoothed it out and kept it? It was odd. I wanted to ask Liam about it, but it was probably still a sore spot. Best to just pretend I hadn't seen it. I slid the invitation back among the pile of papers and left them sitting on the counter.

I went back up to Liam's room, waiting for him to finish getting ready.

When he came out of the bathroom washed and fully dressed, I had to suppress the urge to push him onto the bed and get him dirty all over again. Damp hair, tight t-shirt showing off inked arms, dark denim skinny jeans...

I squinted at his shirt.

"You're going to wear that?" I asked.

He looked down at himself. "What's wrong with it?"

"Do you know how much a shirt like that costs?"

He shrugged. "I don't really remember."

"You do know where we're going today, right?"

"That youth center you talked about...?" he trailed off with a questioning tone.

"Think about how it's going to look when you walk in wearing a brand name shirt like that one."

He continued to look befuddled. "Do you not like the shirt?"

I gave up. Let the rich bastard learn the lesson on his own.

Liam drove us through town under my directions. The buildings became steadily more run down and graffiti became more prominent the closer we got.

"You grew up here?" he muttered under his breath as we drove by a block of abandoned storefronts full of broken windows.

"This place has actually been cleaned up since I last lived here."

He grunted and hit the switch to lock the car doors from the inside. I suppressed a snort.

This was going to be an interesting afternoon.

# 26

"Slow it down, rugrats," a voice called out.

I winced and jumped back as a handful of shrieking kids nearly ran me over. I bumped into Liam. He put his hands on my upper arms to steady me.

"Sorry about that." Jessie ushered us through the door of The Impact Youth Center. She craned her neck and shouted over her shoulder. "I said slow down!"

Liam quirked a brow. "They're an energetic bunch."

Jessie shook her head ruefully. Her brown hair was up in a low bun and pulled away from her face. She wore not a speck of makeup, in contrast with my own heavy eyeliner and lipstick. My brother's girl-friend had that wholesome girl next door look.

Or at least, she did when she worked at the youth center. I'd seen her dressed for her part time job at a dingy dive bar. I'd never seen someone make a complete one-eighty from schoolteacher to biker babe so thoroughly. Standing here in front of me, you never would have guessed she looked just as at home in a leather miniskirt as she did in a cotton blouse.

"You were never that rambunctious as a kid, were you?" Jessie asked Liam.

His green eyes twinkled. "I was worse."

"Somehow I don't doubt that." She gave him a cheeky smile before turning to me. "Thanks so much for coming out to support our fundraiser."

"Of course," I said. "This place means a lot to me."

Jessie didn't know everything, but she knew the center was where I had gotten started with my very first rock band.

"Gael's around somewhere," Jessie said. "I've got him acting as my errand boy today."

She handed me and Liam plastic wristbands in exchange for a wad of small bills.

"These are your passes," she said. "It proves you paid to get in."

"Just like at concerts," Liam said as he examined his.

Jessie beamed. "There's actually going to be a short concert later today."

"Who's playing?" Liam asked, no doubt wondering how a run down non-profit on the rough side of town could have convinced a band to come.

"Some kids at our center put together their own rock band," she explained to Liam. "We thought it was the cutest thing, until we realized how serious they were. Now we're just proud and impressed."

"We'll have to stick around for it." I nodded to a booth where a woman was using face paint to turn a little girl into a cat. "How does this fun fair work?"

"It's two tickets per game or activity," she said. "You can buy them from Anya and Micah over there." Jessie gestured to a table along the wall with two kids standing behind it. "They're both in the band. They'll benefit from this fundraiser, so they were happy to help out."

The table was manned by a tall teen with thick black glasses and a younger looking girl with her hair hiding half her face. They looked to be around the same age as my friends and I had been when we first started our band. I had seen them play before, so I knew he was the keyboardist and she was the lead singer.

"Food and drink can be bought with cash," Jessie continued. "We've got a bake sale with treats the kids have made. If you're hungry for more than just cookies and brownies, a few local restaurants donated some catered food."

"You've really got this whole thing planned out," I said.

"It's not the event of the century, but the kids had a lot of fun putting it together." A fond look spread across Jessie's face. "We're hoping to raise some money to buy more supplies for our art programs. Paintbrushes, blank canvasses, things like that."

"This place only runs on donations?" Liam asked, surprised. "There's no government funding or anything?"

"The government funds standard programming," she said. "Early morning day care, after-school tutoring, things like that. But as for the non-traditional stuff—"

At that, Jessie's brow furrowed.

"Local politicians don't always see the point in giving away tax dollars to painting classes or music lessons," she finished.

"Really?" Liam frowned. "That's complete bullshit."

"It is," Jessie agreed. "Those are some of our most popular programs. But—" she shrugged. "Funding for the arts is usually the first to go, I'm afraid."

Liam's nostrils flared, as if he'd been personally offended.

"How much money are you looking to raise?" he asked.

I had a sudden vision of Liam whipping out his checkbook, right then and there.

"Why don't we go play some games?" I interjected as I linked my arm through his. "You can be all macho and win me a toy."

The frown on Liam's face melted into a soft smile as he looked down at me. "I thought you hated all that macho-caveman stuff?"

"It's for a good cause."

"That game over there has some donated stuffed animals as prizes." Jessie pointed to a wall with dozens of balloons taped to it. People were using plastic darts to try and pop them. Her eyes drifted over my shoulder. An alarmed look appeared on her face. "Stop—!"

"Oomp," Liam huffed as a teen boy rammed into him from behind.

"Shit, sorry, man," the kid said as he righted himself. He looked to be fourteen with long, gangly limbs.

"Language!" Jessie admonished.

"Whoa, hey, you're Gael's sister!" the kid gaped at me. "You're the lead singer of his band!"

"That's me." I hid a smile. I recognized the kid as one of the guitarists in the youth center's rock band.

The kid's eyes flicked to Liam and the awe faded a bit.

"Who invited Douchebag and Gabbana?" he asked.

I nearly burst into laughter. I'd told Liam not to wear that shirt.

"Zain!" Jessie scolded the kid, exasperated. "Be careful who you call names. You'd kill to one day be as successful as Liam Knight."

"Who?" the kid asked dismissively.

I held back a snicker. Liam's expression was hilarious, both confused and affronted at the same time.

"Whatever," Zain continued, ignoring Liam. "I just came by to tell you that Gael said we're almost out of bottled water at the bake sale."

"Tell him I've got some more in the trunk of my car."

He nodded and hurried off to relay the message.

"Sorry about that," Jessie apologized for the second time. "Kids these days."

"It's cool," Liam said, although his lips were twisted into a frown. "I was a little shit disturber when I was his age, too."

"He's actually a really sweet kid," she said. "He's just at that age where he thinks he has to play it cool."

"Do boys ever grow out of that stage?" I asked.

Jessie and I shared a grin.

"Why don't we go get some tickets?" Liam asked, still looking vaguely disgruntled.

I agreed and kept my arm looped through his, tugging him out of the way when stray children ran by us.

"I've never been around so many little tiny humans in my life," Liam said. "How does Jessie deal with it?"

"With great patience, I assume."

"No wonder she's able to handle Gael," he said. "She's used to putting up with bratty kids."

I laughed.

"That's exactly why Jessie and Gael are together," I explained. "My brother's antics had been putting our chances of getting a recording contract at risk. No one wanted to sign a loose cannon. Since Jessie's job is to wrangle unruly youths, I essentially hired her to "babysit" him until we'd sealed the deal. I hadn't expected her to fall for Gael. I certainly hadn't expected my wild, playboy brother to fall for her, either."

"Makes sense," Liam said.

"How so?"

"What boy doesn't dream of getting it on with the hot babysitter?" he grinned.

I snorted. "That's exactly what my brother always says. But Jessie's been good for him. He's been a lot less out of control lately."

"He does seem to have taken on a lot of responsibilities," Liam agreed.

"If I didn't know his girlfriend was the cause, I'd worry it was alien bodysnatchers."

"Surely he hasn't changed that much?" Liam asked.

I thought about it. "I suppose not. He's always taken care of me, always tried to be the mature one when it came to the two of us. He just never took anything else seriously. Our mother was never around to discipline us so he could get away with anything."

"And now Jessie's made him realize that actions have consequences?" Liam guessed.

"I think that's exactly it."

We reached the table selling tickets. The tall boy in glasses was already reaching for a roll of tickets and the cash box.

"Thank you for coming to our fun fair," he said politely with a nod.

"How much are the tickets?" I asked.

"They're a dollar fifty each," the girl piped up. "But you get one extra ticket for every ten you buy."

"How many games are there?" Liam asked, already pulling out his wallet.

The boy paused, seeming to count in his head. "I think we've got twelve booths, between all the different games and activities."

"I'll take three hundred tickets," Liam said.

I nearly choked on my own tongue. Both kids went wide-eyed and gape-mouthed.

"Three... hundred?" the girl asked slowly.

Liam took a handful of bills from his wallet. I tugged him aside as the kid continued staring.

"What are you doing?" I hissed under my breath.

"Buying tickets?" Liam said carefully, as if unsure of what set me off and not wanting to repeat it.

"You're buying more than *four hundred dollars* worth of tickets."

"It's more like four fifty, I think."

"What the hell is wrong with you?" I couldn't help burst out.

"It's a fundraiser, isn't it?"

"That's not the point," I said. "You don't go waving that kind of money around in a place like this."

His forehead creased into a confused frown. "It's a kid's fun fair."

I wanted to smack him. So I did. I smacked him lightly in the chest with the back of my hand.

"Do you really want to go flashing those bills around?" I said. "Do you not remember the abandoned buildings and broken windows we passed by? Most people don't even make that much money in a week's worth of work. Most people here are probably never even seen that much money in one place. The only people who have are drug dealers."

Now it was Liam's turn to look like he'd bit his tongue.

"Are you saying people are going to think I'm a drug dealer?" he asked under his breath.

"No." I scanned the room with a furtive eye. I couldn't stop myself from picking at my nails, flakes of polish coming off under my fingers. "I'm saying people are going to think you're a rich asshole and some of them are going to want to get a piece of that."

A look of understanding finally crossed his face. Understanding and chagrin.

"I thought this place had been cleaned up since you last lived here...?" he trailed off.

"Cleaner, yes. Spotless, no."

"So you're saying I might get jumped and shanked in an alleyway?"

I nearly reeled back. Liam words were like a bullet through my chest. A bullet that shot through the almost-healed fissure inside me, cracking it wide open. Dark tendrils oozed out, slithering between my organs, wriggling their way between my ribs. They congealed in one big mass around my heart, threatening to clamp down and squeeze the life out of me.

Liam couldn't have known how close to the truth he was.

"I didn't even think of it like that." His eyes weren't focused on me. They were now scanning the room warily, just as I had done.

I forced myself to breathe, taking a slow, shallow lungful of air. My fingers and toes tingled, my body both chilled and boiling hot at the same time.

"I'm sorry I'm an idiot." Liam returned his attention to me. His face turned concerned. "Are you okay?"

"I'm fine."

I hadn't meant for the words to sound so curt, but it was hard to talk through my tight throat.

Liam took both my arms gently in his hands, making me face him. I didn't know what he saw in my expression, but his own turned pained.

"I'm sorry," he murmured again. "I should have realized."

His green eyes were so soft, caring. They were like a beam of green light blasting through the darkness.

The dark tendrils writhed and squirmed, fleeing that glow, disappearing back into the fissure. My breathing evened out. I pressed my hands against my thighs, stopping my fingers from picking at the red lacquer on my nails.

"I'm fine," I said. "I just want you to be safe."

"I'm sorry I made you feel otherwise." He leaned forward and tilted his head down.

I put a hand up to still him. "No PDA in front of the children."

He paused, then tipped his chin up and pressed a kiss to my forehead instead of my lips.

I heard a burst of high-pitched giggles from behind us.

"Someone's got a *boooooyfriend*," came a chorus of voices.

I groaned and thumped my head forward onto Liam's chest.

"Great," I said. "Jessie's going to get a hundred letters from angry parents appalled at the inappropriate behavior their children were subjected to."

"Kids gotta learn the birds and the bees sometime."

I stifled a snort of laughter, looking into Liam's eyes again to meet his gaze. He cracked a grin and gestured to one of the booths with a nod of his head.

"Want to go get your face painted like a cat?" he asked.

"I'd much rather see you as a cat," I said. "Cute pink nose, whiskers and all."

"Only if you swear to not take pictures."

"No promises."

Liam took my hand in his and squeezed. I returned it.

The crack inside me began to close. Not completely, and not quickly, but it was closing, growing smaller. Small enough to keep the darkness from escaping.

For now.

## 27

After Liam went back to buy us tickets — only thirty this time, ten times fewer than he'd originally asked for — we wandered through the center, taking part in the various games and activities the kids had put together.

Despite our teasing, neither Liam or I got our faces painted. He did win me a small stuffed giraffe at the balloon dart game, and in return I won him a large stuffed polar bear. I'd played darts at Jessie's dive bar often enough to clean up nicely.

I wondered if Liam would turn disgruntled after I one-upped him at the game, but he accepted his prize with a delighted grin. All afternoon he pecked the bear's button nose to my lips and cheeks.

"If I can't kiss you directly, at least I can give you polar bear kisses," he said.

It was such a cute, childish gesture that it warmed my heart. For all that Liam called himself a sex-god rock star, he was also thoughtful and sweet.

I supposed I shouldn't have been surprised. Even from the start, when we'd first met behind those concert tents, he'd taken the time to reassure and encourage an insecure young woman, a complete stranger.

After we'd spent about an hour playing games, we stopped to buy some food from the bake sale. There were slices of cake and pie, lemon tarts and cookies, along with a host of other sugary treats. I was torn between a slice of blueberry or cherry pie when I saw something that made my mouth water.

"Oh my god, they have double chocolate fudge brownies," I moaned in one breath. I slammed a handful of bills on the table, picked up a large square and took a bite. I moaned again, closing my eyes at the burst of chocolate on my tongue.

"Do you need a moment with that brownie?" Liam asked. "Should I leave the two of you alone?"

I didn't answer, just swallowed and sank my teeth into the soft deliciousness again.

"I suppose it's useless to ask if I can have a bite," Liam said.

"No sharing," I said in between mouthfuls. "Get your own."

"So that's your weakness, is it? Chocolate fudge brownies?"

"Mm-hm," I mumbled.

"Good to know."

The wicked glint in his eyes had me wondering what he was going to do with that knowledge. I had visions of chocolate sauce and naked skin. I hoped that was where his mind was going, too.

I'd just finished the square and wiped my mouth and sticky fingers when a familiar deep voice spoke up from behind me.

"Should've known I'd find you here."

Morris appeared next to me with his girlfriend Natalie by his side. A little stab of pain shot through me, but it quickly passed. I gave the two of them a bright, genuine smile.

"It's good to see you guys," I said. "Are you here for fun or to volunteer?"

"I'm technically working." Natalie clung to Morris's beefy arm. Her long hair was pulled back in a sophisticated braid, which suited her classical, feminine features. Last I'd heard, she'd gotten a part-time job working at the center. "Morris is here for moral support."

Morris cocked his head. "How many brownies you eat so far?"

"Just the one," I said. "But give me time. I only found them thirty seconds ago."

We both went in for a hug at the same time. Natalie beamed, over-joyed that her scheme to reunite us had worked, and that we'd stayed in touch.

When we pulled back, Liam held his hand out to Morris. Morris took it with a careful nod, no doubt remembering Liam's curt behavior. I eyed their clasped hands to see if they either one of them squeezed too tightly in a show of aggressive dominance, but it was simply a firm handshake.

"Natalie, this is Liam," I introduced, knowing that she hadn't yet met him. "He's my new guitarist and—"

I paused there, wondering whether to say it.

Liam held his hand out to Natalie as well. "I'm her boyfriend," he completed for me.

I bit my lip to suppress a giddy smile from spreading ear to ear.

As our two lovers shook hands, Morris stared at me, his eyes inscrutable.

I had to wonder what he was thinking. Was I betraying Harper's memory by dating someone else? Was he worried I'd get hurt just like last time? Was he happy for me, proud of me, that I'd finally moved on?

You could rarely tell with Morris.

"Fraternizing, hm?" was all he said.

"Guess so." I met his stare head on, not backing down. Everyone knew sleeping with a band member was a bad idea, but I didn't care. It was different with me and Liam.

Morris's lips quirked into the barest of smiles. "Good for you."

I returned his smile, relieved he approved. Not that I needed his approval, but he was one of my oldest friends. His support meant a lot to me.

"Ohmigod," Natalie said, eyes wide with recognition. "You're Liam *Knight*." Her breathing turned labored and heavy.

"Nat's got a thing for rock stars," Morris said wryly.

She let out a small squeak. "I don't mean to freak out. I just really *really* liked your band." All traces of sophistication left her as she gaped at Liam.

"Thanks." His smile almost sad. "It's good to meet a fan."

"I was so upset when you guys broke up, I think I cried for three days while playing your albums on repeat a billion times—"

"Nat," Morris said gently.

She snapped her jaw shut with a flush.

"She gets a bit exuberant sometimes," Morris said with an indulgent look. "That's why I love her."

They shared a sappy smile. Normally it would have made me

blanch with discomfort. Now, with Liam by my side, I only felt happy for them.

"The concert is starting soon," Morris said once he pulled his attention away from his girlfriend. "You three go ahead. I'm helping the kids backstage."

Morris looked directly at me, capturing my gaze.

"Make sure Nat gets a a front row seat?" His voice carried a heavy weight.

"Sure." I blinked at his odd tone. "Front and center."

He nodded and left.

"Let's get going," I said. I assumed Morris was up to something, even if I didn't know exactly what, and I wanted to take my duty seriously.

The youth center had a small gymnasium with a raised platform at the far end they used for events like this. Some volunteers had set up rows of cheap and dented aluminum folding chairs to face the stage. People were already trickling in.

I hurried to snag four chairs right in the middle of the front row, three for us and one saved for when Morris got back.

"Morris really loves those kids," Natalie said as we took our seats. "I think that little rock band did more for him than he even realizes. He's such a caretaker type, you know?"

He always had been. Morris and Harper had been the self-appointed mom and dad of our neighborhood. They would take neglected kids under their wings, make sure to keep them away from trouble like gangs and drugs.

They used to joke about which one of them was the mom.

"Yeah," I said, a lump forming in my throat. "He is."

I caught sight of the ticket girl, Anya, the one hiding behind her hair. Her little face peeped out from behind a makeshift backstage curtain hung between two rolling coat racks. The poor thing looked nervous, still ducking her head so her hair covered half her face.

A shy lead singer. It wasn't unheard of. Some of the most reticent musicians came alive on stage.

"How many times have these kids performed?" I asked.

"They've done a handful of concerts, maybe close to a dozen," Natalie said. "We're always on the lookout for opportunities to show off what they can do."

Less than a dozen times. No wonder she was nervous.

Morris appeared behind the girl's shoulder, towering over her tiny frame. He crouched low, getting down on her level, and spoke quiet words. She listened to him with rapt attention.

Her fearful wide eyes soon transformed into a look of excitement and near glee. She gave him a thumbs up, which he returned. He patted her on the back with a large hand and disappeared behind the curtain.

Anya seemed to take a deep breath then strutted onto the stage. The rest of her bandmates followed behind her and took their places, all of them with expressions of both nerves and anticipation.

"Thank you for coming out to our fundraiser," Anya spoke quickly into the microphone in nearly one breath. "Everyone here at The Impact Youth Center appreciates your support and we all believe the arts are important and that all kids should have an outlet for their creativity."

It was clearly a rehearsed speech and her words were rushed, but the sentiment was there.

"Before we start our concert, we want to thank a few people," she continued.

Her voice trembled a bit, but the expression on her face wasn't nervous or anxious. It looked like she was struggling to keep an ear-to-ear grin from spreading across her face.

"Natalie, could you come up here?" Anya asked, looking directly at her.

Beside me, Natalie looked taken aback. I assumed this wasn't part of the planned performance. Maybe they were going to give her some sort of thank you gift or community award.

Natalie climbed the three stairs to reach the top of the platform. She went to Anya with a questioning smile.

I should have expected it. I don't know why I didn't put two and two together.

Morris came out from behind the curtain.

He slowly walked up behind Natalie without her noticing.

He got down on one knee and pulled a small box from his pocket.

Anya grinned and pointed to Natalie that she should turn around.

She did.

Morris lifted the box and opened the lid, displaying a gorgeous diamond engagement ring.

"Will you marry me?" he said simply.

Natalie clapped both hands over her mouth, muffling a choked squeal. Her whole body shook, shoulders heaving with heavy gasps. She looked from Morris to the ring and back again.

"That a yes?" Morris asked, chocolate brown eyes twinkling.

Natalie's face crumpled as she burst into tears, nodding her head furiously.

The entire audience ooh'ed and aww'd, clapped and cheered.

My heart stilled in my chest.

Morris had proposed to Natalie.

My nails dug into my palms.

He was engaged.

I let out a slow, shuddering breath.

He was going to marry the love of his life.

I stood from my chair quickly, nearly toppling it over. Liam looked to me, alarmed.

We'd always planned on Morris being the best man at mine and Harper's wedding.

We'd always planned on Harper being the best man at his.

But Harper was dead.

The crack inside me splintered open. Inky black sludge poured out, so thick and viscous it felt like I would suffocate on it.

Liam whistled. "Ballsy move, doing it in front of everyone like that. What if she said no?"

"She never would have said no," I said numbly.

Liam eyed me, taking in my shallow breathing, noticing the half-moon indentations my nails had left in my palms. He pressed his lips together.

"You're not happy for them," he said in an almost accusing voice.

"No. I am. It's just—"

Harper was never going to stand at Morris's wedding. Morris was never going to stand at ours.

Morris was getting the chance Harper and I never got.

Because Harper was dead.

I rubbed at my nail polish with my thumb, feeling every thin, harsh chip.

"I need to take off," I said. "I'm going to go home and change. This dress is chaffing me."

Liam frowned at me.

"I'll see you at rehearsals tomorrow." I tried to keep my tone even, but the words came out numbly.

I didn't wait for Liam's response. I turned on my heel and ran out.

I ran as I always did whenever the past caught up to me.

I ran as if I could outrun my feelings.

## 28

I arrived late to practice the next day. I didn't want to risk catching Liam alone if we were both early.

I knew he'd want to talk to me after what had happened the previous day. One of my oldest friends had just proposed to his girl-friend — now fiancée — and instead of sticking around I'd made a lame excuse and bolted.

It was becoming a habit. A bad one. But it was the only thing I could think of doing. If I'd stayed, I would have been able to muster up a fake smile and offer them my congratulations. Morris would have seen through it. He knew me too well.

I had to hope Liam bought my excuse. Or at least, I had to hope he wouldn't push the issue. I didn't want him to know the awful memories that had resurfaced the instant Morris dropped to one knee.

I texted Gael I was running late and to start setting up without me.

*You okay?* he'd texted back.

*Slept in,* I'd replied.

*So you picked up some man-candy and had a late night?*

*No! My alarm didn't go off.*

*Sure, sure,* he teased.

He didn't text again for another few minutes, but when my phone pinged again and I saw his message, my heart sank.

*You disappeared yesterday,* he wrote.

I could hear the unspoken question.

*Girl stuff,* I wrote back, knowing that would shut him down.

*Liam looks worried,* he wrote back anyway. *Says he hasn't heard from you. Poor guy probably thought you got into a car accident and were lying dead in a ditch somewhere.*

*Tell him I'm fine.*

*Should I mention the man-candy?*

*No!!*

I turned my phone on silent, ignoring any further texts as I drove to the rehearsal studio.

I was only a few minutes late, but the guys were already practicing without me. I was glad they were taking things seriously.

All music stopped when I walked in as the guys stared at me.

"What?" I asked.

"Late night?" Nathan drawled.

"Why does everyone assume I hooked up last night?" I asked. "Can't a girl sleep in and not have her sex life questioned?"

"You do look a little worn out," Seth piped up. "Bags under your bloodshot eyes, messy hair…"

I hadn't realized it was so obvious I'd tossed and turned all night while fighting back tears.

"I had some trouble falling asleep," I said. Liam's gaze burned into me. I steadfastly avoided looking in his direction. "Let's get started."

Our rehearsal went well, sounding almost as good as we did in concert. You couldn't replicate the kind of energy you felt on stage, but damn, we sure did try. There were no missed cues or off pitch notes.

We played for most of the day, but stopped before fatigue crept in. We'd learned to pace ourselves.

"Good job guys," I nodded as the day drew to a close. "We're getting better and better each time. More polished, more in sync."

"We haven't gone out in a while," Nathan said. "I say we celebrate." He made a drinking motion with his hand.

I hesitated. "I don't really want to deal with a loud, crowded club full of potential fans."

"I know a place where a rock star can get a quiet drink," Gael said, faking an innocent look.

"You just want to see your girlfriend in a leather mini-skirt," Nathan snorted.

"Can you blame me?" Gael grinned.

The rest of us agreed as Seth insisted we call a taxi.

"I don't want to be the DD tonight," he said.

"I'll drive," Liam offered.

We all piled into Liam's car. It was a tight fit, but we made it work. I grabbed a seat in the back. Unfortunately, I choose the exact spot where Liam had tilted his rearview mirror. Every time his gaze flicked to the back window, he lingered on me, expression inscrutable.

Gael gave directions, leading us into a shady part of town. Not as shady as where we grew up, but the graffiti, trash on the sidewalk and tough looking groups of young men lingering in storefronts clearly made Liam nervous.

"I didn't even know there were parts of the city like this," I heard him mutter. "You sure this is the right way?" he spoke up louder.

Gael nodded. "This place is awesome," he said. "You're going to love it."

Knowing how Liam had been brought up, and knowing exactly what kind of bar we were going to, I very much doubted that.

Still, Liam followed the directions and pulled into a parking lot at the back of a dark building. Gael hopped out and headed to the dented metal back door. He knocked in a rapid pattern and the door soon opened with Jessie in the doorframe.

Gael wolf-whistled and looked her up and down. She wore heavy eye makeup to rival mine and a tight black dress with a hemline several inches above her knee. I could see the fresh-faced young woman behind all that makeup, if I squinted and tilted my head.

"Come on in," she gestured. "You're in luck, tonight's karaoke night."

I tried not to wince. Karaoke nights could be hit and miss, depending on who got up there to sing.

We walked down a short hallway and turned a corner, finding ourselves in a small little pub with rickety seating and dirty beer mugs left sitting on empty tables.

Liam's face scrunched up in distaste. "This is where we're drinking?"

"Of course not," I said, holding back a smirk. "This is the public bar. We're going to the special hidden one out back where nobody will bother us."

"It's like the VIP section," Seth said, eavesdropping in on our conversation.

"Thank god," Liam said, no doubt thinking the VIP section would be a little — or a lot — more upscale.

When Jessie pushed open a door that had a "Washroom Out Of Order" sign on it, his face screwed up with uncertainty again.

When we walked into the "VIP section" he made a choked sound in the back of his throat.

This bar was even sketchier than the one we'd just come from. It was the very definition of a dive bar. Sticky floor, tabletops with suspicious stains, dim lighting, and rough-faced biker types playing pool.

"You're fucking with me," he said flatly.

"Nope!" Seth cheered as he bounced over to the bar.

A tall, barrel chested man with a small scar over one eyebrow nodded to Seth as he washed and put away beer mugs.

"What'll it be this time?" the man said in a gruff voice.

Seth clapped his hands together. "I've got a good one tonight," he said.

"This is your VIP bar?" Liam asked in a hushed voice.

"Yup," I said with a self-satisfied smile. "Jessie introduced Gael to the place. Not many people know about it. The owner, Walt, keeps it on the down low. Some of our other musician friends come here a lot, too. No fans or paparazzi allowed."

"It's so..." Liam scanned the room. His eyes landed on the beefy, leather-clad bikers. His eyes went wide, not finishing his sentence. He took a step back. "You sure this place is safe?"

"Define *safe*?" I held back a snicker.

Liam was going to get eaten alive.

"Hey shitface!" someone called out.

Every member in my band turned his head toward the voice.

"That shitface," the guy clarified, pointing to Gael. His group was playing pool in a dark corner, but from the brilliant, fire-engine red hair, I knew it was Cameron Thorne, bassist for the rock band Darkest Days.

My brother's face fell before he forced a cocky grin. "Still don't remember my name, hm? Getting senile in your old age?"

"Fuck you," Cameron said with a good-natured laugh.

Both being bassists, my brother had a sort of love-hate thing for Cameron Thorne. Gael looked up to the man, but Cameron, being Cameron, loved to stir up shit. He knew exactly who my brother was. Cherry Lips had opened for Darkest Days on tour, after all, and they both had mutual friends.

"What are you assholes doing here?" Gael asked him.

"Settling a bet." Cameron held up his pool stick. "You want in? Or are you scared of me kicking your ass in front of your girlfriend?"

Gael tilted his chin up, looking defensive.

"Boys really don't change, do they?" Jessie appeared beside me with a tray of beer carefully balanced in one hand.

"And yet we love them anyway," I replied. "What does that say about us?"

"You can't play pool," Seth called out. He lifted a glass in his hand, a dangerous looking yellow concoction. "We're drinking! Loser has to sing karaoke."

"I thought loser had to drink that godawful poison you come up with?" Gael shot back.

"Knew you were chicken," Cameron tossed out with a shit-eating grin as Gael headed over to Seth.

My brother threw him the middle finger.

We all gathered around a large table with ring stains. Liam followed behind quietly, eyes darting every which way.

But as we played, he slowly began to relax. It couldn't have been the alcohol, since he was sticking to the non-alcoholic version of Seth's godawful mixture. It was probably because we'd been there for an hour and nothing bad had happened yet.

After each of us took several turns we were all pretty buzzed. Three rounds later we'd run out of shots. Nathan was the worst out of all of us, listing sideways in his chair and slurring. We declared him the loser and forced him to get up on stage. Nate was a pretty good singer with great taste in music, so it wasn't like we had to sit through a torturous rendition of a ten minute eighties power ballad.

We were setting up another round when the door to the bar opened and two people walked in, hand in hand.

My blood froze in my veins.

It was Natalie and Morris.

## 29

Natalie had walked through the door, a bright smile on her face and a gigantic rock on her finger. As for Morris, his normally stoic face radiated satisfaction with a hint of smugness.

Liam stiffened beside me.

"Natalie! Let me see it again!" Jessie threw her tray onto a table and rushed over. "It's so beautiful," she sighed as she examined the ring. "The diamond is so clear and sparkling, and the setting is just gorgeous. Take notes," Jessie called over her shoulder to Gael.

I thought my brother might flinch at the thought of rings and marriage, but he blew her a kiss. Maybe I should have been worried about alien body-snatchers after all.

"Hey, Cerise," Morris said quietly.

A wave of nausea came over me. I couldn't face Morris. He'd take one look at me and know I was upset, angry, heartbroken — I was consumed with a dozen different emotions and he'd be able to sense them all.

But I couldn't ignore him, not with everyone else there.

"Hey." I plastered a smile on my face, the corners of my mouth only twitching down slightly. "I'm sorry I didn't get to say congratulations yesterday."

"Can we talk?" he asked.

Bile rose to my throat. I wasn't ready for this conversation.

"I'm sort of in the middle of a drinking game," I said.

"Please?"

*Shit.*

I took in a heavy breath and nodded. "Let's talk somewhere private."

I didn't need the entire bar to hear this.

We went to the back room full of extra chairs and stacks of boxes. There was barely enough room for two people to maneuver around. I turned to face Morris, dreading what was coming.

"I have something to ask you," he said.

I braced myself.

"Will you write a song with me?"

My whirling thoughts halted. I stared at Morris, confused.

"A song?"

"It's the anniversary of..." he trailed off, his brown eyes wounded.

He didn't need to say it. I'd been counting down the days in my head for the last few weeks.

"We should write a song," he continued. "Together. In his memory."

I could feel the mass of darkness roiling inside me, waiting to be released.

"No," I said.

Morris's brow furrowed. "No?"

"I don't— I haven't—" My breath caught in my throat. "I only ever wrote songs with him."

"I know," he said gently. "I was the same. Never joined another band. Not until Kell," he said, referring to his lead singer, the one who'd recruited him to Feral Silence. "But this will be good. For both of us."

"Like... closure?"

He shrugged his broad shoulders. "Whatever you want to call it."

I went silent, thinking it over. Most of the songs I'd ever written had been about Harper. Before his death it was all passion and love and desire. After his death, heartbreak and turmoil and loss.

When comparing the songs between my first band and Cherry Lips, it was like they'd been composed by two completely different people.

And they had been. The current me was nothing like the old Cerise.

Or, at least, I hadn't been until recently.

Something inside me changed as soon as Liam walked back into my life.

I felt... whole.

"Think about it?" Morris said to fill the silence. "I want to write that song with you."

I nodded slowly. "Okay. I'll think about it."

Even as I said the words, my chest ached. That small, miserable part of me kept remembering awful things. I wished I could banish it forever, but it felt like it had been with me for so long. I didn't know how to make it go away.

Morris held out his hands. I stepped into the circle of his arms. One large palm cupped the back of my head. I pressed my face into his chest.

I tried not to feel the absence of Harper's presence in his embrace.

"Morris." Liam's flat voice spoke from the doorway.

I stepped back from the hug, blinking back tears.

"Natalie wants you," Liam told him.

Morris patted me on the shoulder and, after eyeing Liam carefully, went back into the main bar.

"What was that about?" Liam asked.

"Morris wanted to—"

"Write a song with you," he interrupted. "Yeah. I heard." His green eyes, normally so good-natured, were narrowed in suspicion. "I thought you didn't write songs with people."

"I don't normally but—"

"I asked you to write a song with me and you wouldn't," Liam cut me off again. His tone was oddly heated. And not in the good way. "But you'll write one with him."

"I'm thinking about it." I frowned at him. "Why are you acting so weird over this?"

"Why do you think?"

"You're upset because of a song?"

"I'm upset because I walk in here and see my girlfriend with another man," he growled. "An engaged man, might I add."

A shot of disbelief went through me. "And what exactly do you think was happening between us? If you're trying to insinuate something—"

"You won't write a song with me, you won't tell the band about us—"

"Are you mad about that?" I asked, still taken aback by the turn of our conversation. "I thought we agreed to keep it to ourselves for now."

"And how long is *for now* going to last?" he snapped. "Are you just biding your time with me? Are you just waiting for their relationship to fall apart so you can be with him?"

I pressed my lips together firmly. "Liam. I warned you. I won't date someone who has trust issues."

"And I'm not going to date a girl who's in love with another man." His eyes blazed with fury. "I'm not going to date a girl who will end up cheating on me with someone else."

Shock flew through my system, sending me reeling, before I was overtaken by outrage.

"Are you fucking serious right now?" I made my voice low, matching the fire in his eyes with ice of my own. "Did you really just accuse me of cheating?"

"I don't know," he said. "Maybe you're not right now. But how do I know you won't just go running after him the first chance you get?"

My vision went white with anger. "Is that really what you think I'm going to do?"

"I don't want you seeing him anymore."

Liam's words had a sense of finality to them. As if they were the last words he was ever going to say.

But I had a world of words to shoot back at him.

"You don't get to dictate who my friends are," I bit out. "You don't get to come in here and throw a fit of jealousy. And you *sure as fuck* don't get to accuse me of *cheating on you.*"

We stared each other down. The scowl on his face matched my own.

"If you see him again, we're over," Liam said.

My lips curled into a snarl. "We were over the minute you accused me of sleeping around behind your back."

And for once, I didn't regret whirling around on my heel and leaving.

## 30

I told the others I wasn't feeling well and left the bar in a taxi. Gael teased I was getting so old I wasn't able to party like a teenager anymore without getting sick.

But it hadn't been a lie. I did feel sick. My stomach was knotted into a heavy lump. Sharp daggers stabbed through my chest. My eyes burned with the effort to hold back tears the entire taxi ride home.

The moment I stepped into my apartment and closed the door, I slumped against it and let the tears come. I knew my makeup was leaving black streaks on my cheeks but I didn't care. I was lost in a red haze of heartbreak, fury and a twisted sort of self-loathing.

As angry as I was with Liam, I was just as upset with myself.

How could I not have seen this coming? It wasn't the first time Liam's jealousy had caused tension between us. He'd been suspicious of Morris a few times before already.

I should have known eventually something like this would happen.

I threw my purse and phone on the sofa and watched them almost bounce off the cushions and onto the floor. I kicked my boots off with enough force to send them flying against the wall with a thud. I was wearing black socks, the only color I owned.

Liam had been disappointed at the boring color, hoping to tease me about some embarrassing design.

I took in a shuddering breath. I swiped at my cheeks. The back of my hand came back smudged with mascara.

The last time my makeup had been smeared over my face, Liam had wiped it away with a gentle thumb. He'd said my smokey eye was more of a forest fire.

It was hard to breathe around the clenching in my chest. The vise grip threatened to squeeze the life out of me. The tears wouldn't stop falling down my cheeks.

How could things have gone so wrong so quickly?

I wanted to scream until my lungs gave out. I wanted to collapse into a heap of misery. I wanted to punch the wall until my knuckles bled.

I didn't do any of that. I simply stripped out of my clothes and slid into bed, not even bothering to wash my face. A quick wipe with a tissue would have to do.

A shivery-cold feeling began to creep its way under my skin, into my every nerve.

It was happening again.

I'd opened myself up, given everything I had, let myself be vulnerable...

And now that it had all blown up in my face, I was falling apart. Again.

I didn't want to think. I didn't want to feel. I wanted to fall into the oblivion of sleep where Liam's words could no longer haunt me.

*How do I know you won't just go running after him the first chance you get?*

I swallowed around the lump of rage and despair taking root in my stomach.

He couldn't possibly think I might cheat on him. It had to have just been anger over seeing me hug Morris.

But even words said in anger couldn't be dismissed.

I heard my phone ping. I rolled over and ignored it. It pinged again. And again. I flopped over onto my side and grabbed it.

*The fuck is up with Liam?* Gael had texted.

*How should I know?* I wrote back.

*After you took off he got all pissy. Told us to call a taxi cause he was leaving. Fucker left us stranded and drunk.*

*I'm sure you'll manage,* I replied.

*Do you need me to kick his ass?*

*No.*

*Cause if he did or said something stupid, I don't care how talented he is, I'll put my fist through his face.*

*I said no. Everything's fine. I'm going to bed now. Get home safe.*

*Will do.*

I put down my phone.

I stared at the blank screen.

I picked it back up.

I did a search for Cherry Lips. Dozen of blog posts and news articles mentioning us popped up.

I'd kept my promise. As hard as it had been, I'd gone weeks since last checking the rumor mill online. But what did it matter? My promise to Liam meant nothing anymore.

I had to know. Needed to know. People all over the internet were talking about Cherry Lips and not knowing what they were saying was killing me.

I scrolled mindlessly, skimming the words, looking for key phrases like "fucking rocks" or "totally sucks."

I stopped. Scrolled back up hastily.

Someone had posted a photo of me and Liam on stage. It was during one of our brief duets, when he would lean into the mic to sing a few words along with me.

In this photo our eyes were locked onto each other's. His lips were mere inches from mine. It didn't look like a duet at a rock concert. It looked like a snapshot taken moments before a passionate kiss.

The sting of tears hit the back of my eyes again.

I remembered that concert. I'd dragged Liam into a dark office and fucked him senseless afterward. We'd almost gotten caught by the venue manager. We had to pretend we'd gotten lost. Between Liam's undone jeans button and my messed up lipstick, we were pretty sure he hadn't bought it.

Pressing my lips firmly together, I started to read the article accompanying the photo. It was the usual concert review, talking about how awesome we were, our crazy fan base, the accolades we'd received so far, even giving a bit of background on our past as an indie band.

But this article had a few sentences at the bottom I'd never read before.

*On stage with Cherry Lips was Liam Knight, formerly of the band Forever Night, which was on the cusp of hitting it big before Liam left to pursue his own projects. Click here to view a gallery of Forever Night.*

A gallery of photos. Photos of Liam.

I couldn't help myself. I clicked.

There were dozens of pictures taken throughout Liam's early career. In some of the photos he looked as young as he had when I'd first met him. In some he looked the exact same as he did now.

In most of the photos they were on stage, but there were also quite a few with them surrounded by groupies. One girl in particular showed up multiple times, always hanging off Liam's arm. He never looked annoyed at her clinging. In some of the photos he was even smiling softly at her, even as a handful of other women surrounded him.

Maybe she wasn't a groupie. Maybe she was an old girlfriend. I wondered what had happened to them, if they were no longer together. Liam had never mentioned anything about the people he'd dated before me.

I continued flicking through the photos. When I got to the end, there was a another small blurb.

*The former members of Forever Night are now known as Chaotic Neutral. Click here to read a review of their latest concert.*

I hadn't realized the members of Liam's old band were still active in the scene. It made sense. Just because he was content to be a session musician didn't mean they wouldn't go on to form another group.

I clicked the link.

From the photo, *Chaotic Neutral* looked like a normal rock band. Lots of black, mesh, skinny jeans, leather jackets and a hint of eyeliner.

There was the same gallery of photos, both the band on stage and surrounded by groupies. As I scanned the pictures, I zoomed in on the guitarist. He looked like a regular guy, tall with dark hair and a cocky smile. He didn't look like the type who would betray a friend. Then again, Liam didn't look like the type to spit out horrible accusations like he had that evening.

I paused on one picture.

It was the same young woman. That groupie/girlfriend. But this time she was hanging off the guitarist's arm. He was the one smiling down at her. Holding her against his side, hugging her tightly. There was a caption under the photo.

Chad and Paula.

I inhaled sharply.

I recognized her name.

It was the girl from the wedding invitation.

I examined the picture closely, my mind beginning to connect all the pieces.

If she was Liam's ex-girlfriend... and she was now marrying his old guitarist... And it was his guitarist's fault he quit the band...

Had Liam's girlfriend left him for one of his best friends?

I sank back into the sofa cushions, air whooshing out of me.

His girlfriend had left him for another man. Just like his mom had left his dad.

No wonder Liam had trust issues.

I could almost understand his reaction now. If Harper had left me for someone else, I would have had an awful time getting over it.

I stared at the photo, burning her face into my memory. I didn't know anything about the girl but I was mad at her. She was the one who had hurt Liam. It was her fault he had acted so unreasonably.

And it was unreasonable. I'd given Liam no cause to worry. He knew Morris and I were just old friends.

But he'd accused me of cheating anyway.

As much as I understood why that was where his mind had gone, I wasn't about to brush it off. I wasn't about to let him get away with thinking something so awful of me.

It was understandable yes, but I couldn't forget the way he'd glared at me, the way he'd forbidden me from seeing Morris, the way he'd spat out that I might end up sleeping with someone else behind his back...

A pang of anger and heartbreak shot through me.

It didn't matter his reason.

Liam had accused me of something unforgivable.

I didn't know if that was something I'd be able to forget any time soon.

## 31

"Hey, are you guys Cherry Lips?" one of the event staff asked as he poked his head into the artist lounge.

"That's us," Liam and I said at the same time.

I flicked my eyes to Liam. He was staring back. I took in his messy hair, the dark circles under his eyes, the firm set of his clenched jaw.

I turned my head away.

Liam looked as terrible as I felt.

Good. He should feel miserable. He'd brought it all on himself.

Our fight felt like it had taken place months ago, and yet it had only been days. We couldn't put the tour on hold just because the lead singer and guitarist had a tiff. We had to pile into the rented van and sit in silence as we drove to the latest concert. Luckily, this one was only in the next town over, barely a thirty minute drive.

I made sure to beat the others to shotgun. I couldn't stomach the thought of being stuck in the back with Liam again. It was hard enough to keep the tears at bay when I was alone. Being next to Liam only made it a hundred times worse.

"Some local blogger dude says he's here for an interview," the event guy continued. "Wants to talk to you before you get on stage."

All the guys in my band groaned. We'd done a dozen or more of these already, and it was turning into a chore. They always asked the same questions and we always answered in the same way.

"Can't he just rip off the answers from one of those other blogs?" Gael said, only half-joking.

"It's good publicity," I said. "We want people reading about us. Talking about us. The more of these interviews we do, the better."

Gael grumbled, but settled down into the sofa.

My brother had been oddly quiet until now. He kept shooting me careful looks. We hadn't had a chance to talk in private, and I knew he was wondering how I was holding up.

Morris and I weren't the only ones who had been keeping track of the days.

"So can I show him in?" the man asked.

I nodded and he disappeared.

A young guy with a haircut that looked like he'd time traveled from the seventies poked his head through the door.

"Red hair," the guy grinned at me. "Awesome. You're the people I'm looking for."

He walked in and set up a tripod with his phone connected to it. He pointed it at us then took a seat perched on one of the armchairs, not bothering to shake hands or introduce himself.

"I almost interviewed the wrong band," he said. "Those guys opening for you are terribly dull, aren't they?" He turned to me. "So what's with the hair?"

I blinked. "Excuse me?"

"The hair." The blogger pointed at my head. "What's with that color?"

"I like red," I said, nonplussed.

"Yeah, but, isn't it sort of tacky to color your hair cherry red, when your name means cherry and your band is Cherry Lips?"

"Tacky?" I repeated, insulted.

But the guy had already turned his attention to Gael. "Rumor is, you're pussy-whipped now. How's that going for you?"

Nathan made a sort of half-snort, half-snicker sound.

"I'm not pussy-whipped, fuck you very much," Gael snapped. "I'm nailing a hot as fuck chick every night, can you say the same?"

Seth whistled long and low.

"Jessie's gonna kill him," he leaned over and murmured under his breath to Julian.

That got the blogger's attention.

"So Seth, how does it feel to be the runt of the group?" he asked.

Seth's eyes went wide, astounded, before narrowing dangerously. His lips pressed into a harsh line.

"We're not going to sit here and take this bullshit," Liam spoke up firmly. "You need to leave now."

The blogger sized him up and nodded. "Right, you're Liam Knight. Your old band never made it anywhere so now you're just a session guitarist. You ever think about going back to being a real musician, or are you okay with being a has-been?"

Liam's fist clenched and shook. I had no doubt he was five seconds away from punching the guy in the face.

The blogger turned his attention back to me.

"Cerise, I heard you and the drummer from Feral Silence used to be in a band together but you broke up. What happened all those years ago? If you had stayed together, do you think you'd actually be a world famous band by now instead of just a small time act?"

Gael flew from his chair, glaring at the guy.

My throat closed up, all air leaving my lungs.

I'd been trying not to think about it. Trying not to remember.

But of course, today of all days, someone had to bring it up.

Today, on the anniversary of Harper's death.

I inhaled sharply through my nose and steeled myself.

"If you don't have any real questions to ask, you can get the hell out right now," I said.

"If you guys don't want to answer the questions your fans are asking..." he shrugged blithely.

"No one's asking those questions," Gael growled.

The guy popped up from his seat. "Fine, then." He began to put his tripod away. "I'll go interview that boring opening band of yours. I'm sure they'll have plenty to say."

The guy strode out the door, leaving the band to stare at one another.

"What the fuck was that?" Julian asked, so shaken he'd actually joined the conversation for once.

"A fucking asshole, that's what," Seth bit out.

Seth had always been sensitive about being the youngest. For a while he hadn't even been able to legally drink at the clubs we'd played at. Maybe it was time we stopped treating Seth like our kid brother. I didn't want him to develop some sort of complex about it.

My band had more than enough emotional baggage between us already.

I exhaled deeply. My palms were stinging; I'd dug my nails into the flesh again. I forced my clenched fists to relax.

"He was probably from one of those trash magazines," Nathan said. "Just forget about him."

"What if he prints some of that garbage?" Gael asked.

"He can print whatever he likes," Nathan replied. "Our fans won't care and they're the only ones who matter."

"Easy for you to say," Gael said. "He didn't call you out on anything."

"What could he possibly call me out on?" Nathan said easily. "That I'm a slut? Guilty as charged. Can't bash someone who's an open book. Our new guy on the other hand..." Nathan quirked an eyebrow at Liam. "You okay over there?"

I glanced over. Liam's expression was pained.

"Are you going to go on some kind of rampage against the guy?" Nathan asked. "Cause I can find out who he is for you, if you want."

"No. It's fine." Liam shot me a quick look before flicking his gaze back to Nathan. "He's just stirring shit."

"Did he want to shake us before our performance?" Seth wondered out loud. "Maybe he wanted to get into our heads before we went on stage."

"Doesn't matter," I said tightly. "We're going to go out there and fucking rock. All right?"

I looked at each of my guys in turn. My brother, Nate, Seth and Julian all nodded. I looked at Liam last. His face was set with determination. I knew he was recalling the has-been comment.

"We're going to show them," Liam said. "We're going to show them what Cherry Lips can do."

I nodded.

Forget my fight with Liam. Forget my grief for Harper. I had to put those feelings away for now.

This concert, this performance, was all that mattered.

# 32

I stepped out onto the stage in front of a cheering crowd, exuding a fierce confidence, even as a war raged within me.

Sorrow. Today was the anniversary of Harper's death.

Anger. That blogger had pissed me right the fuck off.

Heartbreak. Every time I looked to Liam, I expected to see that familiar cocky smirk he wore. Instead, I saw flat eyes and a grim face.

I grabbed the microphone and looked out at the audience.

They didn't know about Liam.

They didn't know about that blogger.

They didn't know about Harper.

They had no idea anything was wrong behind the scenes.

I wasn't about to let them down.

I suppressed every emotion welling up within me as I sang. I put on my best smirk, my most teasing smile. I strutted around on stage, leaning against Gael's back as he played, draping myself over Nathan as he did a solo, crouching down near the edge to reach out and touch flailing hands.

Even as I took shuddering breaths during the breaks between songs, even as I shook with the effort it took to keep my voice from cracking, I had to hope our fans didn't have a clue anything was different about me.

I had to hope they had no idea how close I was to breaking.

We hadn't changed a single thing in our set list, but up there on that stage, on that night, it seemed like every song was about Harper. About Liam. About losing them both.

We finished the last song of our encore. I stayed out on stage a few minutes longer than I normally did, soaking in the energy of the audience. I was afraid as soon as I walked through that backstage curtain I was going to fall apart.

Finally, I thanked the crowd one last time and left the stage. The band was waiting in the wings for me.

"Fucking showed them, didn't we?" Nathan grinned.

"I think that's some of the best we've ever played," Seth agreed.

I nodded, not speaking.

What if our fans didn't agree? What if they had sense something different about our performance? If that blogger started writing trash about it, if our fans started to turn on us, if the label lost faith in us...

A wave of nausea swept through me before I ruthlessly forced it down.

We all hustled back to the artist lounge to gather our stuff. The guys continued chatting and joking with each other. I grabbed my bag and checked my phone. There was one missed notification.

People were already posting about our concert.

That lump in my gut grew to the size of a mountain.

I couldn't bring myself to read what they were saying.

"There's a cool club not far from here," Nathan said. "Want to go get trashed?"

"Yes," I said, surprising him with my firm response. "I could stand to let off some steam with a drink or two."

Or dozen. Whatever it took to rid me of this feeling, this wretched lump of darkness tormenting me with every breath.

I'd lost Harper.

I'd lost Liam.

I didn't think I'd be able to survive if I lost Cherry Lips.

Seth acted as DD again, complaining under his breath the entire time. We managed to score one of those private VIP booths even without having arranged for one ahead of time. It was sort of a rush, the kind of strings the name Cherry Lips could now pull.

"No drinking games for me tonight," Nathan said. "I've got other plans."

"Scoring with groupies in dark corners counts as a plan?" Gael asked.

"You could try being little less crass about it," Nathan drawled.

"I'm coming with you," Seth said.

Nathan raised an eyebrow. "You wanna be my wingman?"

"No," Seth said. "You're going to be mine."

Nathan gave him a startled look, then chuckled. Seth was rarely up for the kind of pick up games Nate liked to play.

"Let's go score you some chicks, then," Nathan said, throwing his arm around Seth's shoulders and leading him to the bar.

The rest of us took seats in leather armchairs near the glass wall overlooking the dance floor. I made sure to sit as far away from Gael and Liam as I could, which placed me next to Julian. He looked oddly lost without his best friend and constant partner by his side. Seth rarely abandoned him like that.

A server came to take our orders. I got my usual whiskey sour. Liam ordered a plain beer instead of one of his fancy rich twelve-year-whatever drinks.

Not that I was paying attention to what he ordered. He could drink himself to death for all I cared, as long as he dragged his corpse up on stage for our next concert.

"I looked up some info on that dickface blogger," Gael said once we had our drinks. "He does write for one of those trash sites. Apparently his thing is to rile up his interviewees so he can catch them blowing up on camera. We were lucky none of us snapped." Gael eyed Liam. "Although you looked about ten seconds away from pounding his face in."

"I've dealt with worse," he said, "I just hated all that shit he brought up."

Gael clapped him forcefully on the back with a consoling pat. "You're not a has-been. Don't worry about it."

"It wasn't just that," Liam murmured into his beer. "Whatever. It doesn't matter."

I knew exactly what had gotten him so pissed off. The blogger had brought up me and Morris. That was the absolute last thing Liam would want to hear about. He was probably thinking about the two of us right now. Wondering what I was doing behind his back after our fight.

"I can't believe that fucker brought up Morris and the old band," Gael said, as if echoing my thoughts. "Especially tonight."

Julian inhaled a sharp breath and looked to me, surprised. I nodded in response to his unasked question. He gave me a sympathetic look.

"You gonna be okay?" he asked quietly.

"Yeah," I managed to say with a strangled breath.

I found myself rubbing at my nails. The red lacquer was almost completely peeled off at this point. I must have been scratching at the polish all night.

Liam's frown deepened.

Gael continued talking, still angry about the blogger. "It's especially shitty bringing it up, with the engagement and everything—"

My brother cut himself off as I stood quickly, nearly splashing my drink as my fight or flight instinct kicked in. I put a hand on the back of the sofa, fingers digging into the cushions. Gael's eyes went wide.

"Cerise, if you want to just go home, we can do that," he said.

"Running away again?" Liam said. His eyes were dark and flat.

"If my sister is feeling like shit there's no reason she needs to stay here and drink with the rest of us," Gael said.

Liam ignored him and stood to face me with a scowl.

Julian took a quiet sip of his drink and sat back, watching all three of us with rapt attention, although there was concern in his eyes when they fell on me.

"You should just get over it," Liam said, almost spitting the words. His fist shook as he gripped his beer tight. "Morris is marrying Natalie, not you."

A sharp stab spiked through me. I reeled back.

"What the fuck are you going on about?" Gael asked Liam.

"You can't tell me you don't know?" Liam scoffed and gestured to me with the hand holding his beer. "Your sister is still in love with Morris even though he's engaged to another woman."

Gael's squinted at him, then looked down at his drink, as if wondering whether he'd already had too many to hear correctly. He looked back up at Liam.

"My sister isn't in love with Morris," he said with a sort of snorted laugh.

"Could have fooled me," Liam snarked.

"Cerise isn't upset because Morris is marrying Natalie," Julian finally spoke up. His dark eyes were soft as they met mine, but once he flicked them to Liam, they narrowed. "She's upset because her fiancé was murdered five years ago today."

---

## 33

Liam froze, his eyes locked on Julian. I inched backwards, trying to not get their attention.

"Look, it's fine, you didn't know until just now, but today's been really tough on Cerise," my brother said. "My sister and Harper had been together forever and she lost him in a really shitty way—"

"Gael," I snapped. He stopped talking and shot me an apologetic look. He knew I hated when people talked about it.

"I—" Liam's gaze drifted to mine. "Harper...?" He said the words in a hushed voice, dawning horror crossing his face.

"Yeah. Harper."

Liam opened his mouth but nothing came out. I could see his mind whirling, reconsidering everything he'd been thinking up until now.

I didn't want to wait around for him to put it all together. I didn't need to hear his apologies, didn't need to hear his regrets.

I turned to Gael and Julian, ignoring Liam. "I'm taking off now."

"Want me to come with you?" my brother asked.

The offer was thoughtful, but I didn't want to be around anyone right then.

"No. It's fine. I'll grab a taxi."

Gael studied me before nodding. "Get home safe."

I turned and left before Liam could finish processing what he'd just learned.

I pushed my way through the writhing crowd of dancers to reach the exit. I saw Nathan and Seth in the corner chatting up two pretty girls. At least someone was having a fun night.

The bouncer opened the door for me. I stepped out into the cool evening air. I inhaled deeply, trying to calm myself. Trying to stem the tears from falling. Trying to swallow the hurt, the anger, the grief.

I forced myself to shove down the memories that threatened to surface.

I'd spent so long trying to forget how Harper had died. Losing him had been bad enough. Losing him the way I had, knowing exactly how he had been...

It was almost more than I could handle.

I looked down at my trembling hands, at the scratched up polish. I began to shake. I wrapped my arms around my waist, huddling into myself. Oozing black tendrils whirled inside me like a cyclone, and in the very middle was the eye of the storm threatening to suck me in.

I heard someone bursting through the club doors, heard someone call my name.

I couldn't make myself move. My feet were glued to the pavement.

I knew it was Liam approaching from behind me. I heard his heavy breathing, as if he'd run the whole way.

"Cerise," he repeated my name. He went silent, still taking in labored breaths.

I didn't turn to look at him, instead focusing my eyes on the bright headlights of cars as they passed by. They were almost blinding, reminding me of spotlights. My body buzzed like it always did on stage, but there was no high, no rush from performing to go along with it.

"I am so sorry," Liam began. "I don't even know where to start."

"Should we start at the beginning?" I said. "Should we start with you throwing awful accusations at me?"

"That's not the beginning, though," he replied softly. "Is it?"

No. It wasn't.

The beginning wasn't even five years ago.

The beginning was so long ago I could barely remember how it started.

"Morris was never..." I started to say. I tried again. "It's never been Morris. It was always—" A stab went through my gut. "It was always Harper."

"He's the one you were in love with," Liam said, his voice low, pained.

"Childhood sweethearts, everyone always said," I murmured. "We knew each other since we were kids. We grew up, developed feelings for each other. Neither of us wanted to say anything. We were afraid of losing our friendship."

Now that I'd gotten started I couldn't seem to stop. I rarely told anyone this story. The important people in my life already knew and I'd been trying to forget for years.

"Everyone could see we were in love," I continued. "Morris was the one who pushed us together. Literally." I let out a weak snort. "He shoved us into a closet during a game of truth or dare."

I skipped over the rest. The happy memories were almost as painful as the bad ones.

"Harper proposed to me on my eighteenth birthday. No one was shocked. They thought we were too young, of course, and tried to talk us out of it, but they all knew it was going to happen sooner or later. And then..."

My voice faltered, knowing what was next. The storm inside me continued raging.

"Can I ask what happened?" Liam was barely audible over the passing cars. "How he died?"

I shook my head fiercely. "Not died."

I turned to face Liam. I wanted to see his face when I told him.

"Harper was murdered."

A flash of pain shot through his eyes. "Why would someone—?"

"You want me to give you all the gory details?"

"No," he winced. "I'm sorry. That's not what I meant."

"You know my neighborhood was rough. Drugs, violence, all of it." I kept it short, to the point. "A gang wanted Morris to join. He was big, strong, the perfect guy to act as muscle. He refused. Over and over he refused. He'd always protected the neighborhood kids, kept them away from gangs trying to recruit. So they retaliated." I spoke as quickly as I could, words tumbling out of my mouth, knowing that if I stopped I'd never be able to continue. "Harper was late coming home one night. I was so worried. Then a pair of cops showed up at the door. They didn't even need to tell me what had happened. Something inside me already knew."

The tears finally fell. I couldn't contain them any longer.

"Morris was out drinking, partying," I continued. "He ignored Harper's panicked phones calls."

I inhaled deeply and looked up. The evening was clear. Millions of tiny specks twinkled above me. It was more beautiful than the last time I'd watched the night sky. This wasn't a planetarium. This was real. Those were real stars up there, burning bright and hot in the darkness of space. The burning of my eyes, the hot ache in my chest, the darkness at the very core of me, was almost fitting.

I looked down at my feet, unable to take such beauty when speaking of something so ugly.

"They cornered Harper in an alley. Jumped him, knifed him. Left him to bleed out. We didn't know whether it was meant to be a warning, or if they planned on—" I exhaled a shuddering breath. "The coroner said it took more than an hour. Ever since, I've had to live with the fact that my fiancé died slowly, alone and in pain."

"Shit." Liam took a step toward me and reached out, as if wanting to pull me against him.

I held up a shaky hand. "Don't."

He lowered his arms.

"I'm so sorry." His voice was distressed, almost anxious. "I can't imagine what it must have been like, to have to live with that."

"It was hell," I said flatly.

Liam made a movement to step forward, then halted, seeming to struggle with himself. He wanted to hold me, to comfort me.

But I wouldn't have found comfort in his arms. Not anymore.

"I fell apart," I continued. "Morris tried to put me back together, but seeing him only made it hurt more. So he left. And I've been trying to forget about it for years."

Liam couldn't fight it anymore. He lurched forward and took me in his arms, burying his face in my hair.

"I am so fucking sorry," he choked out.

I let him hold me, but didn't return the embrace. Tears still fell down my cheeks, but I was numb inside. Now that the black sludge had completely taken over my chest, my heart, my lungs, my gut, it seemed to have settled. It was no longer a writhing mass. It was now simply a sticky tar coating every inch of me.

Liam pulled back to look into my eyes. I don't know what he saw, but it made him flinch.

"You wanted to know everything from the very beginning," I told him.

He nodded slowly. "I did."

We stared at each other, not saying anything.

He looked away first. "I don't know how to even begin apologizing."

"You could start with, *I'm sorry for accusing you of cheating on me.*"

"I am sorry." He forced himself to meet my gaze. "So sorry."

"You thought I was going to sleep around behind your back with Morris," I said. "Why would you think something like that? Do you really think so little of me?"

"No," he shook his head. "I never actually thought that. I was just upset and worried and jealous and dealing with a bunch of other shit that has nothing to do with you and everything to do with me. I shouldn't have taken it out on you."

"You forbid me from seeing one of my oldest friends. You know how awful that is?"

"I shouldn't have given you that ultimatum."

"No. You shouldn't have."

"I wish I could take it back."

"You can't."

Hurt flashed across his face. "Is there anything I can say that will make you forgive me?"

"I understand you're sorry about what you said. I get that. But I can't be with somebody who doesn't trust me."

"It's not that I don't trust you," he pressed. "I was just dealing with—"

"A bunch of other shit," I finished for him. "Right."

Liam went silent, casting his eyes down.

I rubbed at my nails. Completely smooth. All the polish had been scratched off.

I was done for the night. I couldn't take any more.

"I accept your apology," I told him. "But it doesn't change anything."

I made my way to the curb where taxis were waiting outside the club for drunken partiers ready to leave. I reached for a door handle. I looked back.

Liam was still staring at the ground.

"I'll see you at rehearsals," was all I said.

I slid into the car without another look.

## 34

I didn't tell the taxi to take me home. I didn't want to be alone, but I also didn't want to talk to anyone. I knew the perfect place.

When I walked into Walt's bar Jessie immediately came to my side.

"Whiskey sour?" she asked, her voice full of empathy.

I nodded, knowing I wouldn't actually drink most of it. I didn't want to get wasted. Hanging out at the bar was just better than going home, crying myself to sleep and waking up to nightmares.

I sat on a stool at the far end of the bar by myself. The bar patrons left me alone. They were used to my presence, so walking in wearing a leather corset and knee high boots didn't cause a second look anymore. Besides, Walt, the bar's owner, kept the guys in line. Any inappropriate words or comments and they were out on their ass.

Jessie kept throwing me worried looks so I knew Gael had told her at least part of the story. She spent the night busy with work so at least I didn't have to talk to her.

I'd been there about half an hour, surfing mindlessly on my phone as I nursed my drink, when someone approached the table.

"Mind if I sit?" a young woman asked.

I looked up from the screen.

Natalie stood in front of me. A French braid pulled her hair back from her pretty oval face. My eyes immediately went to her ring.

She lifted her hand to give me a closer look. "It's gorgeous, isn't it?" She let out a happy sigh, her eyes going soft as she examined it for what was probably the thousandth time. "He did a perfect job of picking it out."

"It looks good on you."

And it did. The solitaire diamond in a platinum band had that sort of timeless, classic style perfectly suited to her.

"Do you mind if I sit?" she asked again, gesturing to the empty seat next to me.

Yes.

"No," I said. Go ahead."

She took a seat on the stool, not caring about the cracked leather with foam stuffing peeking out, or the bar's sticky surface. Either she had gotten used to the place by now, or she really didn't mind.

"Can I assume running into you isn't a coincidence?" I asked.

She gave me a sympathetic look. "Gael called Jessie who called Morris who told me that you'd had a rough night."

"You could say that."

"Do you want to talk about it?"

If I didn't feel like talking to my own brother about it, I sure as hell didn't want to talk to Morris's fiancée.

"You don't have to." Natalie's eyes grew sad. "I just know how difficult it's been for Morris recently. Especially today. I can't imagine what you must be feeling right now."

No. She couldn't. Very few people could.

"I can do the talking, if you like," she offered with a small smile. "It's sort of my specialty."

She'd come all the way and was sitting right next to me. I couldn't very well say no without sounding like a bitch.

"What's there to say?" I asked instead. "We all know what happened. We lost someone we loved. It was traumatic. But it's been five years. We've worked through our issues. Today's just harder than most. Tomorrow will be easier."

"Have you?" she asked quietly

"Have I what?"

"Worked through your issues."

I stared into my half-finished whiskey sour. The lemon floated in the drink, bobbing up and down. My trembling hand was making the glass shake. "I thought I had."

But maybe I hadn't. It seemed like every time something triggered my memory of Harper, I pushed it down or ignored it or ran away. I knew those were unhealthy coping mechanisms. Even after years, the wounds still hadn't healed. Maybe they never would.

"I think Morris is right," Natalie said.

"About what?"

"You should write a song together. About him. About Harper."

"All my songs are about Harper."

"Your songs are about pain and anger, grief and loss."

"What else would they be about?"

"Love," she said simply. "Acceptance. Releasing all those feelings you've been suppressing and dealing with them."

"Catharsis," I murmured.

"Yes," she nodded emphatically.

"I don't know..." I said hesitantly.

"I'm sure your fans would love it," she said encouragingly. "You'd probably get a lot of positive reviews."

"Why does that matter?"

"Don't you want everyone talking about how great you and the band are?" She gave me a knowing look. "Don't you want to prove yourself to everyone?"

"You think you know me so well?"

"You're not hard to read," she said. "Everyone knows how hard you work. You push yourself and your band to your limits."

"Since when is working hard a bad thing?"

"It's not, if you're doing it for the right reasons," she said. "But maybe, you're always focusing on your work, you're always focusing something outside of yourself, because you want to try and forget about what's going on inside of you."

"What are you, my therapist?"

"I'm Morris's girlfriend. Fiancée," she corrected herself. "I've seen the same thing with him. He's so dedicated to that youth center, to those kids. He wants to save them from the streets, like he couldn't save Harper. It's a coping mechanism."

I went silent and thought about what she'd said.

Was I using my work to deflect my feelings? It was true I hadn't had nightmares in years. Not since we'd started the band, really. I thought I was over it. I was so focused on hitting it big.

It wasn't until I'd met Liam that all those old feelings began to rise to the surface. I hadn't learned how to deal with them properly, so I dealt with them by running away.

"Morris is so full of pain and anger and grief," Natalie said. "Just like you. But he's found a healthy outlet by helping these kids. He's learned to face his demons head on. I don't know if throwing yourself into your work to distract yourself is good for you in the long run. You're not dealing with your problems. You're suppressing them."

I took a long pull of my drink to avoid having to respond.

Natalie was right. I thought I was over it. I thought I'd come to terms with Harper's death.

But I'd only been ignoring my problems. Focusing on something else.

"Shit," I cursed quietly. I put my head down on the bar, ignoring a sticky spot on my cheek and closing my eyes.

"It's not too late," Natalie said. "There are people out there who want to help you."

"I've been to therapy. I learned all about breathing exercises and overcoming negative thought patterns."

"Therapy is always good," she nodded. "But it's not just that. You've got friends, family, loved ones who are more than willing to help you, talk with you, just be with you when you need someone. I know it helps Morris to have me to talk to during the bad days. You've got people who love you, too. You don't need to handle this all by yourself."

Loved ones.

My mind flashed to Liam.

I'd thought, maybe—

But after the way he'd acted...

"Why did he have to be such an ass?" I muttered.

Natalie blinked. "Who? Morris?"

"No." I shook my head, but it was still face-planted on the bar, so all I managed to do was smear more sticky substance all over my cheek. "Liam."

She made a thoughtful sound. "Morris mentioned something about that. I feel for the guy."

I opened my eyes to squint at her. "Feel for him?"

"He doesn't really like Morris. I get it. I used to be jealous of you, too."

"Me?" I asked, surprised.

"Morris was always talking about his best friend Harper. I found a picture of all three of you. I thought Harper was a girl for the longest time. I thought she was you. It was really hard." As she spoke, the words came out faster and faster, as if she couldn't slow down. "It's really hard being with someone who you think is still in love with someone else. Especially a loved one from the past. How do you possibly compete with that, when there's so much history there?"

I'd never thought of it that way. I knew Liam was worried about me and Morris, but that was ridiculous. We were just friends.

But how could Liam know that for sure? We did have a history together. I had been sad at his engagement.

And Liam did have a history of loved ones leaving him for someone else. His mom had left and started a whole other family. His girl-friend had left him for his best friend.

Still. Accusing someone of cheating on you was horrible.

There were some issues you couldn't just get over.

## 35

I woke up the next morning with a pounding headache. It wasn't a hangover. I hadn't had enough to drink for that. It was from all the worrying and thinking and fretting. I'd barely made it home before dawn, having spent most of the night at Walt's.

Natalie had left soon after saying her piece, leaving me to absorb her words by myself. She no doubt sensed I wanted to be alone, so she hadn't stayed. She'd simply patted me on the back and wished me a good night.

A good night. I wouldn't have called the rest of my night *good,* but I hadn't wallowed in complete misery the entire time, so that was something.

When I slid out of bed and reached for my phone, I saw a dozen missed messages. Most were from Gael, but a handful were from Julian, along with a couple from Nathan and Seth. They were all variations on the same question.

*Are you okay?*

I didn't answer any of them. I didn't know how to answer them. *Yes* would have been a lie, although a reassuring one. But I didn't feel as emotionally destroyed as I'd felt the night before.

Natalie had given me lots to think over.

I'd just come out of the shower and pulled on some clothes when my phone flashed with a missed message notification. My heart jumped, wondering if it was Liam. He hadn't sent me a single message after I'd gotten into that taxi and left him.

But when I checked, I saw it was from Morris.

*Meet me at the youth center,* was all it said.

It had only been sent minutes before. I didn't bother asking what time.

I debated internally with myself. Morris could have wanted to talk about any number of things, and I didn't think I was up to any of them.

But after what Natalie had told me last night, I did want to see him.

*Morris is so full of pain and anger and grief. Just like you.*

I grabbed my bag and headed out.

When I got to the center, I knew exactly where to go. I found Morris in the music room, behind a drum set. The room was soundproof, but as I opened the door I was assaulted with heavy beats and crashes.

The music halted as I stepped in. Morris stood up. He nodded in greeting. Despite the painful aching in my heart, that small quirk of his lips made me smile in return.

"Sorry," he said. "I know this is last minute."

"I wasn't doing anything else."

That technically wasn't true. I was supposed to be at rehearsal. After the previous night Gael was probably half-expecting me to skip out anyway. I deserved one day off.

"Should I bother guessing what this is about?" I asked.

"You don't have to," Morris began.

"No," I cut him off with a shake of my head. "I think it's a good idea. That song. I want to write it. With you. About him."

"About Harper." The pain in Morris's voice matched the pain in my chest as he said the name out loud. "Thank you."

"No. I should thank you. You're right. It's a good idea. Maybe with this, I can finally deal with—" I paused. "Everything. Deal with all that shit I've been pushing aside for years."

"Me, too," Morris said quietly.

"I'll probably be rusty. I haven't composed with anyone else in years."

"It's like riding a bike," Morris said.

"Maybe."

"If it sucks, it sucks," he said simply. "No one has to hear it. This is for us."

"This is for him," I corrected.

"For all of three us, then."

"Gael will probably want to hear it, at least," I said.

"If it's good, he'll probably insist Cherry Lips perform it."

I winced. "I don't know if that would be a good idea."

Morris tilted his head at me. "Why not?"

"Liam—" My throat closed up.

"What about him?"

"I don't think he'd enjoy performing a song like that. A song about Harper. A song composed by both of us."

"I think he would," Morris said.

"You don't know what went down. He..." I trailed off, not wanting to get into it.

"He was jealous of me," Morris said, surprising me. "He thought you were in love with me. He found out how wrong he'd been. Now he feels like shit."

My brow furrowed. "How do you know all that?"

"Liam called me."

I started. "What?"

"He called me," Morris repeated. "Told me everything."

"Why the hell would he do that?"

"To apologize." Morris came out from around the drum set and put his hands on my shoulders, making me look at him. "This was his idea."

"What was?"

"Us writing this song together. I could tell you didn't want to. I wasn't going to push. But Liam convinced me. Told me we should work together. Insisted, even. He said he knew how much I meant to you. How much you were still hurting. He knew I was the only person who would understand."

That speech was the most I'd heard Morris speak at once. The thought that Liam would go so far as to call him threw me off balance. To insist we work on a song together was both disconcerting and heart warming.

Liam was trying, in his own way, to prove he was sorry. To prove he trusted me.

"You want to get started?" Morris asked.

I nodded slowly. "Sure. Let's do it."

Morris got his messenger bag and pulled some sheets of music paper along with two pencils. A piece of card stock fell out along with the papers. Morris picked it up and began to shove it back into the bag.

I recognized it.

"Where did you get that?" I asked.

"This?" Morris examined the card. "A guy I know in the industry is getting married. Nat and I got an invitation a few days ago."

"Chad Emmerson?" I guessed.

"I suppose you would know him. He was in Liam's old band."

And his fiancée, Paula, was Liam's old girlfriend.

A sudden understanding blew through my chest.

Liam had received the wedding invitation between his ex-girlfriend and former best friend just days before he'd seen me hugging Morris.

"Shit," I cursed out loud.

Morris raised an eyebrow. "Something wrong?"

"No. Just—"

No wonder Liam had been so upset. No wonder he'd jumped to conclusions. He'd probably been trying to put the whole thing behind him for years, just like I'd been trying to run from Harper's death.

Then he'd received their wedding invitation and all those old wounds had ripped open.

Liam said he'd been dealing with a lot of shit. Of course. It made sense now.

It really hadn't been about me and Morris.

It had been about him and his ex.

For once, it had been about his pain, his hurt, and not mine.

Among everything else that had been going on, I'd forgotten that I wasn't the only one who'd been hurt.

I wasn't the only one who'd experienced loss.

## 36

Morris and I worked on the song for most of the day. It was as heart wrenching as I'd imagined it would be, but it was also something of a relief.

Through the music, through the lyrics, I was able to express all the things I hadn't been able to say out loud.

I came home and immediately flopped onto the sofa, worn out, exhausted, but with my heart feeling lighter than it had in years. The song wasn't done yet, but it was a start. We'd continue working on it until we got it right.

As I began to fall into a light nap, I heard a knock at my door. A part of me wondered if it was Liam. My heart leaped. When I opened the door, my brother was standing on the other side.

I didn't have time to ask him why he'd come. The moment he saw me, he pulled me into a fierce hug.

"How you feeling?" he murmured.

"Better," I said. "Sorry I missed rehearsal."

"No worries. We all understand. Besides, the rest of us have skipped out for worse reasons." Gael pulled back and looked into my eyes. "The guys are worried about you."

"I'm doing fine. Maybe even better than fine."

"I'm glad. Because if you were still upset over what Liam said I would have punched him in the face for you."

"I know you would have. You don't need to."

"The offer still stands." Gael raised his clenched fist and shook it. "No one messes with my baby sister."

I winced inwardly. If Gael knew the whole story, if he knew Liam and I had been together and he'd broken my heart, Liam would have been done for.

But then Gael said something that surprised the hell out of me.

"Are you going to take him back?" he asked.

I gaped and stammered. Gael laughed.

"Did you think none of us noticed?" he asked. "The way you looked at each other? All those times you snuck away together?" Gael smirked. "You weren't exactly subtle."

"Shit," I groaned.

"No, it's fine," Gael shook his head. "The guys and I talked about it. As long as it doesn't affect the music, we're cool with it." He gave me a soft smile. "We just want you to be happy. And up until a few days ago, you seemed the happiest you've ever been." His smile faded into a glower. "But if Liam did something or said something shitty, then he's out."

"He—" I paused to consider my words. "He said some things. Things that did hurt me at the time. But I think I understand now why he said them. I'm just not sure whether or not understanding why he said them is enough. He still said them. Some things you can't just get over."

"I get that. Some things are unforgivable." He cocked his head at me. "But is this one of them?"

"I don't know," I said truthfully. "I can forgive, but I don't know if I can forget."

Gael hummed thoughtfully. "I had the same problem with Jessie. You know I did some dumb things."

"And she forgave you."

He nodded. "I didn't expect her to, but she did. Somehow, she was able to look past what I did and understand why I did it."

"And that was enough?"

"For her it was. Maybe it's different with you and Liam." Gael shrugged. "But love is love."

"Lo—" I nearly choked on my tongue.

"Are you saying you're not in love with him?"

"I don't— It's not—" I continued to sputter.

Gael chuckled and put a hand on the top of my head, stroking my hair. He ducked down slightly to meet my wide gaze.

"It took me by surprise, too," he said. "I never thought I'd feel that way for anyone. I had you, and I had the guys, and that was enough. But Jessie..." His eyes gaze went distant, tender. He didn't need to continue. From the look in his eyes, I knew exactly what he was saying.

Love changed everything.

My heart pounded heavily in my chest. Was it love I felt for Liam? A jolt of panic shot through me. I didn't know if I was ready for that. As much as I liked him, as crazy as I was for him, love was something else entirely.

Was I even capable of loving again? For a long time, I'd thought my heart had died along with Harper.

Did I even want to love again? Did I want to risk opening my heart, just to have it ripped out of my chest?

"It's okay if you don't know yet," Gael reassured me. "But just think about it. He makes you happy. Before he showed up I would have given anything to see you smile that way again." Gael stopped, hesitating for a moment, as if wondering whether to continue. "I wanted to run something by you," he said. "About Liam. And the band."

I frowned, wondering what he could possibly have to ask.

"What do you think about asking him to join?" Gael asked.

I started. "Join the band? As in, for real?"

Gael nodded emphatically. "Yes. He fits in perfectly with us. We're so much better with him. You know we are. We've never been as good as we have than when we're playing with him. The guys and I talked about it. We're all on board with the idea. We think Liam should be a permanent part of Cherry Lips."

My mind whirled as I contemplated the idea. I knew Gael was right. We were better with Liam.

But bringing him on had always been a temporary thing. All of us knew it. Besides, Liam seemed more than happy with his position as a session guitarist.

"Even if I agreed, I don't know if he'd go for it," I said.

"Why not?" Gael asked. "We all work great together. Why wouldn't he want to join?"

"Every time it was brought up, he seemed not too keen on the idea." Something occurred to me then. "Some bad things went down with his old band. Maybe he just doesn't want to risk things falling apart again."

"Then we convince him," Gael said simply. "If you agree, if all of us agree, then we can make the offer and convince him." Gael pinned me down with a stare. "Do you agree?"

"Aren't you worried?" I asked. "About me and him? Band members dating each other doesn't exactly have a good track record. Look what just happened to us. We're in the middle of this huge—" I cut myself off, not knowing exactly what we were in the middle of. A break up? A fight? "—thing." I finished lamely.

"I was worried at first," Gael said. "But despite what went down between the two of you, you've still both been professional. We've still rocked on stage. I trust you to be adults about it. Besides," Gael chuckled darkly. "There's no reason why we can't just kick him out again if things really go south."

"Let me think about it," I said.

I hadn't talked to Liam since that night when I'd told him all about Harper. He'd apologized to Morris, apologized to me.

But I still didn't know if I could get over the terrible words he'd flung at me.

If Liam couldn't get over his trust issues, I didn't think there could ever be a future for us.

## 37

After Gael left my apartment, I mused on his words while absent-mindedly cleaning the place up. I hadn't done the laundry or the dishes in days. As I stood in front of the sink and washed plate after plate, I couldn't help remembering that time at Liam's house. I'd been trying to clean up with him pressed against my back. Eventually I'd given up and we'd made a beeline to his bedroom.

The memory was both sweet and heartbreaking at the same time. I cared for Liam, so much, but I didn't know how to get that back.

I didn't know if it was even possible.

I didn't know if I even wanted to.

I was just putting the last fork away when my phone pinged. I glanced at it. My hand froze with the fork still grasped between my fingers.

Liam had messaged me.

I debated whether or not to read it. It was late. I should have been in bed already. But I couldn't help myself. I knew I'd never be able to sleep without checking it.

I picked up my phone.

*When you and Morris are done writing your song, I'd love to hear it.*

My chest clenched with a painful ache. Liam was trying. Could I really ask for more than that? I wished I could talk with him in person. I needed to know what was going through his head when he'd said those things.

Without letting myself second guess what I was doing, I grabbed my bag and left the apartment. I made my way to Liam's place, all the while trying to push aside my doubts and worries. I had to say my piece. I had to get it it off my chest.

And depending on how Liam responded, well, that would be my answer.

I knocked on the front door of the huge multi-story house. I had no more polish on my nails to scratch at so I played with the hem of my shirt instead. I hadn't told Liam I was coming over. Maybe he wasn't even home.

I was seconds away from turning around and leaving when the door opened. Liam's surprised expression soon melted into a kind of hopeful look. He stood there, staring at me, his eyes roving all over my face, as if soaking in every details. As if he hadn't seen me in years. It had only been a few days.

"Do you mind if I come in?" I asked.

He gestured for me to enter, the look in his eyes still a bit dazed. I walked through the door and made my way to the kitchen. Neutral territory. I took a seat at the island counter. Liam followed, staying a safe distance away, not crowding me.

Now that I was here in front of him, I was at a loss for what to say. I admitted as much to him.

"Let me start, then," he said. "With an apology."

"You've already apologized," I pointed out. "I accepted it."

"It still needs saying," he said. "I'm sorry for accusing you of cheating on me. It's like I said before, I really never thought that. I was just—"

"I know about Chad and Paula," I interrupted.

Liam's face went blank, frozen. His fists cleaned at his sides. He took a breath in, then let it out slowly. His hands relaxed.

"How?" he asked.

"I saw the wedding invitation in a pile of papers," I explained. "Then I saw some photos of you and her online. It all came together when Morris mentioned he got his own invitation a few days ago." I studied Liam closely. His eyes had darkened, a shadow falling across his face. "You got the invitation to their wedding only a few days before our fight."

He nodded slowly, but didn't say anything further. I continued for him.

"Your invitation was all crumpled up. You crushed it into a ball. Then you smoothed it out and kept it. Why?"

"I thought—" he faltered, then started again. "I thought I was over it. Over her. Over them." He let out a derisive laugh. "I have no idea what they were thinking, inviting me. What they did was awful, but I didn't think they were that cruel. Best I can figure, they hired a wedding planner who invited all their colleagues without knowing what went down." Liam came over and sat down heavily on the stool next to me. He didn't look at me. He placed his hands palm down on the counter, his fingers tapping a staccato rhythm. "I thought I'd put it behind me, what they'd done. I didn't think I was still so affected by it. But apparently not. When I walked in and saw you hugging Morris, all I could think was, it's happening again."

"You thought I was going to leave you for another man," I finished for him.

His hands trembled. "It wasn't just that. I saw them—" He exhaled sharply, a pained sound emitting from the back of his throat. "I walked in on them," he confessed quietly. "I had the ring in my pocket. I'd been waiting for the right moment for weeks. Then I walked in and saw them together." His voice broke as he whispered the words again. "I saw them."

Damn.

It was even worse than I'd imagined. His girlfriend didn't just leave him for someone else. He'd walked in on the girl he was going to propose to in bed with his best friend.

My heart ached with sympathy. I placed my hand on his back.

"I'm sorry," I said. "I can't imagine how much that must have hurt."

"The worst part?" he chuckled darkly. "That wasn't even the first time that happened. I walked in on my mom once, too. Walked in on her fucking that asshole she left us for. I was young, but not too young to know what was going on. That was the catalyst. She knew she couldn't keep it a secret anymore. So she told my dad and took off."

"Oh, fuck," I whispered. I scooted closer and laid my head on his shoulder. "I'm so sorry, Liam."

"I know it's no excuse," he said. "I know I've got shit I have to work on. But being betrayed like that, twice... It's a hard thing to get over. " He ran a hand over his face. "It kind of fucked me up."

I ran a soothing hand up and down his back. "I understand."

"When I got that invitation to the wedding... I went a bit nuts." Liam kept his eyes forward, trained on a point in the distance, as if he couldn't make himself look me in the eye. "Then I saw you with Morris and it was like my worst fear was coming true. The woman I loved was going to leave me for another man."

My hand stilled. My lungs squeezed and released, taking the breath away from me.

Love.

He'd said it.

Liam said he loved me.

I was still stuck on those words, unable to move past them, but he was still speaking, as if he hadn't registered the importance of what he'd just confessed to. As if he hadn't even realized he'd said it to begin with.

"So when I said it had nothing to do with you, and everything to do with me, I meant it. I was upset and jealous and paranoid and I couldn't stop thinking about what Paula had done. What my mom had done. In the back of my mind, I think I was just waiting for it to happen again."

Liam finally turned to look at me. My eyes were still wide with shock at his use of the L word. He cupped my face, brushing a thumb across my cheek gently.

"I never wanted to hurt you," he said. "That's the last thing I would ever want to do. I was just so worried you were going to be the one to hurt me, first. I don't think I could have taken that. If you had truly left me for Morris, I think it would have destroyed me."

I stared at Liam. I stared into those green eyes. Earnest, aching.

I lowered my head to rest my forehead against his. I closed my eyes and took in a shuddering breath.

"I would never hurt you like that," I told him quietly. "I would never betray you. Because I—" I steeled myself. I never thought I'd say these words ever again. But now, looking into those eyes, I knew the truth. "Because I love you, too."

Liam let out a pained sound and crushed me to his chest.

"I am so fucking sorry," he murmured.

"I know," I said. "I understand. And I forgive you." I pulled back, just an inch, until our lips were a mere inch away. "But if you ever say shit like that again, I really will kick you in the balls."

He choked out a laugh before pecking a quick kiss on my lips.

"I wouldn't expect anything less," he murmured.

That small peck, the briefest of kisses, sent a tingle running through me, like a direct line from my lips to the very core of me.

I had never craved him so much, not even before we started dating. I didn't know why. Maybe it was his confession. Maybe it was the real truth about him that made my heart melt. Whatever it was, I had to have him.

I'd missed him so much. I'd missed the man who'd made me pour my heart out to him. The man who had made me believe in love again.

I pressed my lips against his, running my hands up his cheeks to cup his face.

A quick laugh escaped him at my move. His familiar embrace surrounded me in seconds.

I was still trying to wrap my head around everything. But I wasn't going to think about it. Not now.

His grip around me tightened further as he hoisted me off the stool and onto the counter, laying me down as he stood between my legs.

I felt the hard surface on my back. I wrapped my thighs around his waist. He swiped the tip of his tongue across the seam of my lips. I slid my hand into his hair, raking my fingers against his scalp as my heart pounded against my ribcage. I caressed his cheek, the familiar warmth and texture of his skin making my body tingle.

I almost couldn't believe I had him back. It was almost like a dream. A tall, gorgeous, inked dream. But this was real. I could feel it in my bones. I could smell it in his scent. I was touching it. Touching him.

Liam slid the straps of my top down my shoulders, his breath tickling my chin. His hands cupped my breasts, teasing them, pressing them together. I whimpered in his mouth. He moved his lips down. I kept my eyes shut. He left firm kisses in a soft trail all the way down to my chest. Waves of soft pleasure rippled through me.

"I've missed you so fucking much," he whispered.

I bit my lower lip as his warm lips landed on one nipple. Liam kissed the area around it, trapping the other one between his thumb and index finger. My inner walls clenched when he flicked his tongue over one. A light pinch on the other forced a low moan from me.

More kisses across my chest added to my growing need. He was taking his time with me, as if savoring every moment, as if it might be our last.

But it was more like our first. The first time after confessing our true feelings. I wasn't going anywhere, and neither was he. Liam was mine. I was his.

"You're beautiful, Cerise." He pulled me closer to him. "The most beautiful thing alive."

His words made my heart melt. I had no idea how to respond to that. All I could do was pull him into a desperate kiss as the heat in my core spiked.

He pushed my skirt to my waist and pulled my panties down, tossing them away. He unzipped his jeans and reached into his pocket for protection. My heart leaped as an idea formed in my mind.

"Fuck the condom," I demanded.

Liam paused.

"You sure?" he asked, his brows drawing down into a frown.

"I'm on birth control. I'm clean. Are you?"

He nodded. "Yeah. Got tested right after our first time."

"I want to feel you," I told him. "I want to feel you inside me, skin to skin."

He offered me one of his softest smiles. Liam pulled his jeans down his thighs. My gaze shot down his body; I was so eager to see him again. His hard length made my inner walls ache and throb.

My mouth went wide in a long moan as he entered me. The feeling of his bare cock stretching me out was enough to make my whole body tremble. He was back where he belonged, inside me.

A few thrusts later and I was writhing underneath him. His lips were too much for me to resist. I leaned up, reaching forward.

"Get over here." I urged, grabbing a fistful of his t-shirt.

I pulled him down, our lips battled in a hot, fiery kiss. A grunt of arousal left his mouth. I dug my nails into his back. Liam slid his palms down my legs, caressing my skin as he slid into me, again and again.

I threw my head back as waves of bliss shot down my spine. Each long stroke was overwhelming, bringing me closer to my peak until my eyes squeezed shut and I cried out his name. Pleasure crashed through me like a bolt of lightning. I shuddered beneath him, liquid heat pouring out of my very core.

He groaned as my inner walls clamped down around him. His cock twitched violently and he came, spilling himself inside me.

We were still panting when he interlocked his fingers with mine. He pulled me up gently, breathing hard on my skin.

"You're fucking amazing." Liam said, still breathless. "You know that, right?"

"You may have mentioned it once or twice."

He pulled me into another fierce kiss. I still ached and throbbed inside, but I didn't think I could go again. Liam had ravished me too thoroughly.

When we had finally caught our breath, Liam cleaned us both up and helped me off the counter. I stifled a moan as my overworked muscles complained.

Liam pulled me into his arms again. He stroked my long hair back from my face, tucking it behind my ear. His eyes held a sort of wonder, as if he still couldn't believe I was here.

I saw the world in his gorgeous green eyes.

A world I couldn't wait to explore with him.

"I need to ask you something," I said.

His eyes narrowed in concern. "Why do you sound so hesitant?"

"Because I know what you're going to say. But I want you to hear me out and really think about this. Okay?"

"Now I'm nervous," he teased.

"I want you to write a song with me."

His eyes softened. His pressed a kiss to my hair. "I would love to."

"As a member of Cherry Lips," I continued.

Liam's arms squeezed around my waist reflexively. I could feel him tense up.

"We want you to join the band," I said. "And I know it's hard for you. Your old band betrayed you. Your family betrayed you. It's a hard thing to get over. But trust *me*." I pressed both my palms against the sides of his face, forcing him to meet my eyes. "I will never do anything to hurt you. And neither will the others. We want you to be a part of us. We want to be your family."

Liam swallowed hard. His pained eyes bored into mine.

"I don't know if I can," he whispered.

"I know you can." I pressed a soft kiss to his lips. "You just have to trust us. Do you think you can do that?"

Liam's gaze roved all over my face, as if trying to gauge my sincerity. "And if I say no?"

"I'll be sad. We're so much better with you. I know we can do great things together. But nothing between the two of us will change. This is for you. I only want what will make you happy."

"And you think joining Cherry Lips will do that?"

"You need to learn to trust people again, Liam. I think this would be a good first step."

He continued staring into my eyes. I wondered if he would end up shooting me down.

Slowly, carefully, he nodded. "Okay."

"Okay?" I repeated, just to make sure.

The corner of his lips quirked up. "You want to make it official? I, Liam Knight, want you, Cerise Moreau, to be my lead singer."

I threw my arms around his neck and pressed myself against him.

"I promise, we will never betray you. We will always have your back."

His fingers sifted through the hair at the back of my neck as he said three words that meant everything to me. It wasn't *I love you*. I already knew that much was true. These words were even more meaningful.

"I trust you."

# EPILOGUE

The spotlights hit my eyes, blinding me. The roar of the crowd filled my ears. The thunder of bass and drums assaulted my chest.

This was our last concert for the tour. One more song and we'd be done.

I didn't know whether to feel sadness or relief. This tour had taken a lot out of the band. Every one of us was run down, exhausted. But every time we stepped foot on stage, we were renewed. There was nothing like performing in front of a cheering audience of adoring fans.

But it had been a long month or more. Our bodies could only take so much. I knew the guys were ready for a break. So was I.

I just had to do one more thing.

"You guys having an awesome time?" I shouted into the microphone. I was rewarded with a a howling chorus of *fuck yeah*. "We're going to end this one a little different tonight."

I nodded to a waiting guitar tech who took that as his cue. We swapped guitars, electric for acoustic. I took a seat on a small stool. The other guys filed off stage, leaving me alone under a single spotlight.

"This is a new song," I told the audience. "It means a lot to me." My voice only wavered slightly. I cleared my throat. "I hope you enjoy it."

I put my fingers to the strings.

I hadn't planned on playing the song Morris and I had written in public. I didn't think I'd ever want anyone else to hear it. It was too personal. Too painful.

But the moment we sat back and took in the final, completed version, I knew. This song needed to be performed. It needed to be heard.

I needed to play it for Liam.

I needed to play it for Morris.

I needed to play it for Harper.

Most importantly, I needed to play it for myself.

The burning need inside me had nothing to do with the actual song itself. The music was heart wrenching, yes. Touching, sorrowful, uplifting. The song said a million things, and yet in the end, it really only had one meaning.

I was strong.

I was strong enough to face the past without falling apart.

I was strong enough to stare into the darkness and survive.

The others had been right. Closing myself off, running from my demons, was a terrible way to cope.

But I wasn't weak.

I was strong.

As I sang, my eyes wandered over to Liam, watching from behind the curtains. His eyes shone with pride. Even after everything, he still looked at me with wonder. Still looked at me as if I were extraordinary. He looked at me like I hung the moon.

Or as if I were an exploding star, burning in the night sky.

And that was when I realized it.

Up there on that stage, I knew I could take on the world. And it wasn't because I was strong, or because I'd stopped being weak. It was nothing so simple as that.

It was because I was...

Me.

After all these years, I'd found myself again.

And Liam was the one who helped me.

I sang the last few words as the song came to an end. There was a hush in the concert hall, reverent and awed.

Then the audience burst into cheers and shouts and hollers, tears streaming down faces and sobs being wrenched from throats.

I knew exactly who I was.

I was Cerise Moreau. I was the lead singer of Cherry Lips. I was Liam Knight's lover.

And the two of us were going to do exactly as Liam said.

We were going to burn like the sun, together.

# BONUS PREVIEW:

Want more Hard Rock Romance? Continue reading with an excerpt from *Hard Rock Tease* >>>

# HARD ROCK TEASE CHAPTER 1

My heart thumped wildly in my chest. I took deep breaths to try and calm myself. It didn't work. I was going to miss my interview with Etude Entertainment. I was going to lose the best chance I had at getting my foot of the door in the music industry.

The building had too many twists and turns. The corridors all looked the same with their eggshell white walls and marble-tiled floors. Rushing around one more corner, I pushed my way through a set of double doors with shaky, clammy hands. I didn't know which way I was going, but I hoped if I continued on I'd at least find someone to ask.

Light strains of music hit my ears the moment the doors swung open. Piano music. Some of my rising anxiety eased. Maybe there was finally someone I could ask for directions.

Following the music down the hall, I found an open door. A quick peek inside showed me a man sitting at a piano. Broad shouldered, black hair, and tall. Even though he was sitting down I could tell when he stood he'd reveal an impressive height. No doubt much taller than me.

I was about to knock on the open doorframe when the man began to hum. Lithe fingers spidered across the keys, a soft, tinkling melody that complimented the humming. Every so often he would stop to make a notation on a piece of paper laid flat on the top of the piano's surface.

Even without words, the man's singing was lovely. Almost sweet and romantic, somehow. The music made my heart swell, touching something inside of me. Such a sad song, yet at the same time hopeful. There was a longing beneath the light humming.

My rapid heartbeat slowed, my frazzled nerves soothed by the music. Without meaning to, I lost myself in that melody. As a music student, I could appreciate the intricacies of each note. The song didn't sound quite finished. A rough draft, maybe. Still, I could tell the man was gifted.

Hunched over the piano, his shoulders tensed up. He pressed down hard on the keys, fingers now flying. The soft melody turned harsh and aggressive. Whatever loving sentiment the man had begun with, he'd lost it. The music became louder, unpleasant. I could hear unspoken rage in the smash of every key.

The longer the man played the more discordant the notes become, until he slammed his hands down one final time, the music resolving itself in a crash of noise. I jumped, my heart beating a pounding rhythm against my ribcage.

The man buried his hands in his hair, tugging at the strands. He hunched further over the keyboard. He cursed, a quiet, forlorn expletive. Moments later he shot up from his seat at the piano with a flurry, knocking off the papers full of music notes, sending them scattered to the floor.

I took a few steps back out into the hallway, nervous adrenaline racing through my veins.

The man stood in front of the piano, his back to me, chest heaving with every breath. His hands clenched into fists at his sides. He took a slow breath in, then out. Running his hands down his face, he let out a soft, pained sound.

This man was clearly in the middle of an emotional breakdown. I didn't want to interrupt. I took a few more steps backwards, intending to leave before he noticed me.

He bent to pick up the music sheets from the floor. I saw his face for the first time.

All the air left my lungs.

This was a man I'd recognize anywhere.

Blinking once slowly to clear my eyes, I counted to three, making sure I wasn't imagining things. When I looked again, it was still him. Dressed all in black, from his open leather jacket, to his form fitting t-shirt to his tight jeans...

My eyes nearly bugged out. Damn, those were some tight jeans. My stomach muscles clenched involuntarily, an instinctive reaction. A pulse of arousal spiked through my body, warming me from the inside.

My gaze followed his body down further to his heavy black combat boots.

My heart stuttered in my chest.

It really was him.

Noah.

Fucking.

Hart.

All my senses went on high alert.

Noah Hart, lead singer of my favorite rock band Darkest Days, a rock star god, a man I admired beyond all reason, stood mere feet away from me.

My eyes travelled over his body, taking in his long legs, broad shoulders, and messy dark hair. I gnawed on my lip as excitement ran through me. He looked even hotter in person than he did on stage or on TV.

Although I had to be honest, I was sort of disappointed he wasn't wearing leather pants and eyeliner.

Pure misery showed on his face, his expression alight with inner turmoil. I held still, not making a move, not making a sound. I didn't want to disturb him in what seemed to be a private moment.

I also didn't want to risk opening my mouth and freaking out in the presence of one of my music idols.

Noah scooped the papers up, gathering them into some semblance of order. His face was open and lined with pain. The emotion he exuded on stage was just as evident in person. I wondered if he was working on a new song, if this was part of his process.

Something lit up inside my chest at the thought of Noah Hart having trouble writing songs. The fact that it might not come easy to him, despite the wondrous lyrics he wrote and the passionate way he sang, gave me a small bit of comfort. Sometimes it seemed like the work that I struggled with came about so effortlessly to everyone else.

Maybe he and I had something in common when it came to that.

I was still lingering in the doorway, watching him, drinking him in. Dark tattoos peeked out of the collar of his shirt. Enough of his upper chest was exposed to make my thighs clench. One of my shaky hands gripped the doorknob. The other was pressed to my heaving chest, feeling every one of my shallow breaths.

I shouldn't have been so affected. It wasn't like I'd never met this man or his band before. I was a fan, after all. I'd seen them backstage dozens of times. I'd shaken their hands and spoke a few words to each, gotten their autographs and given them my thanks.

I'd even seen a few members of the band up close at a private event, once. Being a music student and having friends with connections in the industry had its perks. Of course, at the time, all I'd been able to do was stare at them, mouth gaping open and blushing. It had been mortifying.

I wasn't going to let that happen again. I had to get out before I made a fool out of myself.

But I had stood in the doorway for too long. I should have left when I had a chance. Noah turned to leave. He froze as his eyes met mine.

Immediately his expression shut down, eyes shuttering. His face went blank, no trace of the pain I'd seen before.

"What are you doing here?"

"I'm so sorry," I replied immediately, shuffling my feet back and forth awkwardly.

His voice was flat. "No one's supposed to be here."

"I-I'm lost," I stammered.

The expression on his face was chilly, except for the lingering frustration in his eyes and the downturned corners of his mouth. He set down the papers he'd picked up from the floor on the piano.

"I'll just... leave," I said weakly.

Noah eyed me up and down slowly. My cheeks flushed with embarrassment at that penetrating gaze. I couldn't help eyeing him back. Damn, but those jeans were tight. I'd heard rumors, but he couldn't really be that big, could he? I could practically see his outline through the rough fabric.

"Do I know you?" he asked.

I shook my head, trying to suppress the heat flaring between my legs.

"I've seen you before." The words weren't a question. "It was at a party. That album release."

My heart sank. The last thing I wanted was for him to recognize me. I didn't want him to think I was just another one of his swooning fangirls. Even if it was true.

"I remember." His eyes narrowed. "You were so starstruck you couldn't say a word."

I fought to shake myself out of my daze. Noah was right. I *had* been struck speechless before. Almost like I was now. I didn't want to let that happen again. I could pull myself together. Definitely. I could totally do that.

"Well. You know." I gestured to him.

He tapped his fingers on the top of the piano in an staccato rhythm. "No, I don't know. What?"

"You're Noah Hart," I shrugged helplessly. Noah. Fucking. Hart. I still couldn't believe it.

"You're a fan?"

I tried to make light of it. "Who isn't a fan of Darkest Days?"

"So the answer is yes?" he asked. "How lucky for you to have stumbled upon me."

I was either lucky or cursed. How could I possibly manage an interview after running into the lead singer of Darkest Days? My heart felt like it might explode out of my chest. My limbs were trembling. My insides were throbbing.

I had to get a hold of myself.

"I didn't mean to intrude. I'm here for an interview."

"This area is off limits to non-employees."

"I'm sorry. I think I got off on the wrong floor."

I hovered in the doorway, unable to make myself walk away.

"You want an autograph or something?" he asked. "I can't imagine why else you'd still be standing here."

"Sorry, I'll just..." I trailed off, breath hitching as Noah strode over.

He moved like a wild animal, purposeful, with a barely restrained edge. As he approached, he scanned me up and down, his dark eyes intense. I felt my nipples tighten and peak underneath my blouse.

His eyes lingered on my chest. I had no doubt he could see the effect he was having on me. I fought back a flush.

"Or maybe you want more than an autograph?"

I folded my arms over my stiff nipples to hide them. "I don't know what you mean."

"Fangirls throw themselves at me all the time. You think I don't recognize that look you're giving me?"

"I'm not throwing myself at you. I'm just standing here."

"Your nipples are hard as a rock."

A sense of shame swirled and combined with outrage inside my chest. "It's cold in here."

"It's almost summer."

"The air conditioning is on."

"Is that why your face is red?"

I put my hands to my cheeks. "It is not."

"I bet your panties are soaked, too."

My mouth popped open, appalled and turned on at the same time. Hearing those words out of this man's mouth made my inner walls pulse.

"Famous rock star or not, you don't get to make comments on my panties."

"Am I wrong?" He took another step forward, crowding me until my back was nearly to the wall. My breathing sped up. I couldn't even tell if I was angry or turned on. "Have I turned you speechless again?"

I inhaled a sharp breath, but nothing came out.

His eyes glinted as he backed away. I let out a wavering whimper, my vocal chords beginning to work again.

Noah gave me a darkly amused look as he walked through the open door. "Good luck with your interview, fangirl."

The moment he left I clung to the doorframe, my knees going weak. Shivers ran down my spine, half in arousal and half in anxiety. I only had room for one thought in my head.

Who exactly was this Noah Hart I'd met, and what the hell happened to my soulful, romantic poet?

# HARD ROCK TEASE CHAPTER 2

I couldn't believe I'd met Noah Hart.

I couldn't believe Noah Hart had been so moody and abrasive.

I also couldn't believe I was actually sitting in the vast foyer of Etude Entertainment with marble floors and expensive leather furniture. My stomach was doing flips, and it had nothing to do with the sexy, gruff rock star I'd encountered.

Well. Maybe it had a little to do with that. Okay. A lot to do with that.

I'd been sitting in the same spot for over twenty minutes, though. Straight-backed to avoid slouching, chin up to convey confidence, thighs pressed together to prevent a flashing incident. I exuded a sense of calm, competence, and professionalism.

On the outside, anyway.

On the inside, my mind gibbered away at me non-stop.

Why were they making me wait so long? I didn't care. This was the opportunity of a lifetime. But what if they decided to go with someone else? Of course they'd go with someone else. I was nothing special.

It didn't matter how long they made me wait, though. I'd sit there forever if it meant I had a chance to work with one of the biggest entertainment companies in the world.

Despite my misbegotten encounter with Noah Hart, I'd wait forever if I had a chance to work at the music label that had signed Darkest Days.

I gave myself a mental shake. No use getting all worked up. I might not even get the job. I'd been left waiting for so long. Maybe they really had forgotten me. I'd been a single minute late. That might have been enough to disqualify me.

Light footsteps sounded down the hallway. I stood up with haste, smoothing down my pencil skirt and blouse. I forced myself to breathe deeply, hoping to wipe away any hint of nerves. Thank god my nipples were no longer stiff with arousal.

A woman wearing a smart pantsuit, in her late-twenties or early-thirties at most, stepped into the lobby.

"Jennifer Young?"

I pushed aside all thoughts of a certain grumpy, gorgeous, and *goddamn sexy* rock star god. I plastered a pleasant smile on my face.

"Yes, I'm Jen."

"Naomi Sera." The woman held out her hand for a shake. I made sure to grasp it firmly. She pulled out a sheet of paper and handed me a pen. "Before we do anything else, you need to sign this NDA."

"A non-disclosure agreement?"

"Exactly. You can't tell anyone the details of what we talk about today."

I scribbled my name with haste and handed it back to her.

"I'm sorry to keep you waiting." Her black hair, cut short in a severe bob, swayed back and forth as she shook her head, an apologetic look on her face. "I had some trouble with—" She cut herself off with an almost exasperated laugh. "Never mind. You'll see soon enough."

My interest piqued, I followed her through hallways decorated with framed vinyl album covers, each one labeled with its recording sale award, either Gold, Platinum, or Diamond. I recognized almost all the names.

"Will I be meeting with any others?" I wanted to get a feel for how this interview would go. Naomi had sounded nice through the emails we'd exchanged, but who knew how many other people would be interviewing me.

"Just myself and..." she paused for a moment before continuing, "... and one other person. That's the reason I'm so late. He was being difficult. You aren't the first person we've interviewed for this posi-tion. The others... didn't work out."

That small hesitation made me nervous. Why wouldn't she tell me who else I'd be meeting with? Could it be one of the big wigs? Someone from the C-suite? And why hadn't the other people worked out?

That question was answered the moment Naomi waved me into an open office.

Scanning the room quickly, I immediately zeroed in on the man leaning against the wall, tattooed forearms crossed over his chest. No leather jacket. From what I could see, the tattoos were random designs, odd shapes and geometrical patterns. If they had any meaning, I couldn't decipher it.

Even with his face turned away and his mouth twisted into a scowl, his presence dominated the room. Although his eyes were averted, he seemed to sense the exact moment I walked in. He tilted his head a fraction of an inch toward me. Dark glinting eyes met mine.

Noah.

"I assume you know who this is." Naomi motioned to him with a wave.

Noah stiffened, shoulders tensing, the only indication of his surprise. "You?"

I straightened my back. I wasn't going to let him know I was rattled. Or aroused. Again.

Naomi looked confused. "Do you two already know each other?"

Noah stayed silent, not bothering to explain, so I did.

"We've met."

He ignored me and turned to Naomi. "Why is she here?"

"She's here to interview for the job."

"She's barely out of school," he said flatly.

"*She* is actually called Jen," I cut in. He was trying to needle me. Trying to throw me off balance, maybe. I didn't know why. His very presence was enough to do that. "I'm not a student. I've graduated college." Only weeks ago, but he didn't need to know that.

"I know seeing Noah Hart must come as a surprise," Naomi told me as we sat down at the conference table. "But we don't want to let interview candidates know too much about the position before they sign a NDA and are officially offered the job."

I resolved to put aside my feelings. I needed to act professional. I couldn't let him get to me. I wanted to get off on the right foot with Noah.

Although I had a feeling *on the wrong foot* was the only way Noah Hart knew how to interact with people.

"As the manager for Darkest Days, it's my job to interview candidates for this position," Naomi said.

I wondered why Noah Hart was part of the interview process. He didn't seem to want to be here at all.

"The professor who recommended you sent us some samples of your work," she continued. "We were impressed. But I'd like to learn more about you personally." Naomi turned to Noah, who was still leaning against the wall, arms crossed over his chest. "Sit."

He did what she said, but turned his head toward the wall, away from me.

"How much do you know about Darkest Days?" Naomi asked.

I forced back a nervous smile. I knew everything about Darkest Days. *Everything.* I didn't know what this had to do with the job, but if they wanted an answer, I'd give it to them. I turned away from Noah and focused on Naomi.

"They're one of the biggest rock groups to come out in the last few years. They've gone Platinum multiple times over. Their latest album won a dozen awards." I wondered how much else to say. Naomi gave me an encouraging look, so I continued. "Industry insiders often remark on their ability to take multiple music genres and blend them together into a hard rock sound that's still commercially accessible. Some say their influence is redefining rock music itself."

"You're familiar with the band and their music," Naomi nodded.

"Good. And what about you? Tell us about your musical background."

My hands went cold and clammy again. I tried to remember the interview tips I'd read online. They all said to sell yourself. I didn't think I had very much to sell. I was sure nothing made me stand out from all the other applicants they'd probably interviewed. I wasn't an expert in anything. I just fooled around with a lot of different instruments. Maybe that could be enough to impress.

"I've been playing my whole life. I started with piano and violin as a child. Later on I learned the cello and harpsichord. I can also play guitar and bass."

Noah shifted, staring at me out of the corner of his eye. When he saw that I caught him, he immediately looked away.

"I'm also a fan of the hammered dulcimer," I continued, starting to feel self conscious. I started playing it because no one else at my academy did. I didn't have anyone to compare myself to. No one to feel inadequate next to. If I was only mediocre it didn't matter as much.

"I'm not an expert by any means, though," I continued. "I wouldn't call myself an expert in any of them, but I can play well enough, I suppose."

"And what about composing?" Naomi asked. "You write your own songs, yes?"

"Yes, although I only started composing in high school." Most of the students at my music academy had been writing music since they were kids. I almost felt embarrassed to have only started in my late teens in comparison.

"A few of your compositions have been performed professionally, your professor told me."

"Those were mostly songs I worked on with other students. I can't take all the credit."

Naomi looked thoughtful. "You went to the prestigious Academy of Orchestral and Performance Studies for college, is that right?"

"Yes, OPUS Academy. I double majored in Composition and Music Theory."

Noah eyed me. "All the theory in the world means nothing when it comes to writing real music."

"Play nice," Naomi admonished.

He looked away.

Naomi continued. "Your professor did say you were one of the brightest students she'd ever taught. She was right to recommend you."

I tried not to duck my head, embarrassed. "She's exaggerating. There are many students much more talented than I am."

"How modest," Noah said under his breath.

"How accomplished," Naomi spoke over him. She made a sharp movement under the table. Noah flinched, rubbing his knee. She continued speaking without a pause. "I'm impressed with your qualifications."

All the praise made me flush. I looked down, wavy long hair falling over my face. "I recently graduated, so I'm not sure how qualified I am."

I could name a dozen classmates who had more talent than me, people who were naturally gifted. I often struggled with my school-work, and even though I loved learning new instruments, it some-times felt like I took forever to become even mildly proficient. I wasn't all that special.

Naomi stared me down for a few moments, a considering look on her face, then nodded once.

"Jennifer, I'd like to offer you this job."

"Are you serious?" Noah said, voice flat.

Naomi ignored him. "Are you interested?"

She said it so matter of fact, I wasn't sure I'd heard right. Had I done it? Was I really going to be working with Etude Entertainment?

The words sank in. Maybe I was more qualified than I thought. Maybe Naomi saw something in me I didn't see in myself. I let out a small choked cough and hurried to reply.

"Yes! Of course I am."

"Wonderful."

Noah sank back into his seat. "Yeah. Great."

Despite his lack of enthusiasm, I couldn't suppress the glee that rose up in my chest. Then the rational part of me gave me a kick. I placed my clasped hands on the table and cleared my throat.

"Although, before I formally accept, I would like to know about the position. What exactly were the others hired to do? And why weren't they able to do it?"

"We need you to write a song," Naomi said.

"That's it?"

Noah scoffed, crossing his arms over his chest. Naomi threw him a vexed look, then turned to me.

"It's not quite so simple. We need you to write a song for Darkest Days."

I gaped. "Are you kidding me right now?"

"Not in the slightest."

"I'd get songwriting credits?"

"No. But you'd get royalties."

My mind nearly exploded trying to imagine the sum of money that entailed. Way more than I'd ever gotten at my crappy part time jobs.

"But the band always composes their own songs," I protested, still unbelieving. "They never use outside songwriters. They have one hundred percent artistic control."

"You're right. August composes the basis of their songs and Noah writes the lyrics, then the guys all work together to flesh it out. But this time, each member of Darkest Days is creating a song solely on their own for their newest album, from composing the music to writing the lyrics. Therein lies the problem."

"Problem?"

"Noah is a lyricist."

I quickly glanced at the lead singer of Darkest Days. That was why he'd been so frustrated at the piano. I immediately felt bad for him. I understood that feeling all too well.

"You can't write songs? Just lyrics?"

I received a withering stare.

"I can write songs," he said through gritted teeth.

"Then why haven't you?" Naomi arched an eyebrow. "You've had months."

Noah averted his eyes.

"I don't care if you've got writer's block or performance anxiety or what, but you need to compose *something*," she stressed.

"Why can't one of the other band members help?" I asked.

He visibly blanched. "I can do it on my own."

"Clearly you can't," Naomi countered. "So if you won't ask the other members for help, we'll come up with another solution." She turned to me. "That's why we needed you to sign a nondisclosure agreement."

So I'd get fortune, but not fame. That was fine by me.

"If you don't want anyone to know, how are we going to explain me hanging around?"

"The same way we explained it with all the others. We'll say you're a consultant brought on to help with producing the album. No one will think it's odd to see you and Noah working together."

"So I'm supposed to work with the lead singer of Darkest Days to write a rock song and pass it off as being composed by him?"

"Exactly. Are you in?" Naomi asked.

I wondered what had happened to all the others they had hired that hadn't worked out. I caught a glimpse of Noah shifting in his seat out of the corner of my eye. He looked irritated beyond belief.

And that was why. Working with this man was clearly not going to be easy.

Especially not when I thought I caught a hint of heat in his eyes when he glanced at me. I couldn't be imagining the quick looks he was throwing my way. Looks that made my heart pump faster, looks that made my head swim.

We'd only just met and he'd already made comments on my *hard nipples* and *soaked panties*.

If I didn't manage to get a grip, this was going to end up being difficult in more ways than one.

Then again, a professional career in music was never going to be easy. I had to take what I could get. And apparently what I could get was a job working with the lead singer of Darkest Days.

I nodded fervently to Naomi.

"Definitely. Yes. I'm very interested in the position. Thank you so much for this opportunity."

"You really think you can work with me?" Noah bit out. "You couldn't even string two words together the first time we met." His eyes fell to my chest again, leaving it unspoken how my body had responded to his.

I fought back a flush and pleaded with my body to cool down. "Well, I have lots to say now. We need to talk about what kind of song you want to write. What kind of sound you're going for."

"I don't need help. And I don't need help from some fangirl."

Pursing my lips, I resisted the urge to snap at him. "Stop with the fangirl stuff."

"Stay out of my way. I can do this myself."

"I've been hired to do a job. I'm going to do it to the best of my abilities."

"I don't need your help," he repeated.

"You've got it anyway."

Noah scowled.

Naomi smiled. "Looks like we've got the right person for the job."

# HARD ROCK TEASE CHAPTER 3

As I left the interview room, Noah was still bickering with Naomi. She had asked me to step out of the room while she and Noah discussed a few details. I wanted to get out of there before I snapped at him again. What a great way to start our working business relationship.

Relationship. I could feel my cheeks heating up. Not exactly the word I wanted to use when thinking about Noah Hart and myself. We would be working together. That was all.

Of course, my body was showing interest in Noah in ways that it hadn't in a long time.

I was torn between terror and excitement. Putting aside the way my insides gushed when I was near him, there was more than one reason why I should feel worried.

It wasn't so much that Noah clearly resented being forced to work with me. I could deal with that. In college I'd been forced to pair up with fellow students who I had nothing in common with, people I might not have chosen to work with, people I might have clashed with in previous years. Still, I'd managed to be professional and had learned to work with people of all sorts.

Working with a lyricist who was dealing with the musical equivalent of writer's block wasn't all that bad in comparison.

It was that I was supposed to be writing a song for *Noah Hart,* lead singer of Darkest Days. Noah Hart, the soulful, romantic poet whose lyrics spoke to my very soul. I was supposed to be writing a song with the man who made me the person I was today. The man who saved me during my darkest days.

It was cliched and dramatic, but it was also true.

And I was supposed to write a song with him.

No way. There was no way in the world I was good enough to do something like that. As far as I was concerned, Noah was a *god.* I was a student barely out of college. Sure, I was pretty good when it came to composing, but I was nowhere near the level it took to work with someone like Noah Hart.

Why had I said yes? Why had I even bothered to show up for this interview? I should have told my professor no. There were dozens of other students I could name who would be a million times better than me for this kind of job.

I gave my head a vicious shake. I couldn't let my insecurities get the best of me. This was the opportunity of a lifetime.

But Noah was right. I *was* a fangirl. I'd been able to hold my own against him so far, but what if I broke down and panted at his feet like my body wanted me to? What if I couldn't control my arousal and embarrassed myself in front of him? What if Noah knew exactly how much I wanted him, and used that against me?

No. I wasn't going to let that happen. I was going to take this chance and I was going to excel. I was going to write the best goddamn rock song the world had ever heard.

All the emotional whiplash was beginning to give me a headache when Noah and Naomi walked out of the room.

"Thank you for waiting, " Naomi told me. "Everything's been sorted. I'll leave you with Noah to work out the details." She shot him a look that clearly said *behave* before leaving.

Noah stared at me with his arms crossed over his chest. "Congratulations," he said. "I suppose you get to live the dream."

"Excuse me?"

"Doesn't every fangirl wish she could sink her claws into Noah Fucking Hart?" he said, using the nickname fans had come up with.

My cheeks flushed, half in anger and half in shame. He wasn't exactly wrong.

"I'm not sinking my claws into anything. I'm here to do a job. I'm going to work with you whether you like it or not."

His eyes were dark and intense. "I don't like it."

"Gee, I couldn't tell. Maybe you should try to be a little less subtle. Maybe try telling me straight to my face that you resent me being foisted upon you. I really had no idea up until this very moment."

His eyes burned with irritation. I bit my tongue. Why had I mouthed off? At least that was better than melting into a puddle at his feet.

"This is my first real job in the music industry," I told him. "I want to do well. You may not want to work with me, but in this case being a fan is a help, not a hindrance. I love your music. I'm going to do my best to fulfill your vision."

"I suppose it might work," he said grudgingly. "You can't be worse than any of the others."

"Why?" I asked with trepidation. "What was wrong with the others?"

"Everything," he shot back. "They had no talent. They were hacks."

"I promise I'll try to live up to your high standards, then."

"Good." He looked away, eyes sliding away from mine to gaze up at the ceiling. "Because Naomi says I have to work with you or else."

"Or else what?" I couldn't imagine anyone trying to tell Noah what to do. Then again, he had listened to her in the meeting. As his manager, she must have had something to hold over his head.

Noah's mouth twisted in distaste. "Or else she'll tell August," he said, referring to August Summers, the band's drummer, main composer and founding member.

"Would that be so bad?"

"Hell yes."

"Why don't you want your bandmates to know?"

He didn't saying anything, his expression awkwardly self-conscious.

Noah was trying to hide his problems from the rest of the band, but I didn't know why. Now it made sense.

"You don't want them feeling sorry for you? Or are you worried they'll think less of you?"

He clenched his fist. "Don't try to psychoanalyze me. We're working on a song together. That's it."

"I know you're a literary genius, but I'm sure the guys don't expect you to be some master composer as well." I tried to reassure him, as if the words of one fangirl would ever hold meaning for him.

Noah shot me a look, almost unbelieving for a brief moment. He stalked towards me, making me back up. He got right up in my face. It would have been intimidating, if it weren't for the fire in his eyes.

I suppressed a shudder as that now familiar heat hit my gut, centering between my legs. It wasn't because he was famous, or because he was talented. This man was capable of setting me aflame, in a way that had nothing to do with his status and every-thing to do with the way his dark eyes pierced me down to my very bones, threatening to scorch me from the inside out. Like he was seeing inside my very soul. Like he could see parts of me that had been buried deep and hidden for years.

Because of his lyrics, I always felt like I knew Noah Hart, even though we'd never met.

When he stared at me like that, it felt like he knew me, too.

"A literary genius? Is that really how you think of me?" He leaned closer, tilting his head.

"Doesn't everyone?" I bit my lip to keep from saying any more. He didn't need to know exactly how I felt about him. He didn't need to know I worshipped him like a god.

He didn't need to know I wanted to lick every inch of his body right then and there.

His eyes fell to my lips. His own eyes darkened, pupils dilating. "No wonder you're so eager to work with me." He flicked his eyes up to mine again. "You got a fangirl crush?" I could tell he was trying to sound sarcastic, but it came out sounding almost curious.

"Crush is a juvenile word," I said, my voice shaky. "Teenagers have crushes."

"Then what exactly do you have?"

"Professional admiration."

He leaned closer, his lips nearly touching mine. "Is that it?"

"Y-yes." I stammered. "What else would it be?"

His eyes were bright and burning. It reminded me of that first moment when I'd seen him sitting at that piano, furiously scribbling down notes on his music sheet, trying to compose but somehow unable to.

My heartbeat raced. That look was the same one I'd seen on stage dozens of times. The passionate poet Noah Hart. That was the man I wanted to work with. That was the man who ignited such desire inside me. The cold Noah I'd seen in that meeting was nowhere to be found in those eyes. I could only see the fire burning inside of them, matching the fire burning inside of me.

His gaze trailed down my face, pausing on my lips again. I wet them unconsciously. His fire raged even brighter. He placed a hand beside my head on the wall, boxing me in.

"Don't get any ideas." His words were low in his chest. "You're going to play music. I'm going to write down lyrics. That's it."

A shiver went through my body. The difference between the coldness in his words and the heat in his eyes had me trembling.

I couldn't keep reacting like this. I steeled myself, locking my shaky knees and straightening my back. I looked him straight in the eye.

"And what kind of ideas do you think I'm getting?"

"The kind all fangirls get when they come face to face with their idol. You're wondering if I'm as big as you've heard. You're wondering what it would be like to have me fuck you."

I nearly whimpered at his words. Warm, wet heat flooded my body.

But despite my inner feelings, I was going to act professional if it killed me. I cleared my throat, trying to steady my voice.

"Don't you get any ideas. I'm here to do a job, not throw myself at some rock star."

"Don't lie." The warmth of his breath caressed my lips. His eyes were dark and glinting. "You're thinking about spreading your legs for me right here and now."

God but he was right. I ached inside, throbbing and empty. The fact that we were in the middle of a hallway in public meant nothing to me. If he made a move right now I had no doubt I'd succumb.

I took in a shallow breath and forced myself to meet his eyes. Despite the longing between my legs, I wasn't going to fall at his feet like all the other girls.

"I'm here to work, not to play groupie." I placed a hand on his chest, putting some distance between us. The heat coming off his body was incredible. I felt every firm muscle of his chest under my palm. My brain threatened to fog up. I filed the sensations away to examine later.

He let me push him away, slowly backing off. I leaned against the wall, trying to fake a casual pose. In reality, I needed something to keep myself upright on shaky legs. He studied me, a curious look despite the heat of his eyes.

"Fine then," he said. "If you're here to work, meet me at eight tomorrow."

"In the morning?"

"Yes, in the morning," he said impatiently.

"Don't rock stars party all night and sleep until noon?"

"Not when they've got an album deadline, apparently," he muttered. "The room you found me in was on the fourth floor. I'll be there working tomorrow." He gave me one last heated look. "Don't be late."

He strode off, leaving me reeling. Leaving me wanting. The quivering in my stomach wouldn't abate.

Noah was so prickly, but those looks he gave me, the words he spoke to me, only caused the simmering tension between us to rise higher with every encounter. He knew exactly what effect he was having on me. He knew I was lusting after him.

And despite his words to the contrary, I had a feeling Noah Hart didn't mind in the least.

# ABOUT THE AUTHOR

Athena Wright is a USA Today Bestselling author of New Adult and Contemporary Romance. She loves to write about rock stars and the girls who tame their wild hearts. Hobbies include procrastination, wasting time on the internet and living out her rock star dreams at karaoke bars. Athena is perpetually on the hunt for her next caffeine fix.

*Find Athena online:*
www.athenawright.com
athena@athenawright.com

facebook.com/authorathenawright
twitter.com/athenawrights
instagram.com/athenawrights

Made in the USA
Lexington, KY
17 May 2018